LAST
GIRLS
ALIVE

BOOKS BY JENNIFER CHASE

JENNIFER CHASE

LAST GIRLS ALIVE

bookouture

Published by Bookouture in 2020

An imprint of Storyfire Ltd.
Carmelite House
50 Victoria Embankment
London EC4Y 0DZ

www.bookouture.com

ISBN: 978-1-78681-894-7
eBook ISBN: 978-1-78681-893-0

To all the police officers and military soldiers—thank you
for your dedicated service to keep us safe

PROLOGUE

"*Hurry*," Candace whispered urgently as she disappeared down the wooden staircase and into the pitch-black basement.

"Wait," was Tanis's breathless reply as she slowed to glance behind her. In just a flimsy yellow nightgown, the damp air from below chilled her bare arms and feet. She shuddered.

The padlock Candace had picked open swung precariously from the latch, ready to drop and awake the rest of the sleeping house. This was a bad idea.

"*C'mon*," urged Candace from somewhere down in the abyss. "*Hurry up!*"

They were going to get caught.

The consequences would be merciless.

Shifting her weight on the wooden landing, Tanis pushed herself onward and pressed her foot onto the first wooden step. And then another. Each footstep creaked beneath her slight weight. She clutched the loose railing and clumsily made her way through the dark until her feet touched cold cement.

Hands fisted at her sides in fear, she frantically blinked her eyes, straining to see through the darkness—to the unknown. It left her powerless. There had been no time to find a flashlight, but it would only capture unwanted attention anyway.

A hand grabbed her arm.

"C'mon, we've got to go *now*."

Candace took Tanis's hand and pulled her toward the end of the basement and around a sharp corner to where a dim light from outside allowed her eyes to begin to focus.

The girls moved as fast as they dared through the maze beneath the old house.

Tanis could only see Candace's long hair flicking from side to side as they ran. At one point, she closed her eyes and relied on her friend's strong will and instinct to get them to safety.

They stopped abruptly at a storm door, the only thing standing between them and freedom. Panting in the darkness, a creak from upstairs lifted both their heads in fear—someone was awake.

Candace lunged forward and grabbed the large bolt locking the door with both hands and pulled. It gave way with a loud clunking sound, and she pushed the bulky door open to reveal the half-moon outside.

Cool air whipped inside, wrapping itself around Tanis's shivering body as she watched her friend take the final two steps—to a new life.

With the moon behind her, and with her arms outstretched in joy, Candace resembled an angel in her white cotton nightgown, her dark hair blowing all around her. "C'mon," she urged again.

Tanis froze. It was as if her feet were cemented to the basement floor. Doubts about running away from the foster home plagued her mind.

They would never stop searching for them—ever.

She and Candace knew too much about what went on at Elm Hill.

How would they survive without any money?

She realized that she just couldn't do it—not now, not like this. She would soon be eighteen and then things would be different—the home would no longer be her prison. She would be legally free. No one would care anymore.

"What are you waiting for? This is our chance."

"I can't... I can't do it. It's just another year," said Tanis. "Not even that long."

"No, we're doing this together. We have each other," said Candace adamantly, shaking her head. "I'm not going to leave you here. We escape together."

"You have to go. You can't stay…"

Candace ran to the side of the house and retrieved a duffel bag, which had been carefully packed and stashed for their escape. Unzipping the top, she pulled on a pair of jeans and slipped on a pink sweater. It was her favorite color, always matched to her nail polish.

"Hurry." Tanis changed her tone. She wanted her best friend to escape the abuse of the home—the authority and focus was always more concentrated on her anyway. Tanis knew that she could endure another ten and half months, but Candace couldn't.

"No…"

"Yes, hurry. I can help misdirect the she-beast and the cops. You'll be safe." Tanis heard the rustle of branches in the distance and looked toward the edge of the property, near the hiking trail, and saw the outline of a man. She had never met Ray, had only seen him from a distance, but he was their ticket out of here. At least, that was how Candace had described him. "Go. We'll meet back in ten months and three days at our secret spot. I promise."

"I will come back for you." Candace's voice faltered. It was clear she wanted to stay, but as she looked to the south she saw Ray waiting; that was all she needed to push forward.

Tears welled up in Tanis's eyes. She knew that she'd made the right decision to stay behind, but that didn't make it any easier. One of them had to stay. It would soon be over. It all would be over.

Candace hugged Tanis tight. Whispering in her ear, she said, "I love you and I'll be back." She gave her a long look before she turned and ran.

Tanis watched her friend move quickly into the shadowed night—and soon disappear altogether.

I love you and I'll be back.

CHAPTER ONE

Five years later

Monday 0730 hours

The diesel engines of the earthmovers and bulldozers roared as they prowled like metal predators on top of the hill and through five acres of dense trees surrounding the mansion. The massive tires left deep grooves in the soil, still sodden after extensive bouts of rain, and various attachments worked to smooth out the terrain and keep rain runoff to a minimum in preparation for demolishing the house.

Loud voices yelled back and forth across the property, directing the action. Three metal containers, each forty feet long or more, sat on the far side of the estate, housing tools, supplies, and some of the more valuable interior pieces of the house such as doors, light fixtures, crown molding, fireplaces, and various pieces of shiplap wood. The new owner, Magnum Development, Incorporated, wanted to save anything that would bring in any extra money, no matter how small. They planned on building three luxury-spec homes on the impressive landscape that would garner more than two and a half million if they could only fight the rainfall and correct the slipping landscape. It was highlighted as a "special project" that they had taken on in addition to more lucrative ventures, but there was still a comfortable profit margin to be had.

Built in 1895 but left abandoned for the last two years, what remained of the house was still known to most around Pine Valley as Elm Hill Mansion. It used to be a safe haven for fostered teenage girls, but now looked more like the façade of a haunted house at a Halloween carnival. Four years earlier, the foster home, which had been a private philanthropy project, had been disbanded by the county and state authorities who had little or no budget to maintain the project after allegations of abuse. The house had repairs and indications that it potentially wasn't safe. The remaining girls were relocated to other homes and soon thereafter the investigation had fizzled and the large house sat vacant.

The historical mansion, with more than 2,000 square feet of livable space, included five bedrooms, two living areas, a parlor, storage, and a library area that had been reduced to a pitiful crumbling mess of empty shelves over the years.

A panicked cry from outside stopped several workers in their tracks as they wrenched a rotting wooden fireplace from the wall. Among them, in jeans, a red flannel shirt and hard hat, was Bob Bramble, the foreman in charge of the project. He looked around, angry at the interruption and keen to get back to work.

"Boss!" yelled one of the employees. "Hey, boss!" the man yelled again, more urgently.

One by one, the booming sound of engines ceased, leaving the area strangely quiet.

"Yeah," Bob said as one of his men jogged up to him. "What is it?"

"We can't get the crowd to leave."

"What crowd?" he growled and craned his neck to see half a dozen people with handmade signs saying "Keep the Elm Hill Mansion" and "Keep the historical house" headed their way. "Oh, brother. Get them out of here," he barked. "We have a job to do! I'm not going to get behind because of a group of idiots."

"But what if they don't leave?" asked the worker, looking at the crowd with a worried expression.

"Then… call the cops."

At the same time, one of the bulldozer drivers jumped from his cab and ran toward them. His face pale, panic in his eyes. "Boss!" he yelled as he increased speed. "BOSS!"

"Crap," the foreman muttered. "Now what?" he snapped as the driver ran over to him.

"There's… it's…"

"Spit it out, Chris… tell me what's going on."

"We found… it's *horrible*, sir…"

Bramble grabbed Chris's arm and gave him a little shake. "Show me. We don't have time for this shit."

The men hurried to the far side of the property where several trenches had been dug. Two other workers were standing side by side staring down the hillside—not moving.

"What's going on here?" Bramble demanded.

One of the men slowly pointed his index finger without saying a word.

Bramble stepped to the edge of the pit and peered downward.

Submerged in the muddy earth, and surrounded by puddles of water, lay the naked body of a young woman—her pale skin like porcelain in the early morning light. Lying on her left side, arms twisted precariously, one in front of her bent body and the other behind. She looked like a broken doll that had been carelessly tossed away. The remnants of a rope dangled from her left wrist. Her long chestnut hair, wet and knotted around her face, covered her frozen expression.

Bramble couldn't tear his eyes away from the body as the sun peeked out from behind a cloud and illuminated her fragile form in a natural spotlight. "Stop working…" His voice caught in his throat. "Stop. Everybody STOP!" He waved his hands, turning around to get everyone's attention. "Stop working. Everybody exit the property now! Now!"

Bramble had never seen a dead body before and the young woman looked painfully close to his own daughter's age. As his team downed tools and headed for the parking area, he bent down closer to the body, carefully moving down the hillside, and strained to see if he recognized her, searching for anything around her that might identify her.

Slipping his hand into his pocket, he stood up, swallowed hard and composed himself—still not fully believing what he was seeing. He knew enough from watching true crime shows on TV to keep the area clear to avoid contaminating the crime scene, but all he could do now was dial 911.

CHAPTER TWO
Monday 0805 hours

Detective Katie Scott kept her pace as she weaved around several clusters of trees on the rural hiking path. Her long dark hair, tied back in a ponytail, swung in time with her fast stride. The cool morning air filled her lungs. It was the part of the day she loved the most; fresh and clear. The forest around her clung to the incredible scent of the mountains after the rain and the leaves were beginning to turn brown. Summer was nearly over and the fall season was fast approaching.

Dressed in dark navy running pants and a lavender hoodie, she could feel the perspiration trickle down the back of her neck. The contrast of hot and cold invigorated her and she pushed her pace even harder until she reached a lookout area at the top of the track with a magnificent view of the valley.

There she waited—still moving her limbs to help keep the blood flowing, catching her breath and enjoying the beautiful pattern the trees, peaks, and valleys formed. The landscape was lit up by the early sun in a stunning canvas of orange and green. A few predatory birds glided around her, searching out small mammals.

It was the perfect way to contemplate what the day would bring, but her mind was never far from her time in Afghanistan as a K9 explosives handler. Nothing would ever totally block those memories—both good and bad—but she was now learning how to cope.

She tried to *cope* every day. To survive. Taking deep slow breaths, Katie felt her pulse returning to normal.

"Hey," came a man's voice lagging up the trail behind her.

Katie turned and smiled. "What took you so long?" she replied lightly.

"You're not the one carrying an extra fifteen to twenty pounds. You left me in the dust. Partners don't do that," huffed Deputy Sean McGaven.

"You asked me to help with your training. I'm not going to hold your hand," she said with a laugh.

"Yeah, well, in case you haven't noticed this isn't the army, no matter what your credentials say." He stopped beside Katie, towering over her with his six-foot six-inch height in matching sweats and hoodie. His complexion was ruddy and his light red hair closely cropped. With his hands firmly set on his hips, he waited for his breathing to return to normal.

"You're doing just fine," she said. "Really."

"Oh great, that's encouraging, just before my heart attack."

"You're not going to have a heart attack. It's always hard to get back into running again."

He turned and enjoyed the view for a moment. "This detective work has kept me confined to an office too much. And..." He hesitated. "Being in the hospital laid up for over a week didn't help. And for some reason, desk work makes me extra hungry. So," he gestured to his stomach area.

Katie stretched her calves and hamstrings. "Don't forget Denise's fantastic cooking." She laughed. Denise worked as a supervisor in the sheriff's department's records division—and McGaven had been dating her for more than six months.

He didn't respond immediately, still thinking about it. "You might have a point there," he joked.

"Don't forget to stretch, *regularly*," she stressed. "And it doesn't hurt to have a good soak before bed—you might want to use some

Epsom salts too. It does wonders for aching muscles and joints. That way, you won't feel so stiff in the morning. Run every other day so that your body can have twenty-four hours of recovery."

He followed her lead and began stretching his legs too. "I hear you."

Katie was lucky—at least that's the way she thought about it. She was working as a detective at a job she loved. When she had returned to Pine Valley after her army tours were over, she was uncertain of what she was going to do next. Return to Sacramento Police Department and work patrol, take some time off, or work cold cases for the Pine Valley Sheriff's Department. She chose the latter and was given the opportunity to head the cold-case unit—a newly formed department—and Deputy McGaven was pulled from patrol to assist. It was the best decision she had ever made.

"Katie?" McGaven asked staring at her.

"Oh, sorry. Just thinking…"

"About the new case?" He finished her sentence.

"Stop doing that," she said.

"What?"

"Finishing my sentences."

"Well… I can't help it."

"Fine. Just don't do it all the time. It's annoying," she said, slowly walking down the trail.

"Isn't it a form of flattery?" He smiled as he followed her back down the hillside.

"Some would think so," she played along. "But, it's still annoying." Katie began to jog slowly back down the steep trail to finish cooling down and to give McGaven a break.

Her cell phone rang.

Katie pulled it out of her pocket. "Detective Scott," she answered. "Yes, he's here. Okay, we're both here now," she said and put her cell phone on speaker for McGaven to hear as he jogged over.

"I'm glad that I caught both of you at the same place," said Sheriff Scott. His voice was serious. "Do you remember a cold case that came across your desk recently, Candace Harlan?"

Katie had to think a moment, but it came to her. "Yes, a missing persons case—actually a runaway from foster care?"

"Yes," he said.

Katie looked at McGaven, knowing what the sheriff was going to say—she caught McGaven's eye and they listened intently.

"I need you and McGaven to get over to Elm Hill Mansion right now. During demolition this morning, they found a body. By description, it's likely Candace Harlan, but we won't know officially until the body is examined. You know the most about events surrounding Candace's case—and I want you to be the first on the scene and to work this investigation."

"We're actually close. Just on our way down the Brown's Hill trail," she said and began walking quickly, McGaven beside her.

"Good. I need you to report to Detective Hamilton immediately."

Katie frowned and stopped, leaving a stilted silence.

"He's been briefed and knows you're on your way. I need you to work the crime scene with him. This was originally a cold case on your desk, so the way I see it, you have first priority to the investigation."

"I'm sure Hamilton has it under control," Katie insisted. She wasn't liked by the detective, and taking over a case like this would do nothing to alleviate the tension between them.

"Katie," the sheriff said, "it's *not* a request. So I would suggest getting to the scene ASAP."

"Yes, sir. We're on our way."

The sheriff abruptly disconnected the call.

McGaven raised his eyebrows. "That wasn't pleasant."

"He's been like that recently," she said. "I can't really blame him, under the circumstances; being the number one suspect in your own wife's murder will have taken its toll. He's just trying to regain his authority at the department again…" She moved faster along the path to get back to the parking area.

"I guess it is tough having the sheriff as your uncle," he said.

"That's an understatement."

CHAPTER THREE

Monday 0955 hours

McGaven parked the unmarked police sedan where he could between hastily parked work trucks, construction equipment and first responders. A number of construction workers, police officers, and people holding signs were obstructing the entrance to the property.

Katie had been informed that CSU were already inside the police-only area waiting for further orders from her. She took a moment in the car to watch the carefully controlled movements of deputies and forensic personnel protecting the crime scene by taping off areas in quadrants and shielding the body with a sheet. Most of the onlookers, including a few protesters that had hung around, pushed against the tape trying to get a look at the murder scene.

Katie opened the passenger door and stepped out, her running shoes instantly sinking into a puddle as the cool breeze whipped through her clothes. "Great," she said, rolling her eyes as she trudged through sticky mud toward the yellow tape area. Neither Katie nor McGaven had had time to change out of their running attire, so they forged ahead without their badges and guns. At first glance, they looked like any nosy onlooker. Luckily, a patrol officer recognized them immediately and let them through.

Katie slowed her pace, taking everything in and scanning the area before making her way toward the body. Bulldozers were frozen mid-operation, towering over her. The stench of diesel masked the familiar odor of wet earth and pine trees, and all around her trenches and heaped soil battled against the run-off of water from all the rain they'd been having recently. To her left were three large metal construction containers—two had their doors wide open, but it was too dark to see inside.

It was a breathtaking site, with stunning views of the rolling valley all around and large elm and oak trees surrounding the house. The slight breeze made a whispering sound as it threaded through the leaves. It was no wonder someone would want to build their home here.

In the middle of the picture-perfect landscape stood the crippled remains of Elm Hill Mansion, clearly of no use or interest to anyone anymore and waiting to be knocked down. The once beautiful pale blue paint was now peeling from the wood in sections, leaving behind a tarnished beige undercoat—a sickly primer color beginning to seep through and take over.

If you squinted your eyes, it was easy to see that the historical house had once been a beautiful and striking manor. Two large columns at the entrance nodded to its grandeur, and several steps led up to a gorgeous double-door entrance with inlaid blue, green, and yellow stained glass depicting birds in the trees, obviously inspired by the amazing views that surrounded them. The doors hadn't been removed yet, but it looked like they soon would be as the porch that had once wrapped around the front and sides of the mansion had already been removed and replaced with caution tape. Pretty windows on all three stories were now a misfit of broken glass and boarding. Around each window were intricately cut wood designs that added a whimsical fringe and decoration. Most were broken, hanging loose or completely absent. The wind, picking up now, caused loose pieces to rattle against the house.

Glancing behind her, Katie saw the small crowd of construction workers and a couple of other bystanders leaning over the yellow tape, trying to get a look at the scene. At least the area had been cleared quickly and there were hopes of preserving the site.

Katie and McGaven kept their course and walked toward the crime scene. Forensic Supervisor John Blackburn was organizing evidence containers and readying himself to take photographs when instructed, but he kept his distance and waited for Katie to get a first look. He nodded as she walked past.

Detective Bryan Hamilton stood next to a deputy, waiting for Katie. His perfectly pressed suit seemed out of place around the chaotic property. He appeared annoyed, running his fingers anxiously through his sparse hair, but forced a short-lived smile as she approached.

"How would you like to handle this, Detective?" Katie asked respectfully, knowing she was treading on his territory and making sure that her presence wasn't going to cause any more antagonism than was absolutely necessary.

H seemed to relax a little. "It's your show, Scott." He then nodded to McGaven behind her.

"We are all on the same side," said Katie. "I'll tell you what I see so CSI can get started as quickly as possible." It was better to include the detective than to alienate him or anyone else at the Pine Valley Sheriff's Department.

Hamilton hesitated for a moment, and then accompanied Katie toward the sheet shielding the trench.

"Who found the body?" she asked, stopping to look at him.

Detective Hamilton turned and pointed. "The construction foreman; well, actually, one of his bulldozer operators." He looked at his notes. "The foreman is Bob Bramble. He's the short guy in the red shirt."

Katie picked him out from the crowd, and then crouched to study all the heavy shoe prints around the area where she stood. "Did anyone go past this area?"

"I don't think so. The foreman had enough sense to stop everything immediately and call the police," the detective said.

There were several yellow markers at the edge of the property marking the beginning of the crime scene. They were at the side of the land farthest away from the house, overlooking the dense forest where the excess water was being redirected. It looked like the bulldozers were bringing more dirt in, in order to even out the area before the final grading and scraping, and the extra rain water had forced the older soil to collapse.

As Katie slowly walked to the edge of the property, she noticed that the earthmoving equipment stopped towering above the crime scene on the flat ground and about ten feet before the final resting place of the body. The activity from the large construction machines had caused the ground to separate. She limited her movement as she paused where she estimated the foreman and other workers had stood.

Pain pressed against her eyebrows as a slight vertigo washed through her vision for a moment.

Hamilton and McGaven waited patiently as she took a few steps to the left and then the right, studying the erosion of the hillside and how the body appeared to have tumbled out. It was unclear how deep the victim had been buried, but Katie wondered if it was a coincidence she was buried at an obvious drainage point.

"Is this extreme erosion after an extra rainy month? Or just the usual?" she asked, deliberately not looking at the body yet. No one offered any type of response, so she scrutinized the surroundings, looking for anything that might have either disturbed the area recently or been accidentally left at the scene.

Her heart pounded loudly in her ears. She felt her hands tremble so she curled her fingers against her palms to mask the movement. Her vision blurred slightly, causing things to appear dull and leaving her equilibrium somewhat off balance.

Not now…

An all-too-familiar prickly sensation travelled down her arms and legs, confirming her worst fear. Anxiety was the curse she carried with her after two tours in the army. Her post-traumatic stress was something she realized that she would most likely have to bear forever. Some days were easier than others—and she hadn't had an episode in almost two months.

Nothing stays away forever…

Standing at the edge of the crime scene, she fought the invisible enemy that raged within her like a silent storm. If she gave in to it, a full force panic attack would ensue where she would not be able to conduct her investigative duties. She knew all eyes were on her, so she made sure that she breathed slowly and steadily. It calmed her nerves and brought down the adrenalin, but her sensations were still heightened, leaving her feeling unbalanced and totally vulnerable. She hated that feeling more than anything else.

This wasn't her first crime scene, but she had only been involved in a handful. It wasn't the thought of a dead body, but rather the reality of another victim. She had seen many victims on the battlefield, from both sides, and there wasn't anything trivial about it. Every life was a story, just as every death was an ending.

Katie focused on the ground to steady herself. Water was still trickling from the opposite edge of the property and then down into the wooded area in several places. Five feet from the leveled edge was the nude body of a young woman, who appeared to have been dislodged and tumbled through a couple of revolutions before stopping in her current position. Twisted. Broken.

Katie reached into her pocket and took out a pair of plastic gloves. Pulling them on to her trembling hands, she prepared to descend the hillside. She took one step and realized that her running shoes would be ruined from the amount of water and mud she had navigated so far. She sighed but continued sideways and with caution, keeping a watchful eye for any evidence, but making sure that she didn't take a fall down the hillside herself.

As she inched closer, something in the mud caught her attention. It was pink and the sunlight made it appear opalescent.

"I have something," she said and leaned in to carefully remove the mud around the object, revealing a long, torn fingernail decorated with pink nail polish. It had been ripped from the cuticle at the base of the nail. It definitely looked real.

Katie looked up and saw John, the forensic supervisor, coming down to her with an evidence bag and a digital camera hanging around his neck. He carefully followed Katie's footsteps in the mud.

Once by her side, he took several photographs for documentation. Behind him, Katie saw that Detective Hamilton was making notes and McGaven watched with intense interest as John expertly recovered the single fingernail and placed it into the evidence bag. He looked at it closely. "It looks like the nail from an index finger—right index finger," he corrected. He looked at Katie, gave a brief smile, and then waited for her to continue before he started photographing the body.

Katie blinked twice, steadying her nerves, then turned her focus back to the body. Her mind whirled questions.

Did the victim fight until the very last moment? Was that how she lost her fingernail?

Why is she naked?

Wouldn't it have been easier to bury the body in the woods where no one would find it?

Katie inched closer. The girl was partially decomposing. Flesh had rotted away from the upper arms, part of her breast and stomach areas, and one side of her face. The back molars were showing through the vacant patches of skin around the jawline.

She studied the girl's face and head. There didn't appear to be any type of blunt-force trauma or any other obvious injuries. She gently moved the long dark hair away from her face to look at the girl's neck. A welted line common with strangulations was visible. She continued to examine the body and found that the girl's right hand was missing the right index fingernail. Wrapped tightly around the left wrist were the remnants of what appeared to be thin twine—now darkened and deeply embedded into the remaining skin.

She didn't want to move the body in any way until forensics took all the photos necessary to document the scene. She wasn't sure how long it had been buried, but it looked to be six months or more, by the level of decomposition. That was for the medical examiner to conclude. The missing persons report Katie had looked over a couple of weeks back indicated that Candace Harlan was reported missing almost five years ago. If the body was Harlan, she definitely had not been dead for five years. More questions attacked her thoughts.

What was she doing back here?

Why?

The Elm Hill Mansion had been vacated for close to two years. Katie studied the area at the top of the property where the estate stood. The shell of the house looked like a prop on a movie set, and suddenly made the entire crime scene feel staged and strangely unreal.

"Detective Scott," said John.

Katie looked over.

"You need to see this," he said. His voice was anxious and that was out of character for the usually unflappable forensic supervisor.

Katie hurried back up to see what he was referring to.

"Look," he instructed and pointed to the victim's back where a word had been carved with deep cuts to the flesh, but it also appeared as if some type of ink was used. The letters were crudely cut, with some exaggeration on the tail of the *g* now blackened, but still clear enough to read.

"What is it?" asked McGaven at the top of the hill.

"I'm not sure," said Katie slowly. She shuddered to think. "I think it says something like 'raccoglitore'."

"Is that Italian?" asked John.

"I'm not sure," she said again. "Wait... there's more." She carefully crumbled away the mud as more letters appeared beneath.

"What is it?" said Detective Hamilton.

"It says," she began slowly. "It says 'raccoglitore di cacciatori'." Katie thought about the words. It sounded familiar to her, but she wasn't sure why. It wasn't gibberish. It meant something. She said, "Does anyone know Italian, or maybe Portuguese?"

"Wait a minute," said McGaven as he retrieved his phone. "Repeat again slowly."

"Raccoglitore di cacciatori," Katie said enunciating the best she could.

McGaven typed in the words on his cell phone and waited. He quickly read the results, stopped and looked at the detectives.

"What does it mean?" asked Katie. Her heart beat faster, not from anxiety but from anticipation of a message from a killer.

"It means... 'hunter-gatherer'."

CHAPTER FOUR
Monday 1230 hours

The words "hunter-gatherer" echoed through Katie's mind in a strained whisper as she continued searching, but the fingernail and body were the only things identifiable at the scene.

Everyone remained quiet while she worked.

"Detective," Katie finally said when she was sure that she'd missed nothing. "You want to come down here?"

Detective Hamilton hesitated and then said, "No, the least amount of disturbance would be best. John, go ahead and document."

Katie thought it was strange that the detective didn't want to be more involved, but was happy that the scene would not be disturbed any further. She decided to continue down and circumnavigate the hill in order to have a closer look around the surrounding area.

"Thanks, John," she said as she passed him, moving down the hillside until she reached flat ground.

Standing at the edge of the vast landscape, Katie wanted to get a sense of the area at eye level, which appeared to go on forever. She had known about the existence of Elm Hill Mansion for as long as she could remember, but had never been to the property—there had been no reason.

In fact, there had been stories of sightings of female ghosts dressed in old-fashioned clothes seen roaming the property when she was in school. No one she knew had the courage to visit. As she got older, the stories seemed to dissipate. It was nonsense, of course, but as she looked around at the isolation caused by endless woods and the sorry state of the house, she saw how it could conjure up those images.

If she recalled correctly, it had been a private home for a long time, and then the owners left and dedicated it as a home for displaced teen girls in foster care. From the style of the building, she estimated that the mansion was early 1900s, but she would find out for certain when she returned to the office. She looked up the hillside, past the body and crime scene, to the dilapidated estate standing watch over the valley below—it was as if it held the secrets to everyone that had ever lived there.

Katie made a slow 360-degree turn, studying the terrain and access areas. It wasn't an easy approach to the property from the wooded trails. The nearest track led west toward a road, which was a solid half mile. The road leading to the driveway would be optimum but the gate below had been locked for some time, so the only other way would be to walk up the steep hill carrying a body. Not likely.

Instinct told her that the house was significant and held many answers to her questions.

Katie walked toward the southern end of the property where a slightly grooved path crossed the open hillside to the level area, which was behind the house. She quickly moved up the path. Weeds had overgrown it but it was still clear to see it had been traversed many times.

She now looked at the back of the house, noticing where the woodwork appeared newer, darker than the front, still had most of its paint and jutted out instead of sitting flush to the back of the house. It was common to add on a bathroom, laundry area, or even extra storage to a house of this age, but she was certain she was looking at the entrance to a basement of some sort. Getting closer, it appeared it had been used as a secured storm door during bad weather, but had become severely neglected over the years.

Katie hesitated a moment as an uncanny sense overcame her. Maybe it was something to do with her anxiety, maybe it was the reaction of being present at the old decaying house, but she wondered if Candace Harlan had used the basement for her escape. She imagined her breaking out in the middle of the night through the basement door and disappearing.

After taking a few photos with her cell phone, Katie pulled open the basement storm door and looked down into the darkness as a musty odor drafted upward, making her take a step back. Wanting to find something that appeared out of place, she decided to take a quick look around.

Katie moved carefully, her sodden running shoes slapping on each wooden stair as she turned on the flashlight application and pointed her cell phone around the room.

Nothing unusual. Cobwebs, dust, and rotting wood. There wasn't anything on the walls or the narrow shelves lining one corner, which were made for mason jars filled with vegetables and fruits. For due diligence, she took a few photographs before turning back.

Back on the hillside, the team had removed the body and were loading her onto a gurney in a body bag before wheeling her toward an unmarked van.

Katie jogged around the property this time and re-entered the restricted area. As she bent down to slide underneath the yellow tape, she glanced at the crowd. She quickly tallied the onlookers and found that there were eleven people. Most bystanders were talking among themselves while the rest were watching as the gurney slowly made its way to the van.

Acting on instinct, Katie took two quick photos of the group with her cell phone. They were all men, but she could easily differentiate the construction crew from the others by their work clothes and heavy boots. There were seven by her count, making it six more men than happened to be near when the police arrived. Two had baseball caps and their hoods pulled up so it was difficult to see their identity easily.

"Hey," said McGaven as Katie arrived back beside him. "Find anything?"

Taking one last glimpse at the crowd, she said, "No. I just took a quick walk around the mansion."

Detective Hamilton caught Katie's attention.

"Here we go," she said, dreading having another conversation with him, knowing that the sheriff wanted her and McGaven to take over the case. It wasn't the first time.

"John and one of the techs are going to comb through the area to see if anything else pops up," he said.

"Great," replied Katie trying to sound upbeat.

"Look," the detective began. "I know that things, well, actually circumstances, haven't been the best, but I wanted you to know that there are no hard feelings."

Katie was caught off guard by his statement. She stared blankly at him.

Detective Hamilton offered his hand to Katie. "Detective, I hear I've been relieved from this investigation and that you are to take over," he said and shook her hand. "McGaven," he continued, and shook the deputy's hand, "let me know if there's anything more you need from me. I will forward you my current notes for the case."

"Thank you, Detective," Katie managed to say. Shocked.

Hamilton began to walk away and then suddenly turned to face Katie. "I know it's more than overdue, but I am truly sorry for your loss."

Katie nodded, appreciating the sentiment and finally understanding why Hamilton was being so uncharacteristically unproblematic about her being assigned to his case. Her aunt's recent murder still hurt her deeply and Detective Hamilton had been the lead detective on her case. Due to the high emotions surrounding the investigation of the murder of her aunt, the sheriff being the prime suspect, the entire police department had been turned upside-down.

"I just wanted you to know," he said and walked away.

McGaven said, "Well, I didn't know that hell had frozen over."

Katie watched the detective direct the bystanders to disperse. "No, I don't believe it has…"

"He put you through a lot of crap during the investigation into your aunt's death. I'm not so sure that all is forgiven from his perspective. But, it's a start," he said, still watching the detective.

"I know… but we need to concentrate on this case," she said, not wanting to think about work politics. "We have a lot of graft ahead of us. First, we need to look at Candace Harlan's missing persons report in more detail."

CHAPTER FIVE
Monday 1345 hours

Katie sat in silence, staring at the road rushing past her window as McGaven drove them back to the Pine Valley Sheriff's Department. It wasn't an uncomfortable quiet, but rather, a familiar respect for the fact each of them was lost in their own personal thoughts of the homicide at the Elm Hill Mansion. They had worked enough cases together to know staying quiet wasn't anything personal.

The body twisted and contorted. The words carved into her back. Katie searched her brain for what "hunter-gatherer" might mean to the killer.

"Katie?"

Did it mean that the killer was hunting for victims? She ran different scenarios through her thought process. Had he killed before? Would he do it again? How was Elm Hill Mansion involved? Did the killer intend for the body to be found, or was it just bad luck with the recent rain?

"Katie?" McGaven said again.

She realized that McGaven had been talking to her. "I'm sorry," she said, and turned to look at him.

"You better be," he replied, cracking a big smile.

"I was just thinking that the killer took a big risk."

"What do you mean? Isn't killing technically taking a risk?"

"Some killers take those precious final moments to pose the body, fulfill a fantasy, or enjoy the silence. But this killer took extra time to carve his message on her back. Because it was important to him."

McGaven took a corner too fast, making the tires squeal.

"Hey, are we late for something?" she said.

"Sorry, this car doesn't handle like the previous one I'm used to. I know that this vehicle is retrofitted for K9 and seems to have more power…" His mouth had turned downward.

"I haven't had a chance to buy a new car yet," Katie grumbled, remembering the incidents that led up to her Jeep being totaled.

McGaven turned into the police department parking lot and around to the private area behind the administration building before pulling into the usual parking place.

Katie opened the door and rushed toward the building followed closely by McGaven. As the heavy door closed behind them, Katie turned to him and said, "I'll meet you in the office in a few. I need to change."

"And shower," he said and hurried toward the men's locker room.

Katie smiled as she passed two female deputies on their way to patrol, and said hello to them.

"Hey, Detective," they acknowledged.

The locker room was deserted.

Katie quickly went to her locker and dialed up the combination lock. With such an unpredictable job, she always kept an additional change of clothes for just this type of situation. A brown suit fresh from the dry cleaners, two blouses, undergarments, and an extra pair of boots. She grabbed two clean towels from the supply area before she stripped down to take a quick shower.

Ten minutes later, she was drying her hair when she noticed a folded piece of paper at the bottom of the locker. She was certain it hadn't been there before. Could someone have dropped it there while she was in the shower? She looked around, suddenly self-conscious, her skin prickling. She walked around the rows of lockers but there wasn't anyone around. There was a white sports sock on the floor that must've escaped someone's gym bag; otherwise, it was completely empty.

"Hello?" she said, just to be sure, before walking slowly back to her locker.

Silence, only interrupted by the ventilation system turning on overhead. Comfortable that she was indeed alone in the locker room, Katie unfolded the small torn piece of paper. It wasn't handwritten. In fact, it wasn't a note at all. It was torn from a larger piece of paper, leaving three legible letters—"ETL"—and on the far corner it said "Express". There was half of a ripped diamond shape on one side. She felt certain the note hadn't accidentally fallen into her locker, that someone was trying to tell her something and she was supposed to figure it out. But she also knew that her inquisitive mind often worked overtime—and that it could be nothing. Not everything revolved around the murders that crossed her desk. There could be a million reasons why this piece of paper had found its way into her locker.

Katie didn't want to break her momentum with the current case, so she pocketed the piece of paper, deciding to discuss it with McGaven later. Shutting her locker, she left the changing room, headed down the hallway and stopped at a familiar unmarked door. A small camera attached to the upper door frame was directed downward at anyone who stood at the entrance. She swiped her keycard and the lock disengaged with a buzz and a click.

The area was the forensic division of the police department, but it felt like another world. Cut off from the outside, with no windows, and the constant hum of the air being circulated, previously gave Katie a strange almost claustrophobic feeling, but now she felt safe and comfortable. She had been given the chance to occupy a couple of empty offices down here to set up the cold-case unit.

As she walked past one of the large forensic examination rooms, she spotted John hunched over a scanning electron microscope, completely unaware of her presence. She paused, wanting to say hello, thought better, and then moved on down a long hallway to her office.

McGaven sat at his desk deep in research on the computer. His short hair had already dried and he looked refreshed now dressed in his slacks and long-sleeved shirt. Katie could smell the lemony shampoo he often used.

"You beat me," she said.

"Well, I don't need to get all dolled up."

"Funny." She dropped her jacket on her desk. "What are you looking at here?"

"I'm trying to locate more about the Elm Hill Mansion, but I'm just finding rumors and ghost stories, nothing that is worthy of the investigation."

Katie pulled the missing persons file for Candace Harlan and grabbed a notebook. "This is Candace's file. It was in a stack with several others I had been considering for our next case. Wow, there's not much to the report."

Turning his chair towards her, he said, "So what do we have?"

"Five years ago, last June, Shelly McDonald, manager at the house, called the police to report that one of the foster girls in her care was missing. Candace Harlan, sixteen years old, five foot seven, 125 pounds, brown hair, hazel eyes, last seen wearing a white nightgown. There were a few clothing items missing, such as her favorite pink sweater," Katie said, reading the basic information and pausing to look at her photograph. Reading down, she said, "It looks like the deputy that took the report was… Deputy Hugh Keller."

"Oh," said McGaven in a dull tone.

"What?"

"Keller was fired about a year and half ago."

"For?"

"Not following orders, using excessive force. He wasn't cut out to be a police officer."

"That's a nice way of putting it."

"Oh, and he was a jerk."

"Okay, that's better," she smiled. "According to McDonald, Candace was there at bed check around 11 p.m., but in the morning she was gone. She said that she thought she ran away with a boyfriend—but didn't have a name."

"How many other girls were there living at the house?"

"It refers to six, including Harlan: Mary Rodriguez, Tanis Jones, Heather Lawson, Terry Slaughter, and Karen Beck. The other girls were all accounted for."

"And none of them knew what happened to her?" he said.

"They spoke to them all. Her roommate, Tanis Jones, stated that Candace was there when she went to sleep and was gone in the morning." Katie frowned. "Wouldn't you think that the roommate would have some idea what happened?"

"Maybe, but maybe she didn't care, or maybe she was sworn to secrecy."

"It says here that Candace didn't have any family. She was given up for adoption—which never happened, so unfortunately she stayed in the foster care system for her entire childhood."

"That's really sad."

Flipping through pages, she said, "There are notations here for other report numbers."

"Let me see."

Katie turned the file to McGaven. "Oh, that means there were police calls to the house. That seems like a lot of calls for assistance."

"How many?"

"Seventeen."

"That's excessive. Make sure we get all those reports and the names of the reporting deputies too."

"On it," he said. "Don't you want to start your profile of the killer?"

"Not just yet. For now I'm more interested in the location, and why the killer thought it was a perfect place to bury a body. Why there and not in some rural area where it wouldn't be found?" She strained her view to see what McGaven had on the screen.

"Okay," he said and turned the laptop so that Katie could see it. "The current owners of Elm Hill Mansion are listed as Magnum Development, Incorporated."

"I've never heard of them."

"Seems Magnum Development, Incorporated, or MDI, is a company with many offices nationwide, but their main offices are in Miami, Florida."

"Interesting," she said.

"Previous owners?"

"Sara and Jonathan McKinzie."

"Local?"

"No. Well…" McGaven stalled.

"Well what?"

"When I try to get their address, or at least mailing address, it's like I'm being taken on a wild goose chase."

Katie frowned and thought about reasons why someone would not want their personal information on public record. "What about the real estate transaction, new ownership, or escrow paperwork?"

"I don't know. I don't seem to be able to find anything right off. It looks like it was paid in cash."

"What is the actual address that the county assessor's office has on file?" she asked.

"I have 403 Elm Hill Road, but…"

Katie read over his shoulder. "But there's also an older address of 407 Elm Hill Road. So… which one is correct?"

"Maybe the property was divided up and there is more than one registered address? I just can't seem to locate them." He sighed. "I can't even find the basic info on the house, like square footage or exactly how much land there is."

Katie stood up and pulled over the movable whiteboard so that they could both see it. "I guess we need to start with what we know right now." She picked up a black marker and began writing down several headings: Crime Scene, Body, Victim, Elm Hill Mansion, and Killer.

"Okay."

"Excuse me," came a voice from behind them.

"Hey, Denise," said Katie, turning and smiling at her friend who supervised the records division.

McGaven immediately stood up.

"Hi," said Denise to him.

"Hi."

"Here's the information from Detective Hamilton from the Elm Hill place." She put the file on Katie's desk.

"Thanks," Katie said.

"And, I was supposed to tell you both that the sheriff wants daily updates—beginning at the end of today."

Katie groaned.

"Sorry to be the bearer of bad news."

"No, you're not," said Katie. "It's just that this was supposed to be Hamilton's case and we don't even know the identity of the victim yet. Well, we do, I guess, but it's not official."

"And on that note," said Denise. "I'll let you two get back to work."

"Bye, babe," said McGaven. "I mean, Denise."

"Bye," she said and was gone.

"Oh brother," Katie said.

"What?"

"You guys are too cute."

"Give me a break…"

Flipping open Hamilton's case file, Katie quickly perused the information. "There's not much here beyond what we already know. Except he has the names of all the workers and the foreman. But…"

"But what?" McGaven asked looking at Katie.

"You said Magnum Development?"

"Yeah."

"Here, it says that the demo company is Edison, Fullerton, and Taylor Demolition Company."

McGaven scrolled through the computer. "I don't see that name anywhere connected with Elm Hill Project."

"Maybe it's nothing, but…"

The internal office phone rang.

Katie picked up the receiver, "Scott."

"Detective Scott, this is Dr. Dean."

"Yes, Dr. Dean, what can we do for you?" Katie's heart skipped a beat. For the medical examiner to call her this quickly, it meant something very important.

"Do you have time to come to the morgue?" he asked.

"Of course, we'll be right there."

"See you soon," the medical examiner said. "Bye." He hung up.

Katie returned the phone to its cradle on the desk.

"What?" McGaven impatiently asked, waiting for her response.

"We've been summoned to the morgue," she said.

CHAPTER SIX
Monday 1545 hours

At the morgue, Katie and McGaven rushed around the corner and down the hallway where they almost careened into a couple of morgue technicians heading in the opposite direction. Whether Dr. Dean had their first clue or their first dead end, Katie couldn't wait to hear.

Once they entered through the main door, they automatically slowed their pace as Katie led the way down the hallway, through large double doors, and then on toward one of the examination rooms where she spotted Dr. Dean leaning over a desk writing notes, their victim's body exposed on a stainless steel exam table beside him. Katie instinctively felt the urge to cover her, to keep her warm and give her back some dignity.

"Dr. Dean?" said Katie quietly, as though she might wake the sleeping girl beside her.

The middle-aged doctor looked up and smiled. Taking his gold-rimmed glasses off, he greeted them. "Ah, Detective Scott and Deputy McGaven. Please come in."

Returning his glasses, he finished signing a few documents and then closed the file, looked up and removed his glasses once again. It had been a while since his last haircut, which left his curly dark hair too long and unruly. Underneath his white lab coat, his usual choice of work clothes were a Hawaiian shirt, khaki cargo shorts, and rubber sandals. "Thanks for meeting me here so quickly."

"Have you been able to confirm her identity?" Katie asked. She wanted to get right to the point—the sooner the better.

The doctor took a deep breath and said, "Yes, and no."

"I'm sorry?" she said, her enthusiasm dwindling.

He grabbed one of the folders labeled Candace Harlan and retrieved some dental x-rays labeled "Crossroads Plaza Dental" and placed them alongside a set of x-rays already attached to the light board.

Katie glanced at them. She wasn't sure what she was supposed to be seeing but studied each dental map as if she did.

"Here are Candace Harlan's dental records; she had some work done about ten months ago. And here are the dental images I took from the body brought in earlier."

Katie tried to hide her excitement that Candace had been alive just ten months ago, not to mention her first lead – a visit to the dental office.

"But, here's the problem. The victim *isn't* Candace Harlan."

Shocked, Katie responded, "What?" Everything in her calculating investigative mind said that the murder victim was Candace Harlan. The location. Her approximate age and size. It all made sense. It had to be her.

"I know, it threw me at first too. But…" He pointed at both sets of x-rays. "The victim's incisors are different, with a slight imbalance here on the left side, and she still has her wisdom teeth, unlike Candace Harlan."

McGaven studied them. "They don't match."

"I'm sorry, but you've lost me," Katie said, still stunned.

Dr. Dean smiled. "The woman you see on the table isn't Candace Harlan." He shuffled through more paperwork. "Like Candace, your victim is a healthy female, between twenty and twenty-five, five foot seven inches tall, 120 pounds, hazel eyes, but she is *not* Candace Harlan."

Katie nodded.

"Okay…" started Dr. Dean. He moved the table at an angle and began his dissertation on his findings. "This is my preliminary examination, but I think it will help you both get started on the investigation and give you a direction. I've already emailed you what I'm going to tell you now and I will update you when the autopsy and toxicology reports are finalized."

"Of course," she said, her voice sounding a bit hoarse and tinny in the room.

"Cause of death—asphyxiation by strangulation. It appears that a thin twine of some type was used. Similar to the twine tied around her wrist. I've forwarded this information to John to see if he can get a better clarification for you. And… of course, manner of death, I'm ruling a homicide."

"Was there any other trauma to the body? Injuries? Sexual or otherwise?" she asked.

"No," he said and politely waited for her to ask more questions.

Katie studied the body, noting the missing skin and decomposition. "How long do you think she has been dead?"

"About two to three months based on decomposition, the condition of the body, and soil type. I'm not familiar with the area she was recovered from, but I know we've had an unusual amount of rain these past few weeks so that could change that estimate, give or take two weeks."

"These bare areas," Katie said, pointing to patches of missing flesh. "Is that normal after being buried in the soil underground for that amount of time?"

"Generally speaking—yes."

"What about…" began Katie. She paused and then said, "Can we see her back?"

"Of course."

Dr. Dean rolled the girl to one side so Katie and McGaven could see her back. Katie pulled her cell phone from her pocket and took a quick photo of the writing.

"What do you think made those marks?" she said.

"Hard to say, but it was definitely done post mortem. The blood had already stopped pumping, which made it easier for the killer to make the letters with less bleeding and no movement."

Katie leaned closer.

"If you look at it magnified it's not a clean cut you would get from a precision instrument like a scalpel. It's thick with a blunt or a curved side." He read the words out loud. "My Italian is minimal, but it's something about a tracker?"

"Close. It means hunter-gatherer."

"Wasn't there an old movie called *Hunter-Gatherer*?"

Katie looked at McGaven as the doctor let the body lie on its back again.

He shook his head. "I don't know, but I'm going to check everywhere."

"There you go," the doctor said. "I'm sorry, but I'm late for an appointment. Do you need anything else right now?"

"No, I think we can get started."

"Nice to see you both," he said, looking directly at Katie.

"Thank you for the speedy information, Doctor."

"My pleasure. I wanted you to know that your victim isn't Candace Harlan as soon as possible," he said and left the room.

Katie took another look at the body before she headed for the door.

"So, Candace Harlan is still missing?" said McGaven following her.

"Afraid so," she said.

"So is it still our homicide? I mean, it's not one of our cold cases."

Katie sighed. "Technically, you're right. We need to talk to the sheriff."

"I was afraid you were going to say that."

CHAPTER SEVEN
Monday 1935 hours

Katie drove the unmarked police cruiser up her long driveway and cut the engine. She sat behind the wheel and didn't move at first. It was only Monday and she was already exhausted. Glancing at her watch, it was later than she realized. A familiar sound interrupted her musings over the new homicide. The distinct bark could only belong to a German shepherd. Loud. Rapid. And at times incessant.

"I'm coming, Cisco," she said, popping out of the car and trudging toward the front porch of her farmhouse carrying her thoughts about the case along with her physical things.

Opening the front door, the sleek black dog with wolfish amber eyes bounced with happiness around her, barely allowing her to enter the living room.

"Hey, big guy. You have a good day?" she said. Her voice only made him even more excited. She dropped everything she was carrying by the front door as the eighty-pound dog circled several times around her and then bounced up and off the couch before he began to settle down. A few high-pitched whines and a look as if to say "where have you been?" followed Katie into the kitchen where she set to work preparing his meal.

"Sorry I'm so late today. We have a new case. At least, I think it's our case," she said, watching him gobble down his food and remembering the times she had fed him when they were on tour in Afghanistan—outside, in tents, and various other makeshift camps. Not all those memories were traumatizing. She had been paired with Cisco and made friends there she would keep forever. They were all bonds that could never be broken. She was grateful that her uncle was able to call in some favors and coordinate Cisco's release back to the US—as a hero dog after several tours and dozens, if not a hundred, of explosive finds. Katie had lost count.

Katie hurried to her bedroom and quickly changed into a comfy pair of pajamas. She was going to get to bed early tonight, because tomorrow was going to be a long day at work. There were so many things running through her mind that she just wanted to get sleep over and done with so she could get started.

A cold nose touched her hand; Cisco nuzzled her as if to tell her that he had missed her and wanted her to stay with him.

"Okay, let's go outside."

The dog padded along behind her to the sliding door leading to the backyard. She opened the door and Cisco dashed outside. The area had been specially fenced for him, to keep him safe and happy, but in a way that still allowed for the beauty of the rural setting to be enjoyed. Solid pine trees skirted the ten meandering acres, some even fifty feet tall. Mature lemon and orange trees grew along one side of the property along with two large walnut trees. In between were blooming bushes and flowers that had been planted originally by her parents—specifically her dad. He had loved the outdoors, and wanted to make his yard and surrounding property as bountiful with nature as possible. In her mind, he had succeeded. Once her childhood home, the house passed to her after her parents were killed in an accident when she was a teenager. Cisco and her uncle were her only family now.

Katie stood on the patio and took in the crisp air filling her lungs, allowing her to unwind—remembering fond times when she was young—playing and running around the acreage. She shivered slightly, but it helped her to focus on the moment instead of what had happened in the past. She watched as Cisco made his usual rounds of checking the fence and some interesting bushes, did his business, and finally returned to her inside the house.

Glancing at her watch, she had a few minutes before her 8 p.m. forty-five minute virtual session with Dr. Megan Carver. The psychologist had made special arrangements with Katie for online bi-monthly sessions. It was important to have the meetings on Mondays, per Dr. Carver's instruction, due to the fact Katie's anxiety was generally higher at the beginning of the week.

Katie opened the refrigerator and took out some cold chicken leftovers from the night before and quickly ate a piece. She would make something proper to eat after her session.

She moved to the living room, sat down on the couch, and opened her laptop. Feeling more relaxed with the comfort of being at home, she took a couple of deep breaths and keyed up the app to wait for Dr. Carver's call. She tried to push the images of the victim out of her head, but the ominous carved letters glared back at her.

Cisco edged his way closer to Katie on the couch and tucked his body in tight next to her.

A high-pitch ringing sound emitted from the computer. On the screen, it read: *Megan Carver, LCSW MFT.* It was exactly 8 p.m.

Katie accepted the call and a window popped up showing a woman with dark brown hair loosely pulled back away from her face. She put her glasses on and smiled. "Hi, Katie," she said.

Katie smiled. "Hi, Dr. Carver."

"Are you ready?" the doctor said.

Katie nodded. "Yep."

"Why don't you start by telling me about your day today?"

Katie tensed. "Well, it was rather eventful."

"What was the first thing that you did today after leaving the house?"

"Well, I went for a run with my partner McGaven." She smiled. "He's trying to lose a few pounds and asked me to run with him."

Dr. Carver wrote down some notes that Katie couldn't see. Looking back at the computer, she asked, "How were you feeling on your run?"

"Fine."

"Did you experience any out of place feeling or strong emotions?"

"I don't think so. I love running—it's my way of creating time and space from everything else."

"But you shared it with your partner?"

"Yes, but…"

Dr. Carver waited patiently for Katie to explain.

"It's different," Katie finally said.

"How?"

"It's… just different. It was more friend time instead of alone time." Katie began to feel a pressure build in her chest. She took a deeper breath, trying to relax.

"So, you chose to run with your friend, your partner. He's important to you?"

"Of course."

"I know that you told me that he had recently been involved in a shooting and that he spent time in the hospital."

"Yes." Katie readjusted herself on the couch. She wanted to run, unsure of where, but just run away. The feeling haunted her. The room seemed to shrink around her, making it difficult to breathe.

"How did it make you feel?" the doctor gently pushed.

Katie wasn't sure how to answer. She had all kinds of feelings: discomfort, dread, fear, anxiety. What did the doctor really want to know? Feeling uncontrollable emotions were a part of everyday life for Katie. Anxious energy shuddered through her body.

Dr. Carver kept her eyes on Katie. She pushed again, "How did it make you feel when Deputy McGaven was shot and ended up in the hospital?"

"How do you think it made me feel?" Katie's voice cracked slightly under the pressure. "I felt responsible. What if he..." She couldn't finish the sentence.

"Died?"

"Yes. What if he had died?"

"You would feel responsible?"

"Of course."

"Did you push McGaven to make the decision he did?" Her voice was calm and therapeutic.

The doctor's calmness made Katie angry. She had no right to question how she had felt during the shooting incident. McGaven chose to follow Katie into a trap she had set up to draw out a killer. It had been his choice, but he had helped to save her life too.

"Katie, you know that you're only responsible for yourself and not for the decisions that McGaven or others make."

"Yes..." Katie pinched back tears. "But I'm involved. It's what partners do. They have your back. I made an impulsive decision because I didn't want anyone else to suffer the consequences..."

"You can't carry the burden for everyone else... otherwise, there's a breaking point. You can't carry that. You have to give yourself permission to take care of yourself. To grieve when necessary. To give yourself a break."

"You don't understand. If the roles and situation were switched, I would have done the same thing for McGaven—without hesitation. And that's... and that's why it hurts so much. I've lost too many friends and family." She leaned back and let tears roll down her cheeks. Grabbing a Kleenex from the table, she dabbed her eyes.

Cisco, feeling her change in energy, sat up and pushed even closer to her. He nuzzled the side of her face.

"Take a deep breath, Katie," Dr. Carver said, never breaking from her calm and even tone.

"I'm sorry." Katie was fighting to keep her emotions in check. "So, yes to your question. I feel responsible for McGaven being shot. I feel responsible for him being in that situation in the first place. I knew that he would be fine, but it dredged up so many situations. Such vivid recollections from the battlefield—like I'm still there. I saw death. I saw suffering. Too many times I was the last person a dying soldier saw before they passed. I cannot stop this endless loop of people I care for... dying..."

"You know that McGaven is fine. He's alive. He's well and he's still your partner?"

It amazed Katie how unfazed Dr. Carver was by her outburst. The muscles in her face didn't twitch. "Of course."

"You must take one thing at a time—right?"

"Yes."

"It's not about your partner—that's not why you came to see me—but it's a good place to start. You work together. He's your friend. Enjoy that. Let the heaviness of "what if" or "what might" because of previous experiences go. It will take time. Write down every uncomfortable thought you have—it will be helpful for you to read and look back on."

"I know what you're telling me is correct, but it doesn't feel that way," said Katie, feeling suddenly exhausted and wanting the day to be over.

"That's okay," she said. "Let the feelings come, and we can address them together, and then finally let them go. You will begin to feel better—I promise."

"You make it sound easy." Katie nervously laughed. "One, two, and three..."

"It isn't," the doctor said flatly. "But, I know you're strong and I know you'll get through this and move forward with a healthy attitude."

Katie nodded. She knew that the doctor was using a recent situation as a gateway into the more deep-rooted and traumatic experiences that truly haunted her. Start small and then move to the bigger obstacles. She'd do the same in Dr. Carver's position.

Let the feelings come…

Move forward with a healthy attitude…

CHAPTER EIGHT
Tuesday 0730 hours

Katie and McGaven sat alone in the patrol briefing room waiting for Sheriff Scott to make an appearance. They had been summoned early to meet with him. The room was set up like a classroom with chairs and desks in neat rows in front of a podium, computer screen and large blackboard. The soft buzz of the overhead fluorescent lights was the only thing keeping them company. It cast a yellowish hue, making everything seem ugly.

It was unusual to meet in the large room instead of in the sheriff's personal office. Katie tried to figure out what her uncle had in mind. It obviously had to do with the Candace Harlan cold case and the fact that the latest homicide victim wasn't her. She tapped her foot trying to combat the anxious energy charging through her and pushed away any early signs of her silent enemy.

She glanced to McGaven. He sat at attention, spine straight, with his eyes forward; always ready and waiting for whatever came next. Katie was about to say something to him, but decided to stay quiet.

The main door opened and Sheriff Scott seemed to hesitate before entering the room. Katie heard low voices in the corridor. Finally, the sheriff opened the door wide and was followed by a tall, striking blonde woman, in her forties, wearing a dark suit. Next came Detective Hamilton, John Blackburn from forensics, Lieutenant Commander Reyes, Lieutenant Sanders from the detective division, and the head of internal affairs. It was quite the ensemble.

Katie felt her pulse kick up another gear as the group filed in and took their places near the podium—this wasn't going to be pleasant.

The door opened again and several deputies and a few other detectives filed in quietly and took available seats in the audience around Katie and McGaven.

The tension was palpable as Sheriff Scott moved behind the podium to begin. Katie noted that her uncle looked strong. His tanned face, chiseled features, and greyish cropped hair made him handsome, but his demeanor today really made the crowd sit up and pay attention. It had taken him a while to move through the grieving process after his wife's murder, but it made Katie happy to see that he was beginning to thrive once again as the department's respected leader.

"Thank you, everyone, for coming. I'm sorry it was last minute, but rather than leaving messages, I wanted to do this in person. This department has been through a lot of changes as well as challenges of late. I wanted to talk to you in person to thank you all for the overwhelming support I have received during my most difficult time…"

Katie watched intently as her uncle addressed the room. Her arms tingled, a sign of a big change coming.

"And for that I want to thank you—each of you," he said. He then turned and gestured to the woman in the suit standing closest to him. "This is Dorothy Sullivan, our new undersheriff. She will be taking the place of Samuel Martinez, who has recently resigned."

Katie watched Sullivan with curiosity. Expensive outfit, perfect coifed blonde hair, three-inch heels, studded stone earrings, and a diamond ring worn on her right hand. She looked professional, but Katie had a difficult time imagining her doing the rounds in a police officer's uniform or engaging in a shootout.

The sheriff continued, "She comes to us from the Fresno Police Department with an amazing resumé where she implemented new patrol and detective protocols to help ensure safety for our officers while increasing patrol for the neighborhoods. Her background in police and community proactive safety and Neighborhood Watch has been receiving positive results in many other jurisdictions as well. She's been a patrol officer, homicide detective, and SWAT officer. She will oversee some of the patrol and detective operations here." He moved out of the way and allowed Sullivan to approach the podium to say a few words.

"Thank you, Sheriff Scott. I won't bore everyone and take up your time, but I want to say that I'm looking forward to meeting and working with each one of you. I've met with Sheriff Scott on several occasions and we have the same vision for the department. I cannot wait to get started and we can work together to make Pine Valley Sheriff's Department one of the best in the state of California. Thank you."

Katie looked at McGaven who seemed just as surprised as she was at the sudden announcement.

"Okay, patrol, you are dismissed," the sheriff stated.

As the group began to filter out of the room, Katie and McGaven stood up to leave as well.

"Scott and McGaven, not you two," Sheriff Scott stated. There was no inflection in his voice except business, which made it difficult to know if he had good or bad news for them.

They moved to the front line of desks and took a seat to wait and hear what their fate was at the department—and more importantly what was going to happen to the cold-case unit.

"First," the sheriff began, "we want to commend you both for your exceptional work in solving cold cases for the department and the community, especially in such a short period of time. Your efficiency and creativeness have been exemplary. But…"

Here it comes…

"It has come to our attention that certain protocols have recently been taken without the proper channel of authority's authorization.

Detective Scott, even though the department commends you on your hard work and unfailing dedication, we cannot overlook some actions on your part…"

Oh crap…

"Taking an investigation into your own hands by trapping a killer and putting your partner and forensic supervisor in the line of fire is never acceptable. All without proper protocol and chain of command. Your personnel file will reflect these lapses in judgment, but it will in no way demote or change your current position. The reason why we have such chains of command is for your safety. I cannot emphasize enough how important it is for a law enforcement officer to follow the rules and get the proper authority to go through the proper channels. If we don't follow simple rules, then we will be faced with chaos and potential loss of life."

Katie fidgeted in her seat, but never averted her gaze from her uncle. She didn't dare look at anyone else but she knew all eyes were on her.

"Now, on to the real business at hand," the sheriff said.

What the…

"Since the latest homicide victim hasn't been identified yet, but is not Candace Harlan the missing girl we first assumed her to be, this puts us in an unusual situation. We have decided, after careful consideration, due to the information available and the work already done on the Candace Harlan's missing persons case, it should be headed up by the cold-case unit. If they deem additional help necessary, it would be proper to provide it."

Katie let out the breath she didn't know she'd been holding. She tried to wrap her brain around the fact that she was reprimanded and a permanent record of her conduct in trying to find her aunt's killer would be lodged in her file, but she was still being given a recent homicide to investigate.

"Is there any problem with taking the case?" the sheriff asked.

Katie blinked and said, "No, not at all."

"Good. Of course, John and Detective Hamilton will be available to you as well."

"Yes, much appreciated." Katie finally made eye contact with the rest of the group. John cracked a slight smile although Detective Hamilton's serious expression was hard to read.

The sheriff went on to explain that they had to continue writing daily reports and submitting them to him and internal affairs. Katie's mind went numb, still trying to work out what was going on. When the sheriff had finished, he excused her and McGaven and began talking with the other members.

Katie tapped McGaven on the shoulder and they just were heading out of the room when Undersheriff Sullivan stopped her.

"Detective Scott?" she said, her voice low and direct.

"Yes?"

"I wanted to tell you in person. I've read your file and the cases that you've closed. And I'm impressed—*really* impressed," she said.

"Thank you, ma'am."

"And I really would like to chat with you sometime about profiling and victimology."

"Yes, of course. I would like that," said Katie, not really meaning it, but wanting to be polite nonetheless.

"Good. We'll meet up soon." She left.

In a whisper, McGaven said, "New friend?"

"Looks like it."

Katie and McGaven hurried through the door and down the hallway.

"I'm sorry about the reprimand," he said.

"I'm not."

"C'mon, I think you'd be a little bit bummed."

"No."

"Yes you are."

"Okay, maybe a little. But I would do what I did again in a heartbeat."

CHAPTER NINE
Tuesday 0845 hours

Back in her office, Katie plunged herself into the investigation with renewed energy, filling out the lists of what they knew—even though the murder investigation had already started with an unexpected twist. Once she was finished scribbling on the big whiteboard, she stood back to take it all in from afar.

"I'm struggling too," said McGaven, reading her mind. "Trying to get my wits around everything so far, especially after that meeting."

His voice startled Katie, who had been concentrating so hard she'd forgotten he was in the room. "Our murder victim is our main objective," she said. "But everything we know up to this point about Candace Harlan is also important. They are connected—somehow." Her voice trailed off. She was stumped for the time being.

"What are the odds that a murder victim dumped at Elm Hill Mansion would so resemble Candace Harlan's profile?"

"Well," said Katie. "We need to start at the beginning."

"Meaning?"

"The missing persons report and the crime-scene location."

"Candace Harlan and Elm Hill Mansion." He nodded in agreement.

"Exactly," she said as she flipped open the missing persons file and studied her notes. "We don't have much from the missing persons report and the crime scene creates more questions than answers."

"Isn't that the way every investigation begins?" he said, trying to sound optimistic.

"Okay, wise guy. Have you found anything more on the house yet?"

"It looks like it was built in 1895, but that's all, so far."

"I could visit my friend Shane Kendall, the archivist at the county building, to search for anything about the house and property."

"Sounds solid," he said, typing something, hitting the "enter" button and sitting back to wait for the search engine to churn. "Oh."

"Oh? What does that mean?" she said.

"The house manager, a Mrs. Shelly McDonald, maiden name Shelly Deville, is serving five years for burglary. Most likely be out in two."

"Great. She might give us information in return for a good word to her parole officer. Her relationship status?"

"Looks like she was married to a Douglas McDonald and divorced ten years ago. No information regarding any contact after that."

Katie stood up; her muscles were tight and a numbing headache pushed against her sinuses as she tried to see a way through all this partial information. "We need to have Denise run a report for those requests for police assistance at the house, and… can you find out the social worker, or social workers, who placed girls at that home?"

"On it."

"If you can, we also need to find out who worked at Elm Hill Mansion. There had to be a cook, maid, groundskeeper, or someone besides the manager. They could be listed as county employees."

"I'll get on this right away, but it might be a bit of a waiting game for responses."

"Maybe Denise can help?" she suggested.

"Denise is awesome," he said as he sent an email to request information.

Katie turned to him and smiled. "She definitely is…"

"I ran background on Candace Harlan, but there's nothing after the time she stayed at Elm Hill."

Katie frowned, looking at her notepad. "Well, let's go see what Crossroads Plaza Dental has to say."

Looking up, he said, "Road trip?"

"You bet, let's go."

Katie drove with McGaven straight to the local dentist, not bothering to call ahead of time. She knew that Candace Harlan was a patient there from the x-rays forwarded to the medical examiner's office, and she wanted to acquire as much information as she could on Candace's last known whereabouts while she waited on other leads.

Pulling into the Crossroads Plaza shopping area, Katie easily found a parking place. There were three cars around back, probably employees, and two customer cars in front.

The building was large, square, one-story, and had many windows. It was a pretty structure with low-lying shrubs and a few late-blooming flowers hanging in baskets near the entrance. Two benches faced each other where patients could wait, and stenciled on gold strips by the door were the names Dr. Thomas Elgin, DDS and Dr. Francis E. McAlister, DDS.

"Dr. Elgin is Candace's dentist," she said and opened the wide glass door.

Inside, the air conditioner was on full force, which seemed strange since it was fall and the weather wasn't at all hot. She caught the immediate smell of a disinfectant and other chemicals. The large waiting room had several couches with big pillows and a dozen chairs in rows. There was one man sitting in the corner waiting.

He looked up from his magazine and gave Katie a once-over—it wasn't clear if it was because she was a woman, or the fact that she had her badge and gun visible.

Behind a plexiglass barrier was a young woman with short brown hair, oversized glasses, and a neat blue uniform. Pinned to her top was a smiling bear face with the name Cara beneath.

The woman looked up and saw Katie and McGaven. "Hi… Can I help you?" she said, forcing a smile though her eyes were glued to McGaven's gun.

"Hi," McGaven said, taking the lead and looking at her name tag, "Cara."

She smiled.

"I'm Deputy McGaven and this is my partner Detective Scott. We're from the Pine Valley Sheriff's Department. We're here following up on an investigation. I wonder if you could help us?" he said with a smile.

"Sure," she replied enthusiastically.

"Is Dr. Elgin here?"

"Yes, he is, but he's in surgery at the moment."

"I see. Well, I'm sure you can help us."

"I'll try," she said and nervously laughed, glancing at Katie for the first time.

McGaven leaned against the counter like he was going to tell her a secret. "Our medical examiner just requested some x-rays for a Candace Harlan. And we need a little more information. Can you do that for us?"

"Well… I don't know…" she stammered.

"We can get a warrant, but who wants to go through all that?" he said. "We just want to know when her last visit here was."

"Well… okay…" she said and keyed up the computer. "You said Candace Harlan?"

"Yes."

Cara clicked through several screens until she found what she was looking for. "Okay, yes, I see where her dental records were requested for ID." She gasped. "Is she…?"

"We don't know. That's why we need more information. You are really helping us by doing this."

Katie hoped that McGaven wasn't laying the charm on too thick.

The doors opened and a woman with two little girls entered. They found a place to sit down and wait after finding some toys in a basket in the corner.

The receptionist left the desk and went to the files.

One of the little girls approached Katie. "Excuse me."

"Yes?" she said, bending down to the little girl's level.

"Are you a policeman?"

"Yes, I am."

"Where's your uniform?"

"I'm actually a detective. We don't wear uniforms like the police officers on the streets."

"Oh," she said. "Is it scary?" She watched Katie with large blue eyes and an innocent expression.

"Well, sometimes. But that's why I have a partner. We take care of each other."

"Oh. Okay, thank you," she said and then skipped back over to her mom and sister.

Katie smiled and moved her focus back to McGaven and the receptionist.

"Okay, here's her file," she said, opening it. "Ms. Harlan was here at the beginning of the year in February. She had a crown fixed and complained of teeth sensitivity."

"I see," said McGaven. "Do you remember her?"

"No, I'm afraid I don't. She came in on a Thursday and that's my day off."

"What's her address? We need to double check that we have the right one," he said and smiled.

"Oh, uh, it looks like 1457 Green Street."

"Darn. That's the address we have. Did she happen to leave an emergency contact?"

Cara scanned the paperwork and said, "Yes, she listed Amy Striker. The phone number is 555-2711 and the address is the same."

"Thank you, Cara. You've been very helpful."

"Thank you, Deputy," she said, eyeing him. "I hope you solve your case."

Katie and McGaven turned to leave and that's when she saw the two little girls sitting side by side, each with a book. They had slightly different hair styles, but they were twins. It suddenly hit her. Katie touched McGaven's arm before they exited the dental office. "*Twins*," she said. "What if Candace Harlan has a twin?"

He shrugged. "I guess it's possible. But how?"

"Don't you see? That's why the victim looks so much like Candace. Ask the receptionist if there is another patient, a family member by the name of Harlan. I know it's a long shot, but it's the only thing that makes sense. A doppelganger, a twin, maybe a cousin, but I think the victim might be related to her."

Katie went outside and waited for McGaven. She paced the pavement, running everything through her mind. It was a long shot, but a sister, or a twin, was a possibility, even if there was no mention at Elm Hill Mansion about a sibling.

McGaven exited and said, "You're right, Katie. I'll give you kudos for this. Cara said that Candace's sister, Carol Harlan, was also a patient, and they usually had appointments on the same day. There was an outdated contact number as well. Probably a fake one to begin with."

"There was no indication from her file that she had a sister."

"Maybe she didn't know she had a sister until after she left Elm Hill?"

"Maybe they were separated when they were babies? And reunited?" she said, thinking about all the possible reasons. "Okay, let Dr. Dean at the examiner's office know that he needs to compare the dental records of Carol Harlan."

"On it," he said, retrieving his cell phone. "I'll run the system for everything on Carol Harlan as well."

Walking up to the car, she said, "We also have an address now, 1457 Green Street."

"That's in the Parker Division," he said, looking at his phone. "Looks like the Edison something company is the one doing the construction project. I'll know when I get in front of my computer."

"Maybe we'll find Candace Harlan now," she said.

CHAPTER TEN

The beginning of third grade was an exciting time for me—being eight years old was a new adventure. I would soon be beginning more academically challenging work—feeling like a real student instead of a child idly entertained by a teacher among a classroom of idiot children. My days were filled with the wonder of learning.

English.

Math.

And learning history made me the most content.

I was the happiest when I was away from home. It was the opposite for most kids, but not me. Not in the least. I imagined flying away to a better place—a magical place.

My home was a nightmare that had transcended into my waking life—every single day I stepped into the lion's den praying that I would be okay—and not eaten alive. It didn't matter what had happened that day—how fun it was, how good it was, how happy I was—as soon as I walked through the front door of my house, everything changed in an instant.

As I jogged up to the front porch with a heavy backpack slung over my right shoulder, dread always filled me. I glanced up at the outside light where the light bulb had been smashed and not replaced. Tiny remnants of the bulb still evident around the step corners were a constant reminder. The filthy step and worn-out doormat were the only things that greeted me.

The joy of school and all the new things I had learned faded away, replaced suddenly by deep despair and unwavering darkness.

My small hand gripped the front doorknob hoping it would open this time. I slowly turned it, and to my surprise it was unlocked. It was never unlocked. Ever. Gulping for air, I slowly pushed the door inward, but it jammed, only opening two inches. Something wouldn't allow for it to open any farther. I could barely breathe. I pushed harder with all my strength, but it still wouldn't budge.

I knew why.

CHAPTER ELEVEN

Tuesday 1345 hours

Katie and McGaven took turns driving. Katie often liked to ride quietly in the passenger seat reflecting on new information and clues they had gathered. Katie knew McGaven's moods as he no doubt understood hers.

Today, however, she wanted to feel the steering wheel gripped beneath her fingers. The strength of the V8 engine roaring under the hood, catapulting them towards their next lead and keeping her focused. The case was complex and she knew that they would need to peel away the evidence one layer at a time.

Katie's hands shook slightly in anticipation, as she took the appropriate exit from the freeway and slowed the car's speed to take the uneven roads leading up to the Parker Division.

"What's with the roads here?" she asked, breaking the silence.

"It's been like this for a while. I'm assuming they will re-pave them when the development is finished."

"Hmm," she said, watching for areas where she could pull the sedan in and park.

Parker Division was made up of six roads from north to south intersected by three roads going east and west. Most homes still had dirt front yards as well as some final finishing touches on the porches and frames around the windows yet to do. But there were others still entombed with heavy plastic, unfinished and exposed.

Katie kept driving and found an open area that hadn't been surrounded by temporary cyclone fencing. She eased the sedan down the street.

"So where's 1457 Green Street?" asked Katie. She slowed the vehicle even more, scouring the area. "Seems strange here with all these empty houses and no one actually working. Like a ghost town."

McGaven craned his neck, searching too. "Did they take the day off?"

"Shouldn't we see work trucks from Edison, et al?"

"Wait," said McGaven and pointed. "What's that?"

There were three construction trucks parked in front of two unfinished homes that were being framed in. Stenciled on the doors was *EFT & Company, Construction & Development*, referring to Edison, Fullerton, and Taylor Demolition Company.

"There's Green Street," she said, making a right turn and stopping when they came to 1457. The address had been spray painted on the curb. "Doesn't look like anyone is living there. No one is living in any of these houses yet. Why would Candace Harlan use this address? She couldn't have pulled it out of thin air."

"Not likely."

Katie parked. "Let's go look at a house," she said flatly as her nerves buzzed at a low level in her arms. She didn't like being in an unknown area without knowing exactly what to expect—she was glad that McGaven was with her.

Opening the car door, "Okay…"

Both of them stepped out onto the street and did a slow inspection of the neighborhood.

Katie shut her eyes for a moment to let her other senses check for anything out of place. It was a trick that she had honed in the army. There was no birdsong, which seemed strange. The subtle breeze rattled the heavy plastic covering the windows on the house across the street. Opening her eyes and looking down, she noticed that the street was exceptionally clean without so much as a piece of paper or leaf out of place—nothing blew along the ground.

"It is 1457?" asked McGaven with a hint of skepticism to his voice.

"Yep."

"Just double checking," he said, filling the tense silence with chitchat which wasn't customary for him.

"This is the address. Let's check it out."

"I'll take a loop around the perimeter."

Katie nodded and headed toward the front door.

Walking across the landscaped yard, she felt her boot heels sink slightly into the typical dirt/sand combination of California soil. The windows and doors had been recently installed. The trim was freshly painted white to contrast the dark blue of the house. The smell of paint charged her senses as she stepped up to the front door painted red with a small window at the top. She stretched her body and stood on her tiptoes to see inside. It was empty, and there were missing appliances in the kitchen. There was no sign of anyone living there—ever.

She walked around to the large living-room window and peered inside. It was empty but the carpet had been installed recently—there were still company-branded stickers at the corners. Random pieces of garbage were scattered all over the floor. It was clear that the final clean-up hadn't been done. This was a brand-new house and was almost ready for its first residents—no doubt about it.

Katie heard footsteps coming along behind the house. They were too quick and light to belong to McGaven. She hurried around the corner to find a man dressed in a dark hoodie and dark pants walking her way. His face was obscured by the sweatshirt hood pulled tight and he stopped dead when he saw Katie, then turned and sprinted away.

"Wait!" she said, breaking into a sprint after him. "Wait! Sheriff's department! Stop!"

The faster she ran, the more he increased his speed. As Katie pursued, she couldn't help but think that she had seen this person before.

But where?

Katie pumped her arms faster, wishing she was in her running shoes.

That's it!

When they had been at Elm Hill Mansion, she had paused a moment before entering the crime-scene area and glanced at the group of onlookers. She was sure that there had been a person matching the general build and dress of the guy she was now chasing.

Her heart pounded with effort and adrenalin as she chased the man around two houses and through a backyard. Jumping over some leftover pieces of drywall and empty paint buckets, she had to use all of her running endurance to keep up.

Katie kept her pace with the fleeing sprinter, but she wasn't gaining on him. Then he ducked behind a house, pushing over a pile of supplies stacked high in the front yard and causing her to slow to avoid an ambush. Crouching down and pulling her weapon, she approached the six-foot-high pile of scaffolding boards with caution, directing her gun in front of her. Inching to the corner, she peered around to the other side.

No one was there.

After a few tense seconds, she inched around to the other side.

It was deserted as well.

Relaxing her arms slightly, she lowered her weapon. Second-guessing herself, she thought maybe she had been chasing a teenager instead of someone that had been at the crime scene.

Then a dark blur darted out nearby and headed out toward the road again.

Katie bolted, running as fast as she could and jumping every obstacle in her path, weaving around discarded drywall, two-by-fours, and dozens of buckets of paint like she was being chased by wolves.

Catching sight of him again, she slowed her pace, realizing as she looked around that she was traveling in circles. Was he trying to direct her somewhere? But why? And where? She regretted not alerting McGaven to her chase and wished that she had Cisco with her to track him. It would have been more efficient, and safer to have the dog by her side.

She heard a crash nearby. The noise rattled her nerves, making her grit her teeth. With her heartbeat pounding in her ears, she pushed herself harder, running towards the noise. Just as she was about to turn a corner by one of the freshly painted houses, she almost collided with a burly man carrying tools and a large bucket.

Katie stopped abruptly, barely missing him.

"Hey, lady, what are you doing?" said the man with an angry tone. "Why are you here?" he demanded, noticing the Glock 19 she held lowered in her right hand.

"Detective Scott, Pine Valley Sheriff's Department," she said, winded and a little bit unnerved at the sound of her own voice. "Did you see a guy come through here wearing dark sweats and a hoodie?"

"Nah, no one here like that," he gruffly answered. "Even you shouldn't be here—officer." His gravelly voice turned sarcastic with an emphasis on *officer* and she couldn't help but see that he didn't want her anywhere near the construction in progress.

Katie glared at the worker. "And you are?"

He smirked and slowly drew out his answer. "I don't have to tell you nuthin'."

"That's right," Katie fired back. She could smell his sweat and pungent deodorant mixed together like a stink cocktail. "You don't have to say anything to me, but I can get a patrol car here in five minutes and they will take you in…"

"Oh yeah. For what?" He leered at her and gave her a once-over.

"How about for obstruction? Evading a police officer. Or, how about I take a look at your permits?" She stood her ground, not really going to do any of those things, but the stocky man didn't know that.

Katie remained quiet. It was a useful technique that worked most of the time when she wanted someone to be helpful or honest with her.

"Is there a problem, Detective Scott?" said McGaven calmly from behind her.

"I'm going to ask you again. Did you see someone wearing a dark tracksuit with the hood pulled up?" she said, hoping that being outnumbered would make the man more talkative.

"No, not today," he said slowly.

"What do you mean 'not today'?"

"We've had some problems with stealing. Probably kids. Tools have gone missing. Things have been moved around."

"What kind of tools?"

"One of our tool boxes was pried open and some of the hand tools were taken. Small stuff like screwdrivers, hammers, stuff like that. None of the expensive power tools were touched."

Katie thought about it. Maybe he was right, it was kids. "What's your name?"

"Carl."

"Carl what?"

"Carl Brown."

"You work for Edison?" she said.

"Yeah."

"So what's the timeline here?"

"For what?"

"To finish these houses."

"By next month."

"To put them on the market?"

"No."

"No?" she said.

"They've already been sold."

"We did a check on a house on Green Street. It doesn't show that it has been sold."

Brown shrugged. "That's what they told us."

"Have you ever heard of Magnum Development? MDI?"

Shaking his head, he said, "No."

Katie decided to use a bit of charm and said, "I'm sorry, Mr. Brown, for coming down hard on you. But, I have one more question," as she holstered her weapon.

"Don't worry about it." He shrugged. "I guess."

"Do you know who either Candace Harlan or Amy Striker are?"

"No, should I?"

"Have you ever heard the name Harlan?"

"Like I said, nope."

Katie watched his reaction and it appeared to be genuine. No hesitation. No averting of the eyes.

"If there's anything out of the ordinary, can you call me?" She gave him her business card.

"Sure," he replied, reading the card.

"Thank you." Katie turned and faced McGaven before carefully stepping around the area. He had been waiting patiently in the background, like a bodyguard, keeping quiet until needed.

"What's going on? Why did you bolt?" he asked.

"I saw this guy following us and when I tried to talk to him, he ran."

"What did he look like?"

"I couldn't really tell. He had a black hoodie obscuring his face. And he was really, really fast on foot."

They walked back toward the house on Green Street.

"Anything about him seem familiar?"

"Yeah, I think he was at the crime scene."

"Maybe a fan of the police?"

Katie said slowly, "Maybe, but I think he was after something else. Or knows something that we don't know about the case."

"Like what?"

"I don't know," she said. "Find anything interesting about the house?"

"Nada. It's just like the rest of the places. The crew is finishing up the interiors and soon people will begin moving in."

They reached the car and paused.

"Mr. Big Guy back there said that all the houses have been sold."

"Really?"

Katie opened the car door. "So if they have been sold, why can't we find anything?"

"You know how slow these things work. Maybe all the information hasn't been entered into the system at the title company and assessor's office." McGaven studied his partner. "What? You've got that look. I don't know whether to be happy or brace for the worst."

Katie smiled. "Well, I know that property taxes wait for no one. There's must be a record somewhere."

"I saw a real estate sign down the street for MayFare Realty. I'll dig around there."

"We need to find out why Candace Harlan and Amy Striker are somehow connected to this house on Green Street."

CHAPTER TWELVE

Tuesday 1530 hours

Katie leaned over McGaven's shoulder as he ran through several police reports for Carol Harlan. To their surprise, there were numerous reports for vandalism and trespass, but nothing else popped.

"It looks like these charges were all dropped," McGaven said.

"All those dates are from several years ago, nothing current," Katie said, discouraged. Reading on, she said, "Actually, it looks like Carol was kicked out of places where she was sleeping. It makes sense that she was homeless." Reading on, she said, "What about the contact information she gave?"

"It looks like 1477 Spring Street."

"Why does that sound familiar?" she said.

"It's because it's the government building downtown. It's common for inmates to use that address when they are transient."

"Okay, what about Amy Striker?"

"Nothing on her. And the phone number 555-2711 is not a working number—of course."

Katie sat back in her chair feeling a bit defeated. "Why the name Amy Striker?"

"It could be a purely made-up name or a name from the past. An old childhood friend. A neighbor. A fictional character in a book. It could be just about any name that she wanted to use."

Katie sighed. "You're right." She grabbed her phone. "I just can't help but think that hooded guy is somehow tracking us." Looking at the image, "Who are you?"

"What's that?" asked McGaven.

"I took this photo when we entered the crime-scene area at Elm Hill just for documentation."

"Send it to my email," he said.

Katie sent two photos to McGaven.

With a few keystrokes, he enlarged the images. "Hmm," he grumbled.

"What?"

"Why is it when you need to see an identity of somebody—they are standing in the perfect position with the lighting to make it next to impossible to identify who they are?"

Katie pushed her chair next to McGaven and scrutinized the screen. She let out a breath. "Maybe if I had waited another second or two, there would be a better photo. But, we're assuming that that hooded guy is the same guy I chased at Green Street."

"Look at the build," he said.

Katie saw the guy had his hands in his pockets and had shifted his right shoulder to further obscure his identity. "Yeah, he appears to be like the guy I chased. But look at how he turns his body to make sure that his identity isn't seen."

"It's like he knows where the potential cameras are."

"Who would know instinctively how to do that?"

"Well, criminals, for one."

"What about someone who understands camera angles?"

"You mean like a photographer—or a model, I suppose. Interesting."

Katie looked at the second photo with other people. "Look at how everyone else is oblivious to anyone watching them or photographing them." The others were leaning in and craning their necks to get a better look at the crime scene. "It's a huge contrast between hooded guy and the others. He doesn't seem to be curious about the scene, but cautious."

"Well, we have plenty more information to dig through," he said.

Katie glanced at her board and realized that they really needed a confirmation that the body at Elm Hill Mansion was Candace Harlan's sister—Carol Harlan. She also had a sinking feeling that they were missing something—or someone.

CHAPTER THIRTEEN

Tuesday 1845 hours

Katie searched for 1188 Spreckles Lane as she slowly drove by the brightly painted houses. It was a nice older neighborhood with cottages that had been remodeled and nicely kept up. It was pretty and inviting. The sidewalks were neat and tidy, as were the grass and bushes. Green was the color of the day, after all the rain they had received made the landscape pop.

"Eleven eighty-eight, where are you…" she muttered to herself and glanced at the tiny piece of paper with the neatly printed address once again. No explanation. No other notes of direction. Just the address. Even her GPS wasn't any help.

Katie drove the police sedan around the block again. "What am I missing?" she grumbled. "There's eleven eighty-six and eleven ninety… where's…" That's when she saw it. A small yellow house tucked back behind two towering trees down a single long driveway. It had climbing vines and two large lemon trees.

She parked her vehicle on the street and got out.

Small stepping stones ran along the side of the drive leading up to a detached single-car garage. The instant aroma of orange blossoms and another sweeter smell filled the air—even though it was late in the season. It reminded Katie of long summers when she was young—before going back to school.

There was a pounding noise coming from inside the small house—like a tool hitting a pipe. Rhythmic and constant. The closer she came to the front door the louder it became.

The front door was wide open.

"Hello?" she said.

"In here," came the reply.

"Where?" she laughed and stepped inside.

"Here."

The tiny cottage had a nice-size living room filled with moving boxes, and she spied where there were most likely two bedrooms and a small bath between them.

"I thought you were a detective," the muffled voice said from another area.

"Just clearing the other rooms first..."

Katie turned to the left and around a corner, finding herself in the small kitchen. White cabinets, a half-size refrigerator, a small butcher block island, and two long countertops rounded out the area. From underneath the sink two legs and part of a torso were visible, the banging sounds continuing.

"What, are you a plumber now?" she said.

The man pushed himself free from under the sink. Chad was still wearing his Pine Valley Fire Department uniform. "What took you so long?" he said.

"This isn't the easiest place to find."

He stood up, his sparkling blue eyes fixed on her. "What do you think of the place?"

"I... I like it. It's cozy." She didn't know what else to say. It was tiny, but there was definitely a significant amount of charm.

"Yeah, I know. Small, but affordable. After I do some repairs, I'll be able to flip it and get something bigger. But for now..." He gently pushed Katie backward and planted a long kiss on her lips.

"Is that your Chad hello?" she giggled.

"Is that your gun?" he countered with a sly expression.

"Sorry, the gun and badge are a part of the package."

"It's nice to see you," he said and kissed her again. "Really nice."

"I thought we were having dinner. This doesn't look cook friendly yet."

"How does pizza and wine sound?"

"That sounds great."

"Great." He retrieved his cell phone.

"Oh, I almost forgot."

"What?" he said.

Katie smiled genuinely and said, "Congratulations on your new house."

As they relaxed on the sofa eating their favorite combination pizza and sipping a nice red wine, Katie felt relaxed. It was the first time in a couple of days that she'd taken a breath and didn't feel rushed, stressed, or ready for something unexpected to jump out at her.

Chad studied Katie and said, "What's up?"

"What do you mean?"

"I've known you long enough to know when something is bothering you."

Katie chuckled. She had always loved Chad, even when she didn't know it herself. Growing up with such a great friend through happy and terrible times was something that she had cherished. She sighed.

"I heard about that girl's body found at Elm Hill Mansion. I figured it was going to be your case," he said, waiting patiently for her.

"Yep, you guessed correct. It was already one of my cold cases, actually—that's why it's our case. It's actually more complicated than that."

"Sounds fair enough."

Katie took another drink of wine and paused. "Yes, but I can't help but feel that I'm stepping on toes…"

"Why? Hamilton again?" He had known that Hamilton was the detective in charge of Katie's aunt's murder case.

"Yes, but…"

"But what?" he said and moved closer to her.

"There's a new superior that will be watching me… it's so…"

"Annoying?"

"I was going to say disheartening… I know that the cold-case unit is new, and that I'm still considered a rookie in some ways, but this new undersheriff definitely has her eye on me."

"Her," he said. "Oh, I get it. A little competition."

"No, it's not like that. I just got the feeling that she wants something, that she's going to try to be my buddy— I wonder if it has to do with my uncle, but maybe I'm totally off about that. That doesn't work when you're a cop—you don't pal around with your superiors."

Chad shook his head and said, "It might be nice for you to have a woman on your side—even someone in the brass."

Katie looked away and thought about all types of scenarios, how they would go down, and none of them seemed good in her opinion.

"Look," he said. "Just keep working your assigned cases and you'll be fine—you always are. And as for your uncle, he's a big boy and can handle himself." He put down his wine glass and said, "As for me, I'm only interested in one detective—a *hot* cold-case detective."

"You're right," she said, feeling the wine relaxing her body. She leaned in to kiss him.

Her cell phone rang.

"Great," Chad said irritated. "Can you ignore it?"

"Yes." And then, "No, I better get it." Katie reached over near her jacket and retrieved the cell phone. "Detective Scott," she said as Chad nuzzled her neck. Listening intently, she frowned and bit her lower lip. "I understand. Yes, I know where it is." The call disconnected from the third watch commander.

Chad straightened up. "Let me guess. Work."

"Yes." Her mind was already one step ahead. "They've found another one."

"Young woman?"

"Yes."

CHAPTER FOURTEEN

Tuesday 2015 hours

The calm Katie had found in Chad's arms dissipated as she raced to the crime scene. Two women found murdered in two days was highly unusual and extremely disturbing. She couldn't waste any time. She knew that the Harlan case could go in many directions, but another dead woman with ties to the Elm Hill Mansion couldn't be coincidental.

The daylight had fizzled and with an almost moonless night due to the heavy cloud cover it would be near-impossible to search a crime scene in any real detail. The dark shadows in between the trees stretched as she drove, creeping into her thoughts.

When she reached Stately Park, there were already a half dozen patrol cars securing the area around the hiking trail and helping the crime-scene unit carry large freestanding lights over to the crime scene.

Katie had never worked an outdoor crime scene at night before and it made her nerves rattle and her mouth go dry. Willing her anxiety to stay at bay, she focused as best she could on the task ahead. Questions plagued her mind.

Did the victim suffer the same injuries?

Would there be the same disturbing message carved on the victim's back?

Could they have a serial killer on their hands?

She ran over in her mind what she needed to pay particular attention to when looking for evidence in the dark. She'd need to work more of a spiral grid than a typical cordoned zone search to assess the area. The first impressions of a crime scene were usually the most important, so she'd have to use all her senses to capture as much as she could in the dying light.

Parking in an available area, Katie saw McGaven and a few familiar patrol officer faces in the crowd. He approached her car just as she got out of the driver's seat and they hurried together towards the entrance to the hiking trail.

"How did you get here so fast?" she asked, switching on a large flashlight she'd grabbed from the trunk.

"I caught a ride with Deputy Anderson. Everything okay?"

"Fine. Why do you ask?"

"No particular reason," he said. "But your blouse is undone…"

"Just stick to crime scenes," she said, clutching her shirt underneath her jacket and trying to hide her smile.

"Noted, Detective."

Katie watched the patrol officers set up lights along the trail which led down to the creek. They went some way to illuminate the area, but the contrast and color of the trees and surroundings were muddled in the darkness. There were more shadows than light.

With all the rain they'd had in the past few weeks, the creek was higher than normal going into the fall season. The sound of water rushing along the rocky bed grew louder and louder as they approached the crime scene, blocking out the voices around them.

As Katie picked up her pace, McGaven slowed to allow Katie to take point and survey the body and immediate crime scene alone. As always, he hung back to cover the areas of entry, exit, potential evidence, and anything deemed unusual or possibly left by the killer.

As she approached the body, the crackling sound of police radios faded and voices all around her lowered to a muted tone. She blocked out everything that might interfere with her concentration and focus. Refining extreme focus was something she had learned in the army—it kept her attention expertly sharpened and alive.

This time, Katie decided that she wasn't going to stop and speak with Detective Hamilton first, but forge straight ahead while she still had a little light to work with. She needed to stop worrying about the other detectives and keep her attention on her orders from the sheriff and on the investigation.

The crime-scene techs were readying themselves and waiting for the order to document and collect evidence. They nodded at her as she made her way around several large trees until she reached the yellow tape.

The sound of running water from the creek increased in volume again as she felt a slight mist spray her face where the intensified humidity hit cold air. Her boot heels started sinking into the soil; it took her total concentration to keep from falling down or slipping into the creek.

Why did the killer pick this spot?

Was it because no one would hear the girl's screams or pleas for help?

Katie stopped abruptly and sucked in a breath as her eyes adjusted to what was in front of her. Approximately three feet away, illuminated in a yellow pool of lamplight, lay the naked body of Mary Rodriguez, lying on her side, eerily reminiscent of the other victim. Her arms were tied behind her back, one shoulder protruded upward, horribly discolored as if it had been dislocated, and her face looked directly at Katie with open eyes. Her expression was that of torture and pleading—Katie had difficulty keeping her eyes locked on the body.

Steadying her trembling hands, Katie slipped on a pair of gloves. To the outside world she appeared calm, but her anxiety was always ready to wreak havoc on her nervous system during accelerated times of stress.

There were no obvious footprints or drag marks around the body, which seemed strange: either the killer expertly covered his tracks or had some way of tossing the body without any evidence of detection.

Unusual.

Disturbing.

In Katie's peripheral vision, she saw Detective Hamilton talking to McGaven. She knew that there were others around, but tried to block everyone out and focus only on the victim.

She leaned down to examine the girl's wrists tied behind her back. There were numerous deep red and purple marks with areas of dried blood on her wrists and up her forearm, indicating that she had been restrained for some time before she drew her last breath. Her neck was also ringed with the same type of ligature marks, which indicated she had been strangled. There was no sign of decomposition—just the beginning stages of rigor mortis with the stiffening of limbs. If Katie had to guess she would estimate this poor girl had been dead less than a few hours, but the medical examiner would confirm in the report.

She noticed that the victim's short blonde hair had dark roots and showed areas of damage with patches missing from her scalp, as if the killer had pulled the hair out forcefully in a struggle.

Taking in the positioning of the body one final time, she carefully moved the torso to one side so that she could see between the girl's shoulder blades and down to the lower back. The body's stiffening limbs made it somewhat difficult, but Katie managed to see what she dreaded most—hand-carved letters on the skin with slightly running ink that read 'raccoglitore di cacciatori'.

Hunter-gatherer.

Katie now knew that it was a distinct possibility they were dealing with a serial killer hunting and gathering victims…

The crime scene was in an out-of-the-way location and the killer seemed intent on dumping the body at this exact site. There were no visible footprints or drag marks and it didn't seem likely that the rain had washed them away. Did the killer travel to the creekside in some type of boat, like a canoe or row boat? As she studied the body, it made her wonder why at that spot, naked and with the message.

Why? For the drama? Not to be found straightaway? Wouldn't it have been more efficient to leave the body on the trail or in the parking lot? In some ways, the crime scene appeared planned due to the preparations it took to get the body there. And in other ways, it appeared haphazard to dump the body beside a creek.

Katie stood up and did a quick 360-degree sweep to double-check for footprints in the dirt or surrounding landscape, but the night was closing in and the evidence technicians were more apt to catch anything that was initially overlooked by detectives.

"What do you think?" asked McGaven over the sound of the rushing creek water. He had done his own inspection of the scene and now waited to compare notes with his partner.

Katie turned to him and said, "We have another 'raccoglitore di cacciatori'." Her tightly knitted eyebrows and slightly downturned mouth told him everything he needed to know about the seriousness of the case they had been handed.

"Hunter-gatherer," he replied to himself.

"Who called in the body?" Katie asked, raising her voice.

"Avid hiker whose dog got away and then found the body," he said.

Katie looked around the body for pawprints, but saw nothing. If a curious dog had found the body, there would be dozens. "Was it an anonymous call?"

"Yes."

"Man or woman?"

"It was unclear."

"Unclear?" she said. "What do you mean?"

"It was one of those electronic voices."

"You mean like for the hearing impaired?" she said.

"No, like the person used an electronic voice changer. You can buy these devices almost anywhere where electronics are sold."

"Very clever, so the caller wanted to disguise their voice," she said, still scrutinizing the area once again. "The killer called it in, probably due to the fact that the creek levels are rising, wanting to make sure that the body was found where he left it. Couldn't wait until tomorrow when a hiker might stumble upon it. The body might've washed downstream by then." She took a step back, still troubled by the scene. "Why is this location so important to the killer and what does it have to do with the teen girl's foster home at Elm Hill Mansion?"

McGaven didn't immediately answer, but finally said, "I'll put in more searches on the usage of hunter-gatherer, where it originated, books and movies that used the saying, and anything that refers to it."

"I agree. Anything that would help to profile the killer." She squatted down and looked at the restraints again. "Why these particular girls? What connects them besides the foster home? Too much trouble went into dumping the body here for it to be unimportant. If you can, maybe search notable crime scenes where bodies were found by water, like a creek, river, and even the beach. Might try other counties too."

"Okay, that's quite a reach but I'll see what I can come up with."

Detective Hamilton approached.

"Nice to see you, Detective," said Katie cautiously, still not completely convinced that the detective didn't have a bone to pick with her.

He nodded. "We weren't able to find any other evidence around the scene aside from the body."

"The body itself has quite a bit of evidence. Can you double the search area, and search again in the morning?" she asked. "That would mean someone would have to guard the area until sunrise for the chain of custody to stay in play."

Hamilton started to object, but then agreed. "Of course." He hurried towards the officers to make sure that they complied.

"At least right now, it's not completely clear if it's the primary or secondary crime scene. Given there are no signs of a struggle in the earth, I'd say she was dead when she got here and this is the secondary scene," she said, more to herself, trying to get facts straight in her mind. Looking at McGaven, she said, "Did you find any other access points?"

McGaven said, "There are only two possible ways someone could have brought a body and disposed of it." He gestured to the area where they had entered down the trail. "The way we came in or... a small back trail that intersects to another main trail. And I guess from the water too."

"Is it easily accessible?"

"Fairly—depending upon how they transported the body or if she walked to her final destination. Anyone could use these stairs and it leads to another easy trail next to a parking lot. There are only eight stairs."

Katie followed McGaven as he used a flashlight to illuminate the area to the far northeast corner where a set of stairs had been formed out of heavy four-by-fours with low bushes on either side. It had been heavily traveled which meant that, along with the rain, finding fresh, singular shoe impressions would be impossible. The stairs were in good condition even with the recent amount of rain.

Katie turned and called back to Hamilton, "Detective, please have this area searched and documented as well."

"Will do," he said.

It was unclear to Katie if he wasn't happy about her taking over the investigation, but in the end, it didn't matter. What mattered was finding the killer before another woman was murdered.

In a low tone to McGaven, she leaned in and said, "We need to look at the history of the girls who stayed at the Elm Hill Mansion."

"How many years?"

"At least back ten years from the closure date. Rodriguez and Harlan were in their twenties."

"I'll get on it in the morning."

"Oh, we need the names of people who worked in or around Elm Hill."

"I'll get on this right away, but it might be a waiting game to gather all the information."

Katie sighed.

"What?"

"I don't think this victim is going to be our last…"

CHAPTER FIFTEEN

I kept my head held low because I had to walk around the house to the backyard hoping a neighbor wouldn't see me pass by their window. It would raise unwanted questions.

I pushed through the side gate and headed to the back door. Hesitating a moment, I opened it. Relief filled me. Quickly stepping inside the house and shutting the door behind me, I made my way down the hallway lined with expertly stacked piles of discarded boxes, newspapers, and magazines as high as the ceiling. The path was barely wide enough for me to slip my way to my bedroom. I moved as quietly as I could—tiptoeing in silence.

Hurrying past the bathroom, which hadn't functioned in over a year, made me cringe with shame. The piles of clothes and various household items that covered every surface in every room weren't mine, or my mother's. I wasn't sure who they belonged to, but they took up space everywhere, smothering us.

I finally made it to my bedroom. To the twin mattress on the floor in a corner where I kept two boxes filled with my only possessions. I cherished them. I quickly sat down and began to take an inventory of my books and homework as quietly as I could.

"There you are," said my mother, standing at the doorway partially obscured by the haphazard junk towering around her.

"Hi, Mother." I didn't lift up my eyes to look at her. I couldn't. I didn't want to.

"Watcha got there? You weren't going to share with me?" she sneered. Her voice, coarse and high-pitched, rattled me. I winced. She held a

cigarette between her left index and middle fingers that were deeply stained a rust color by the nicotine—her nails were painted a horrible pink but it didn't make them look any better.

Taking a long drag, she exhaled, allowing the smoke to swirl around her head like a fancy headdress, and finally dissipate somewhere in the cluttered room. "You think that your books are going to make you smarter? Huh? Do you? Why do you mock me with that attitude of yours?" she accused with her tone penetrating my brain—my soul.

I couldn't get her voice out of my head…

CHAPTER SIXTEEN

Wednesday 0130 hours

Katie was on her fourth cup of lukewarm coffee and it didn't seem to make any difference to her energy levels or performance at one thirty in the morning. Her body acted as if it was moving through waves of sludge as her mind whirred through the few leads they had at the moment. She wasn't getting anywhere. At least not anywhere fast.

"Okay, I finally got it. I had to wake a few people up to be able to search the right county database, but I've got it now," said McGaven, sleep deprivation weighing heavy in his eyes.

Katie stood up straight and waited patiently for the list.

"There are six names of the last girls who resided at Elm Hill Mansion before it was permanently closed two years ago."

Katie leaned over McGaven's shoulder. "Remind me," she said sleepily.

"Okay." He hit a few keys and a list appeared.

Candace Harlan
Mary Rodriguez
Tanis Jones
Heather Lawson
Terry Slaughter
Karen Beck

"And employees," he said.

Shelly McDonald, house manager (live in)
Margaret Adler, housekeeper and kitchen manager
Elmer Rydesdale, grounds keeper and maintenance
Tatiana Wolf, tutor

"All girls given up for various reasons including deceased parents, incarceration, and repeat offending."

"How sad for these young girls," she said. "But now, we need to locate them."

"It will take some time. Here are some notes I received from…" he looked at his notes, "Jerry Weaver, who was one of the child protective officers at the time. He remembered some details, but will have to follow up when he gets in to work."

"Like?"

"Like the fact that Mary Rodriguez was the most outspoken and most difficult of the group. She had been in juvenile detention for theft, prostitution, drugs, and a few other things, but the judge gave her another chance and, instead of jail, the opportunity to live at the foster home."

Katie flashed back to the image of Mary's lifeless body dumped by a rushing creek, to the pleading expression on her face.

"Also Tanis Jones and Candace Harlan were tight. They went everywhere together and always had each other's back when one of them got in trouble at the house."

"We need to talk with Ms. Jones and find out more information about the girls and see if her recollection is the same as the social worker's."

"Mr. Weaver will get us copies of their old files tomorrow."

"Good."

"He also said that the cops were called out to Elm Hill at least twice a week and there was one officer that seemed to take a special liking to one of the girls."

Katie sat on the corner of her desk. "Let me guess, Candace Harlan."

"Bingo."

"And the officer was Hugh Keller?"

"Yep, just received the information now."

"Anything else?"

"Oh, he did say that the girls regularly complained about the abuse from McDonald. They referred to her as a 'she-beast'."

"Can we find anything about the allegations of abuse? If the girls regularly complained, wouldn't there be reports of arrests or anything? Even replacing McDonald? That seems disturbing to me," she said. "It seems that money was an issue keeping the house updated and safe."

"I don't see anything referring to more information other than allegations, but I'll keep digging."

Katie read over the report quickly. "Ah yes, the so-called she-beast, Mrs. Shelly McDonald. Since she's in jail, I guess I know where I'm going tomorrow."

McGaven pushed his chair back and stretched.

"Take off. You're exhausted and I'm spinning my wheels here. We'll start again early tomorrow morning, which is only a few hours from now, with fresh eyes and fresh coffee."

"I need to get out of this chair more often." He smiled, trying to suck in his waist.

"Well, you want to go to the women's correctional facility or the county basement of archives tomorrow?"

"That's a tough choice."

"We'll have a nice little chat with Mrs. McDonald first and see what she has to say about her time as manager at Elm Hills Mansion—and who she has been talking to."

CHAPTER SEVENTEEN
Wednesday 0945 hours

Katie turned off the freeway and headed toward the correctional facility just outside Sequoia County. She had tossed and turned the entire night with the faces of both dead girls swirling in her mind. Their bluish lips and glassy eyes kept taunting Katie, blaming her for not having the answers and warning her that the killer was smarter and more cunning than anyone she had ever dealt with before.

It wasn't the first time that Katie had dreamt of the dead. When she had witnessed a soldier die on the battlefield in Afghanistan, her first experience of death, his dying words would forever be burned in her memories—both in the daytime and dreams.

Don't leave me… I don't want to die…

"Have you heard anything I said?" asked McGaven who had been reading Shelly McDonald's rap sheet out loud to her. He looked disheveled, drinking an extra-large coffee from a Styrofoam cup, and balancing several files and reports on his lap.

"I'm sorry. Do you mind repeating it again?" she said.

"At least we have one thing in common."

"I hope we have more than just one," she countered.

"We both look like something the cat dragged in this morning."

Katie laughed. How true. "Keep reading about Mrs. McDonald."

"She's no stranger to the criminal justice system. She seems to love helping herself to other people's things; jewelry, clothes, phones, food, and here it says she walked out of a superstore with a DVD player."

"Ambitious."

"She's managed to have a lot of her sentences reduced or dismissed."

"Interesting. Do you have a photo?" Katie said.

McGaven shuffled through papers. "She's forty-nine, five foot eight, blonde hair, blue eyes." He turned her booking photo toward Katie.

"Ah, makes perfect sense now," she said.

"What?"

"She's pretty—about middle age—but pretty nonetheless. Probably used to getting what she wants. Wonder why she took the job overseeing those girls?"

McGaven shuffled more papers. "The longest job she's had… was about two years. She moved a lot. Maybe this job was perfect; a place to live, fairly remote and she's in charge. She only had six girls to look after."

Katie turned the police sedan down a narrow road leading up to the facility. It was only just wide enough for one large bus to pass. The overall landscape changed drastically. The endless razor cyclone fencing a bold contrast to the gentle sweeping slopes and pine trees they'd just passed. The land around the prison was barren, as if they had landed on the moon or some uncharted territory.

"Here we are," she said.

"Yep, when I first started on the force I used to transport prisoners from the jail to here." He studied the area. "Nothing's changed."

Katie followed the signs for visitors and law enforcement personnel. There were several police cars and a transport van already parked, but she managed to find a space. She grabbed her small notebook, but left behind her cell phone and personal items.

McGaven followed Katie's example, emptying his pockets of personal items but keeping a file folder with notes and information.

They both exited the vehicle and adjusted their suit jackets, covering their badges and guns, before walking to the visitor entrance.

Standing at the first entrance waiting, Katie spied three cameras all focused on visitors and the parking lot. Goose pimples ran down her arms and the back of her neck; an alert system within her, warning her that she was entering a potential enemy territory and that several secure doors would be bolted behind her—with no easy escape if something went terribly wrong.

"Identifications, please," came a voice.

Katie and McGaven showed their badges in the direction of one of the cameras.

"Detective Katie Scott and Deputy Sean McGaven are here to interview inmate Shelly McDonald," she said.

There was a pause and then a loud buzz unlocking the first set of doors.

Katie pulled the door open and they entered. She expected it to be cooler than outside, but it was, in fact, warmer and the air was quite stale.

A correctional officer waited for them in a booth behind bulletproof glass. He barely looked up as he said, "Relinquish your weapons," as he must have had said hundreds of times before to various visiting police officers.

Katie looked to her right to find a long row of locker-type storage units. She put her Glock 17 inside one of the cubbyholes, closed the small door, and retrieved the key. Putting it into her pocket, she waited for McGaven to do the same.

They waited for the next set of doors to open for them. There were several sets of metal detectors as a last resort before visitors moved deeper into the prison. As they walked through one set, briefly waiting to hear the loud metal doors secure behind them leaving an echo bouncing off the walls, they were immediately faced with another.

When they finally reached the area where the interview rooms were located, Katie concentrated on her breathing and ran questions through her mind. Thinking about McDonald's character, she thought it best for McGaven, as a man, to take point on the interview.

Another correctional officer joined them and unlocked a door.

Katie put her hand on McGaven's arm. She whispered quietly to him, "I want you to run the interview, okay?"

His eyes widened but his demeanor told her that he understood. "You got it," he said.

Katie would be merely an observer but would intervene if necessary to move things forward or to pose a question that hadn't been asked.

They moved into the small room with a metal table stationed in the middle with two chairs on one side, and a single chair on the other.

The door closed behind them.

Katie took her seat next to McGaven and waited. She glanced around the room, which seemed unexpectedly clean. The four off-white walls appeared to have been painted recently.

They didn't wait long to hear the door unlock and a guard entered, escorting Shelly McDonald in a prison jumpsuit. She looked a bit older than she did in her mug shot, but nonetheless, it was easy to see that she'd tried to hold onto her looks, even in prison. Her hair was neat and she wore some makeup.

The guard guided her to the empty chair, unlocked her handcuffs and left the room, closing the door quietly behind him.

Shelly looked at McGaven, smiled, and then brought her focus to Katie, scrutinizing her for a moment, before settling her attention back on McGaven.

"Mrs. McDonald," he politely addressed. "I'm Deputy McGaven and this is Detective Scott. We're working a homicide investigation."

The woman's eyes lit up and she dramatically leaned forward as if to hang on every word McGaven said. "What does that have to do with me, darlin'?" she said with a slight southern accent.

McGaven referred to his notes, but Katie knew that he already had memorized most of the information. He wanted to cut eye contact to keep the woman interested. "You were the managing caretaker for the Elm Hill Mansion home for foster girls? Correct?"

Her demeanor changed; leaning back, she stiffened her posture. "Yeah," she said. "I never thought I'd hear about that place again."

"You didn't like your job?"

"It was okay, if you like spoiled brats."

"Why did you take the job?" he said.

She shrugged. "Nothing better. Steady paycheck from the state. Plus, it was a place to sleep."

"Do you remember a teen by the name of Mary Rodriguez?"

Katie watched Shelly closely to see if there were any subtle changes in her posture, any reflexes.

"Of course. She was one of the better ones."

"Why do you say that?"

"She never gave me any trouble," she said, carefully moving her fingers through her hair as if she was looking into a mirror.

"What kind of trouble?"

"Not doing chores, mouthing off, or sneaking out to have sex with who knows who. You know, stuff like that."

"What happened when the girls got into trouble?"

"They got disciplined, of course. Is that what this is all about?"

"No, ma'am. We're investigating the homicide of Mary Rodriguez. Her body was found last night alongside the creek in Stately Park." He paused.

"Well… I don't know anything about that. Don't get me wrong, that's terrible, but I know *nothing* about it. How could I?" she said and then gestured to her surroundings.

"After the closure of the mansion, had you had any contact with any of the girls?"

"No." She became agitated and picked at her chewed fingernails.

"Had you heard anything about any of the girls after the closure?"

"I told you no. Nothing. Why would I?"

Ignoring her question, McGaven said, "What about Candace Harlan?"

She stopped fiddling with her hands and looked directly at McGaven. "What about her? She went missing. Actually, she ran away. That's all I know—never saw her again."

"Was she one of those troublesome girls?"

Shelly didn't answer. She went back to fidgeting with her hands and fingers.

"Was she one of those spoiled brats?"

"Why are you harassing me?"

"It's a simple question, Mrs. McDonald. Was Candace Harlan well behaved?"

"Why do you say that?"

McGaven kept his intensity. "It's a simple yes or no question. Was Candace Harlan one of those brats?"

"She was…"

"She was what?"

"She was the girl that led the other girls. Know what I mean? The others wanted to be her and wanted to be her best friend."

"Okay, I can understand that, but—"

"She was different," she said.

"Different how?"

"She just was, that's all."

"Who was her closest friend?" McGaven asked.

Shelly leaned back and some of her forced charm came back. "That's easy, Tanis."

"You mean Tanis Jones?"

"Of course. They were inseparable. They also shared a room."

"I've read the missing persons report. You stated that you thought Candace ran away with a boyfriend. Do you remember who?"

"I don't know who he was or his name. Just like I told the police officer that took the missing persons report. I. Don't. Know."

"Tell me, Mrs. McDonald… would you know why someone would want Mary Rodriguez or Candace Harlan dead?"

"What…?" She squeaked out, barely able to keep her composure. "I don't understand. Candace is… dead?" She spoke in a tone just above a whisper.

"Does that shock you?" he said, not wanting to disclose anything about the body not being Candace, but most likely her sister.

"She… it's just that…"

"Who visited the girls? Who did they run to when they sneaked out at night? And why would anyone want them dead?"

"Why would I know? Isn't that your job to find out?"

"How long had you been dating one of the police officers that would get dispatched to the mansion?"

"I don't know who you're talking about." She glanced at Katie as if to say, "Aren't you going to back me up, us women have to stick together?"

McGaven straightened his paperwork and neatly deposited it into the file folder.

"You're leaving?" she asked with a hint of regret in her voice.

McGaven brilliantly paused and looked directly at Mrs. McDonald. "Do you understand how important a homicide investigation is?"

"Of course."

"More young women could die."

She remained quiet, fighting with her conscience or whatever she was trying to hide.

"And do you understand that I can't waste time—"

"Of course I do."

"Then start acting like it and answer a few simple questions."

"I'm telling you the truth," she insisted.

McGaven rose from his chair. He towered over Shelly McDonald. Katie followed McGaven's lead and got up from her chair, heading for the door.

"Wait," she said, urgently. "Look, I did things back then I'm not proud of—drugs, loose sex. But I swear to you that I don't know where those girls went or with whom."

"And were you seeing one of the responding police officers?"

"Yes," she slowly said.

"Name."

"Hugh Keller."

McGaven tossed a business card on the table. "If you remember anything that might help in the homicide investigation, we might be able to help you sometime." He turned to the door and knocked twice. "Guard."

Katie and McGaven walked out into the parking lot. The sun had broken through the low-lying clouds and it had turned warmer.

"That was something back there," Katie said. "You played her brilliantly."

"I learned from you. Straightforward. Make them think that you already know the answers. And of course, keep them off balance."

"Oh no, I'm not taking credit for that performance. That was all you." She smiled and got into the car.

"I just figured that she wasn't going to give us anything, but she gave up the cop's name—Hugh Keller. He had a choice of either resigning from the force or going to jail."

"Doesn't sound good." Katie backed up the vehicle and sped off down the narrow road leaving the correctional facility.

"He's managing a bar on the east end of town. Hopefully he's learned to take his job a bit more seriously."

"Makes sense, with his previous behavior, that he got involved with McDonald. Pretty woman, loose attitude, and well…"

McGaven frowned and said, "I've heard stories about him from other officers and I had a few interactions with him personally. I wanted to punch him out, but didn't."

Katie glanced at McGaven. He seemed to manage to surprise her more with every investigation. How lucky she was to have a great partner, with such integrity. "Still waiting for the final autopsy and forensic reports to come in for Mary Rodriguez, but we have plenty to do."

"I'm still trying to run down family, place of work, or residence for her. It seems like these girls are invisible. It's probably why it's so easy for them to move around undetected."

"Yeah, well, not to the killer. He's tracking them down somehow. And if he's going after the final six that means there are four more potential victims." That thought angered and even terrified Katie because she didn't want to waste any time while another girl was murdered. She stepped on the gas pedal harder, wanting to get back to the office and coordinate their next move.

"Why do you think the killer murdered them after all these years?" he asked.

Her cell phone sounded. Katie quickly read the message: *Victim positively ID'd as Carol Harlan.*

CHAPTER EIGHTEEN

The blue paint spilled across the kitchen counter and dripped onto the cracked linoleum floor. It was an accident, of course. I had a school project due and there wasn't any more time to complete it. I didn't have a friend's house to go to. No one could know how I lived—with a vicious hoarder who hated everything about me. When I got older, I would leave and never come back. I waited desperately for that time.

There she was, standing there seething over the mess even though the entire kitchen and living room was filthy, cluttered with stuff occupying every available space—jam-packed. It didn't matter. She didn't see it. She only saw the paint that I had spilled.

"What have you done?" she hissed.

"It was an accident."

"What have you done?" she spat again, taking a long gulp from a plastic glass filled with straight vodka. Her long dank hair, peppered with grey, hung loosely around her face.

"Please, it was an accident. I'll clean it up." I could smell the alcohol on her breath from where I stood.

"Why do you always do this to me?"

I began wiping up the counter with used paper towels as fast as I could—the only thing I could find within my reach.

I felt the tears well up in my eyes, but willed them not to roll down my cheeks. I couldn't let her see me cry. Never. Never. Ever. Again.

"You know what this means," she said with a hint of glee in her voice.

"See? I'm cleaning it up," I begged.

"You think I like punishing you?"

"Please, no. I promise it won't happen again."

"I'm sorry, but what kind of mother would I be if I let you get away with this?"

"No."

"Go," she said.

"Please, no," I begged again. But I knew what would happen next. I had to go to her room, which stank of the heavy perfumed fabric spray she used to cover the stench of the trash we lived amongst, sickly and sweet.

"Go…" she commanded, pointing her bony discolored finger.

I put down the paper towels and walked obediently to her bedroom. That was where she kept it. The special bamboo stick that she would beat me with. Thrashing and thrashing until she was too tired to continue.

She wasn't the only one who broke my heart—just the first…

CHAPTER NINETEEN
Wednesday 1430 hours

Katie had dropped McGaven back at the office after she had received a call from Shane, the county archivist and researcher. He said he had found many of the original plans and contracts pertaining to Elm Hill Mansion.

As she drove, Katie reflected on the new information from Shelly McDonald and wondered if it was pertinent evidence, or mere gossip. It didn't really matter at this point; they needed to run down every lead no matter where it took them.

First, they needed to understand more about Elm Hill Mansion because both victims were connected to it, and it seemed to be steeped in rumors and abuse allegations that didn't amount to anything, but that now required some factual answers. Katie needed to know the truth.

She pulled into the parking lot for the Sequoia County Office Building and made her way to the building and planning department. Opening the grand doors of the old building – which was dated 1884 and still had the historical provenance to prove it – stunning vintage stained glass greeted her as she took the stairs to the second floor, even though she would eventually end up in the building's basement where the files were kept.

Shane was waiting for her at the top.

"Hello, Detective," he said as he adjusted his gold-rimmed glasses. "It's so nice to see you again."

Katie smiled. "My pleasure. I know who to go to when I need more than just the property information from the Internet or the County Assessor's Office."

"The Internet is so incomplete, even though most people try to use it entirely for their research. That's the first mistake. Just because it's on the Internet, certainly doesn't mean it's correct."

"That's what makes my job more complicated," she said. "Lead the way."

"Of course." He gestured.

Katie followed Shane to the back area of the planning and building department and over to a set of old wooden stairs leading down to the basement. Tucked away behind a door that looked like it should lead to a storage cupboard, the staircase and handrails were part of the original building and creaked loudly as they descended. Katie imagined how the early county clerks must've walked these stairs carrying handwritten documents before filing them accordingly. A string of small light bulbs was the only thing that lit the way, swinging slightly as they passed by and casting strange distorted shadows on the walls and steps.

"The county has promised to install more up-to-date lighting, but somehow, they don't make any time or money in the budget for it," he said.

"I don't know... I think it adds atmosphere to the building," she said. But in truth, it made her edgy.

Katie followed Shane to a rickety landing and then down four more steps to the basement. His thin frame easily navigated the stairs as he must have travelled up and down them thousands of times.

Once in the basement, the air temperature drastically dropped and there was a hint of moisture to it. Overhead automatic fluorescent lights flickered into life and filled the dank space, making it easy to see. There was also a light breeze from some type of air con or cleaning system pumping filtered air into the area and keeping the temperature constant. There were no windows, making you unaware if it were day or night outside.

The large room had been shuffled around since Katie had last been there. Large filing cabinets, architecture drawers, open cubbyholes of all sizes, stacked banker's boxes with perfectly printed names and corresponding letters and numbers, two large mahogany desks, two desktop computers with large scanners, and a long backlit table for spreading out reports and architectural drawings.

"You've been busy since I was last here," she said. "Wow, I'm impressed."

"I've finally had some help to move things around." He moved over to one of the computers. "I've just about finished scanning everything from the county from historical properties and houses pre-1930s. It's taken a while, but now everything is in the county's database—it's not open to the public yet though." He gestured to the empty stool. "Please," he said.

Katie was still taking everything in and marveling at how much work it took to organize it. "You've done such a tremendous job, Shane—the county is so lucky to have all of this history."

He smiled shyly, avoiding her gaze as he tapped a few keys, bringing up several black-and-white photographs.

Katie took a seat next to him and readied her notebook.

"Here is a photograph that was taken by a local photographer, Edison Evans. He took many of the area's landscapes and buildings. Anyway… this is a photo of Elm Hill Mansion located at 403 Elm Hill Road just after it was built in 1894."

"I thought it was built in 1895."

"The house was finished in 1894, but the landscaped grounds weren't completed until 1895. The property actually takes in 403, 405, and 407 Elm Hill Road, but its official address is 403 Elm Hill Road."

"Amazing…" Katie said as she studied the photographs, noticing how much smaller the trees were. Each image was from a different angle. The mansion was so beautiful and grand, situated high up on the hilltop. The details of the doors and windows were like something out of a children's story book with intricately cut flower designs and fringing in common art deco motifs.

There were several photos showing a parlor with a fainting couch and two high-back chairs, an ornate fireplace with the same designs as the windows, and a simple bedroom containing an iron bedframe with a quilt folded neatly across the bottom. Then a photo of two people standing just outside the front door next to one of the main windows on the front porch.

"Are they the original owners?" she asked.

"That's Emily and Frederick Von Slovnick. They were immigrants who came to this country from Germany. Frederick made his significant amount of money in railroads and the building industry. He built that huge house for Emily where they planned on having many children."

Katie studied the couple. They stood stiffly next to one another, side by side, arms straight down at their sides, wearing what most likely were their best outfits. Emily had on a dark dress, ankle-length, buttoned up with a light collar, with dark buttoned boots. No jewelry was visible, not even a wedding ring. Frederick wore a loose-fitting dark suit with a light-colored tie and a slim-fitting rounded hat. The couple both looked solemn and serious.

"Are there any photos with their children?"

"That's where history gets convoluted," he said.

"What do you mean?"

"Emily became pregnant several times, but she never was able to carry the baby to full term. All the babies were stillborn."

"How awful."

"But, I couldn't find any death certificates to support that—until…"

"What do you think happened?"

"Well…" He clicked to more photographs, these showing a horse-drawn carriage pulling a hearse.

"Did they die?"

Shane clicked on a newspaper article dated 1911 from the *Sacramento Bee*: *Couple Dies in Unknown Circumstances: Five baby corpses found buried in backyard.*

"I've never heard about this before, aside from the usual high school rumors about a woman in a long dress wandering around the grounds like she was searching for something." She laughed. "When kids got bored of that, no one ever really talked about the place until it was donated for the project to house troubled foster girls."

"From everything I've been able to find out from newspaper articles and family history online, it appeared that Mr. Von Slovnick poisoned his wife's after-dinner drink and then took his life as well. You would assume because of the loss of the children, but I can't find actual proof. That drives me crazy."

"Sounds more like a movie plot."

"You could see how stories and gossip could easily take on lives of their own over the years."

"Definitely." Katie quickly reviewed the photos again. "This is fascinating stuff, but what does it have to do with the foster home?"

"Two things. This is where it gets a little interesting. Here's the list of owners since the Slovnicks." He pulled out a piece of paper from a file showing a dozen names and gave it to Katie. "Nothing unusual, except the fact that most only owned the home for short periods of time, a year, three years, and most never lived in it until Sara and Jonathan McKinzie who lived there for almost twenty years. They then sold to MDI, Magnum Development, Incorporated."

"Do you have any contact information for the McKinzies?"

"Yes and no."

"What do you mean?"

"I'm sorry, I don't mean to sound like I'm taking you on a wild goose chase. I couldn't find anything else about them. It's almost as if..."

"They're ghosts," said Katie. "Sorry, I couldn't resist. It most likely means that they were bogus names. But why?"

"Keeping identities hidden usually means that they have something to hide..."

"Something criminal," she said. "Well, thank you, Shane, it's been interesting as usual. I'm not sure how this fits into the two homicides yet—if at all."

"Detective, I told you I had two things."

"Oh yes, what else do you have?" Her thoughts were already a couple steps ahead, wanting to hear what Dr. Dean had to say about the Rodriguez body.

Shane got up from the desk and pulled out two sets of architectural drawings. Katie joined him, peering over his shoulder as he unrolled the plans.

"Here are the original plans for the mansion," he said, showing Katie the dates and the different pages depicting the plumbing, electrical, and the different stories of the house. "Now, here are the plans that were submitted for permits."

Katie looked at both and they seemed the same—the dimensions, floors, and general layout. She didn't immediately see any difference. But her eye caught the staircase, something *was* different. "The staircase," she said.

"Good eye, Detective. You're correct. The staircase area was actually made smaller."

"Why?" she asked.

"I don't know. To make more storage space, perhaps, or to make the stairs more aesthetically pleasing? I don't know, but I thought it was worth bringing to your attention."

Katie scrutinized the drawings for a moment.

"Have you been inside the mansion?" he asked.

"I took a brief walk around the mansion and property, and looked at the basement."

"You might want to check out the staircase next time you are there. You know, sometimes in houses of this age they would build extra storage, a narrow staircase for servants, or a small servant's quarters. The Slovnicks seemed to have enough money to pay for a servant or nanny."

She nodded, taking it all in as he pulled out a large legal-sized envelope filled with a stack of paperwork. "Here you go, Detective. I made copies of everything I had and what we've talked about."

"Thank you so much, Shane, for your hard work. As I've said before, I wish everyone who helped with criminal investigations were as thorough and professional as you."

He smiled and couldn't quite keep Katie's gaze. "Thank you, Detective."

"Oh, I have a question for you but... you have to keep it *confidential.*"

"Of course," he said, perked up, his eyes wide with wonder.

"I don't know if this means anything. I wouldn't normally leak this confidential information so early in the investigations, but since the Elm Hill Mansion has such a colorful past I just thought..."

"It's okay, Detective—really. I swear, I won't tell anyone."

Katie smiled and said, "Do the words 'raccoglitore di cacciatori' mean anything to you?"

Without hesitation, he said, "It means hunter-gatherer."

"You know Italian?" she asked.

"Yes, and Spanish and German."

"Does hunter-gatherer mean anything to you—besides the obvious?"

"There's an old book series that was written in the late 1940s based on one young man's experiences of finding his way in life— where he fits in and what his life means. He travelled the cities, rural areas, and many countries to try and find himself. It's quite interesting and a bit unsettling. It's called *The Hunter-Gatherer: One Man's Journey.*"

Katie was temporarily at a loss for words. "You say this is a book series from the 1940s?"

"Yeah, I like old stuff, what can I say? It's actually well written by… the author's name escapes me. Sorry."

"How many books are there?"

"Uh, four or five. No wait, six books."

Katie jotted down some notes. "You definitely have what it takes to be a detective, you know," she said, though numbers raced through her mind: six girls in foster care, six books in the series, and five buried stillborn babies. Could there be some connection there?

"Nah, I love it right where I am."

Katie took the envelope from him. "I believe you're right. You are right where you should be." She turned to leave and said, "If you think of anything else, you know how to reach me."

"Yes, Detective—I will certainly do that. Good luck. Do you need an escort back to the main floor?"

"I can manage, thank you." She turned to leave, gazing at all of the historical information around her and still amazed about all she had learned about Elm Hill Mansion.

CHAPTER TWENTY

Wednesday 1635 hours

Katie rushed back through the forensics division of the sheriff's department to meet up with McGaven, but stopped when she heard voices coming from John's office. Glancing in, she could see two technicians and John having a meeting, so she kept moving to her office at the end of the hall.

The office door was slightly ajar, and she could hear low voices from within. Her gut instinct put her on high alert as she pushed open the door. Leaning on the corner of her desk was Undersheriff Dorothy Sullivan, dressed in a deputy uniform instead of her expensive suit and spike heels. Her makeup had been pared back a little too.

Both McGaven and the undersheriff turned to Katie as she stood in the doorway.

McGaven raised his eyebrows at Katie, implying that he had no idea why the second highest officer at the sheriff's department had paid an unannounced visit to their cold-case office.

"Detective Scott," the undersheriff said. There was something in the way she pronounced "Scott" that made Katie cringe.

"Undersheriff Sullivan?" Katie replied.

"Oh no, Sullivan or Dottie is just fine," she said and smiled broadly as she stood up, several inches taller than Katie, even without her heels.

Katie returned a smile as she dropped her briefcase and the large envelope from Shane on the desk. "Is there anything that we can do for you?"

"Oh no. I'm just making the rounds and talking with everyone—getting acquainted. I wanted to see how the cold-case unit operated. Very clever use of space here. It's great, actually," she said looking around and gazing at Katie's whiteboard scribbled with notes and next leads. "I won't keep you two. I can see that you're busy." She hesitated before exiting, as if on cue. "I appreciate your reports on the Harlan homicide. Keep up the great work." She turned and then faced Katie directly. "How's lunch sometime next week?"

"Uh, sure." Katie tried to sound enthusiastic, but she wasn't looking forward to being chatty with her boss or having a "girls' lunch" either.

"Your uncle said how much you like burgers, so let's meet for burgers then."

"Of course. Text me the date and time," said Katie.

Undersheriff Sullivan left.

"Well, that was exciting," said McGaven, not looking up from the computer screen.

Katie put her index finger to her lips—giving the signal to remain quiet for a moment. She peered out the door and everything was clear. "She's gone now."

"Katie made a new friend," said McGaven teasingly.

"Thanks. Why don't you go instead?"

"C'mon, a burger power-lunch will do you good."

"Yeah, no."

"Here's info and background on the girls," he said and handed Katie a sheet of paper. "To add to your murder board."

"Okay. Wow, not a lot of information."

"I was a bit surprised too—but they were essentially thrown away, taken into foster care and thrown back out. I couldn't find a residence for Tanis Jones, but there's her last place of employment. It's something."

Katie began writing an overview of the young women who were the last to stay at Elm Hill Mansion. "Okay, Tanis Jones works at Sunshine Gifts & Antiques. We'll have to pay her a visit. Heather Lawson moved out of state to Kansas and there are no records for her. Terry Slaughter – no information. She has quite a few aliases. And Karen Beck committed suicide in prison."

Katie stood back and sighed.

"What's up?" McGaven asked.

"Just looking at the short lives of these young women. How things could have been different if they had homes, families, someone who cared. It just makes me sad."

"For all intents and purposes, we have to move forward assuming that Candace Harlan is alive," he said slowly. "Heather Lawson and Terry Slaughter, too." McGaven scrolled through pages of information. "I believe that Lawson and Slaughter most likely changed their names. It will be difficult to find them, but we can, if needed."

"Unless one of them becomes our next victim," Katie said sourly.

"Hey, you're not getting all negative on me now," he said.

"Never." She studied the board. "We need to talk with Tanis Jones."

McGaven looked up. "Let's go."

A buzz alerted Katie that there was a text. She glanced at her phone and saw that it was from Chad, but dismissed it, promising herself she would get back to him later.

"Have we received any emails from forensics or the medical examiner? We need to talk to him about Mary Rodriguez." Katie hadn't had a chance to open her messages and knew that McGaven was always cc'd on any reports.

"Nope."

"What about that CPS officer? Has he called you back?"

"Wait a minute. Oh yes… Jerry Weaver, CAPSW."

"That's quite a title."

"It means he's a certified advanced practice social worker and CPA officer."

"We need for him to get us all the information about the last six girls at the Elm Hill Mansion."

"I've put in another call to him. We keep missing each other, so I gave him your number as well."

"Good. Updates… okay, let's see what kind of evidence picture we get here…" she said and began printing her newest information.

McGaven read as she wrote.

"So, the mansion was actually built in 1894 with the landscaping completed in 1895. It is 403 Elm Hill Road."

"Okay, makes sense."

"The original owners were German immigrants Emily and Frederick Von Slovnick. He made a considerable income in the railroad and building business—so he built this beautiful mansion for his bride."

"That was a big deal back then."

"This is where it gets unusual. According to available records, Emily had several miscarriages with no living children. Then Frederick poisoned his wife and took his own life."

"Wow, tragic," he said.

Katie stepped back and said, "The only thing that seems to stand out about the house is that the building plans differ—from the original to the submitted. It seems that there is a discrepancy in the staircase."

"Placement or size?"

"It's actually smaller now."

McGaven thought about it for a moment. "We'll have to check it out and see what's what."

"Okay, this is who we have so far…" she said, and continued her lists.

Current People of Interest:

Unknown man/boy *that Candace Harlan met and ran away with.*

Robert (Bob) Bramble *– construction foreman for the Elm Hill Mansion Project. Found body.*

Amy Striker—*emergency contact for Candace Harlan (dentist office)—address 1457 Green Street at the Parker Division.*

Unidentified man *– hooded runner at Parker Division.*

Tanis Jones—*only local foster girl. Last place of employment (current) Sunshine Gifts & Antiques.*

Shelly McDonald—*in prison, confirmed that there were disciplinary actions and police were dispatched. Linked to Deputy Hugh Keller.*

Sara and Jonathan McKinzie *– previous owners of Elm Hill Mansion.*

Deputy Hugh Keller—*dispatched to Elm Hill Mansion domestic disturbance, disturbing the peace, missing persons report. Implied relationship with Shelly McDonald? Was relieved of duties just after the mansion closed down for good. Works as a bartender at The Well.*

"I think that's about it for now," she said. "It's—" She stopped talking and struggled with her lists.

"What's wrong?" McGaven asked.

"I'm not sure."

"Well, we'll just have to keep pushing forward and see what shakes out. This isn't all of it—just what we know now."

"I guess you're right. Have you found out anything else about 'hunter-gatherer'?"

"Just what you have, but I'm searching social media, blog sites, and chat rooms to see if there's any connection with special groups or crime sprees—anything of interest. I'm also searching the tri-county area for other homicides that might resemble ours."

"As a stroke of luck, I asked Shane at the county archives if 'hunter-gatherer' meant anything and he said that there are six books in a series with that name from the 1940s about a young man and his travels."

"That's interesting and convenient. Those books sound so abstract, but I'll see what else I can find out," he said.

"The killer taking the extra steps to carve those words on his victims' backs—and his fascination with Italian. Says something…"

"Like he's crazy."

Katie chuckled. "No, it says something about his life, an event, or his childhood."

"You mean some defining moment?"

"More like some type of a lifestyle he hates or loves, the way he was brought up, or something that isn't so obvious. But it is big for him." Looking back at the board, she said, "Everything has been set in motion because of Candace Harlan. We find out where she is and I think everything will begin to fall into place." Glancing at her watch, she said, "Let's get out of the office."

"I thought you'd never ask."

"John is having some type of meeting with his tech so I can't ask him about the evidence, and I haven't heard from Dr. Dean about Mary Rodriguez's autopsy. And it's a bit too early to catch Hugh Keller at work… So let's see what we can find out from Tanis Jones. We may need to have patrol check in on her periodically. I want to make sure she and the other girls are safe."

"On it. I'm still trying to track down Heather Lawson and Terry Slaughter."

"Oh, and I have a surprise for you," she said, smiling and gathering up her keys, phone, and notes.

Standing up and slipping his jacket on, he said, "Can it get any better?"

"Cisco is going to join us."

"That's epic."

CHAPTER TWENTY-ONE

Wednesday 1705 hours

A light mist filtered over the countryside, covering the sky and making the hour seem later than it was. The leaves were falling at a quickened pace and the usual brilliant shades of nature's greens were just a bit duller than normal. Katie flipped on the windshield wipers and grumbled that the blades were in dire need of replacing as every swipe made a grinding noise and streaked her view.

A soft whine emitted from the back, as Cisco's head and attentive ears pushed their way in between the driver and passenger's seats. He gazed out the window and began to softly pant.

"I hear you, big guy," said McGaven as he peered through the streaky windshield. "I hate rain too."

"It's not rain. It's barely misting," said Katie as she punched the accelerator and they rocketed down the road.

"Where's the fire?"

"Everything in a homicide investigation is a fire—that's homicide 101."

"Yeah, well I want to get there in one piece."

"Haven't you always?" she said.

"Point taken."

Katie drove toward a popular tourist area where many visitors stopped to buy supplies and gifts before heading off on various hiking trails and to local camping areas. She slowed her speed at the high street and began searching for a little shop called Sunshine

Gifts & Antiques amongst many quaint shops with colorful banners fluttering in the breeze.

Spotting a parking spot, Katie said, "This place is as good as any," and swung the car into the place with ease. For a moment she watched as a couple walked by slowly drinking coffee from a local java house and stopping to admire a window display before moving on. Cisco put his muzzle to the open crack of a back window trying to get a noseful of all the wonderful smells of the streets and people passing by the car.

Scanning the small shops, Katie and McGaven quickly found the gift shop and entered. Pushing the door open, a high-pitched three-step chime alerted the staff that someone new had arrived. The shop was small, but filled with gifts of every kind: key chains; journal books; candles; postcards; toys; jewelry; books; T-shirts and aprons printed with silly phrases. These items filled every inch of the space and most of the walls.

"Hello?" said Katie patiently waiting.

The smell of incense was sickly and overbearing. Katie hadn't given any thought of her anxiety in more than a day, but being in a cluttered store made her uneasy. Her mind kept flashing to the smell of smoke and burning buildings, making her tense and lightheaded. Once that uneasy feeling had been released, she knew what followed—fight or flight.

As usual, McGaven stayed near the door in case someone tried to sneak up on them or do a runner.

"Hello?" Katie repeated, her voice sounding funny and far away in her ears. She had the strong urge to run out of the store and just keep going.

Not now…

A shuffling noise came behind the counter and a short woman wearing a tie-dyed dress in a dizzying array of blue, yellow, and pink appeared. She had too many colorful bangles on her wrists and every finger carried an oversized ring adorned with colorful stones. Her eyes slowly scrutinized Katie, taking in her badge and gun. "Yes, can I help you?" she said with a forced smile.

Katie knew it wasn't Tanis Jones because the woman was easily in her sixties.

"Hi, I'm Detective Scott from the sheriff's department. And this is Deputy McGaven. We were given information that a Tanis Jones works here."

"No," the woman replied. "I don't know anyone by that name."

Katie watched as the old woman could barely keep her eye contact and it was clear that she was lying. "I'm sorry, but who are you?"

"I'm Mandy, the owner of the shop."

"Nice to meet you, Mandy, but we have received credible information that Tanis Jones worked here, or still might be working here. Are you sure she isn't here?"

"I'm sorry, Detective."

"I tell you what. Here's my card with my personal cell phone number on the back. If you happen to remember Tanis, please give this to her." Katie put her business card on the counter. "Tanis is *not* in trouble, by any means. I would like to speak with her about her friend Candace and anything that she tells me is confidential. Alright?"

The woman nodded but made no move to pick up the card.

"Thank you, Mandy, for your time," she said and left with McGaven.

Once outside, Katie said, "Now we wait."

"What? You think that she's going to give your number to Tanis Jones?"

"Trust me. I know a thing or two about people who are distrustful about the police. I bet she's calling Tanis right now."

"Twenty bucks."

"What?" she said.

"Twenty bucks that she doesn't contact Tanis."

"You're on. Double or nothing that we hear from Tanis in an hour."

"Detective Scott, you have a bet. Now what?" he said looking around.

"A very late lunch."

Katie and McGaven stepped out of the deli after finishing their food. Katie carried some extra turkey and bacon in a napkin as a snack for Cisco.

"Well, somebody is going to owe me twenty bucks," said McGaven looking at his watch. "It's been about an hour."

"It's been forty-one minutes," Katie corrected.

"Okay. We'll wait another nineteen minutes."

Katie opened the driver's door and fed a very thankful German shepherd his treats. "Good boy. I didn't forget about you."

Katie's cell phone rang. "Scott," she answered.

McGaven stepped forward, waiting to hear who was calling.

"Is this Detective Scott?" the woman's voice asked.

"Yes." Katie looked up and down the street, trying to see if she could see Tanis Jones.

"I heard that you wanted to talk to me."

"Is this Tanis?"

There was a hesitation. "Yes."

"I have a few questions about Elm Hill Mansion and Candace Harlan. And the other girls if you feel up to it."

Tanis didn't answer.

"Ms. Jones?"

"I know that you have questions, but…"

"I can promise you that it will be discreet."

"I don't want to end up in court."

Katie looked at McGaven, biting her lip. "I don't see that happening. We're trying to get some background information. Please, Ms. Jones, it would be very helpful in our homicide investigations."

"Investigations? There's more than one?"

"Yes, I'm afraid so. We're still identifying the second body—but we believe it was one of the girls at Elm Hill."

"No…" she said, her voice weak and fading.

"Where can we meet you?"

"If you go up the street past the real estate office, there's an alley. Take it and there will be stairs at the end. My studio is up there."

"We'll see you in a couple of minutes."

The call ended.

"Damn, I'm out twenty bucks," he said.

Cisco barked and suddenly darted from the car.

"Cisco!" Katie yelled after him.

The black dog trotted up the street and took an immediate right to the alley.

"Where the hell is he going?" said McGaven.

"I think to Tanis Jones's house."

The partners jogged up the street and turned up the alley, following the dog's trail. There were two dumpsters and the intense aroma of the back kitchen of a bakery.

"He better not be tracking a doughnut," McGaven chuckled.

"Cisco," Katie said again, ignoring McGaven's comment.

A painfully thin woman peeked out over the railing as the dog zoomed up to greet her. Cisco nudged her hand and she bent down to meet him, petting him constantly. "You are beautiful," she said.

Katie recognized the woman as Tanis, older than her twenty-three years, thinner than expected, and her hair had been dyed with red and brown streaks. She was about to say something but stopped. Cisco seemed to have a calming effect on her as she spoke to him quietly.

"Is it okay if we come up?" Katie asked.

Tanis nodded.

Katie and McGaven slowly ascended the stairs. "I'm Detective Katie Scott and this is Deputy Sean McGaven."

She shyly invited them into her home.

"That's Cisco. He's a retired military dog," Katie said.

"A war dog?"

"Yes."

Tanis said, "You were in the military?" She sounded surprised as she studied Katie.

"Two tours in the army with Cisco here. We were an explosives K9 team." She smiled and sensed that it meant something special to Tanis, but she didn't push to find out more.

"Please come in," she said.

The studio apartment had been decorated in a similar style to the gift shop with bright colors and plenty of knickknacks. Katie figured that the owner was letting Tanis stay there.

A folded futon took up one corner of the room and there were two mismatched fabric chairs on the other side. At the other end was a small kitchen with a microwave and hot plate and then a closed door which she assumed to be the bathroom.

Instead of standing awkwardly at the threshold, Katie took a seat in one of the chairs. She eyed McGaven and he took the other. They patiently waited.

Tanis quietly petted Cisco and then sat on the makeshift couch with the dog nearby. She pulled her bare feet under her to get comfortable. "What did you want to know, Detective?"

Katie had all sorts of questions she wanted to ask, but as she watched the frail young woman petting Cisco, she hesitated. "Well..." she began. "You lived at Elm Hill Mansion?"

"Yes."

"How long did you live there?"

"Since I was thirteen," she said.

Katie assumed that to mean about five years. "What was it like there?"

Never looking up from Cisco, she said, matter of fact, "It was like living in a jail waiting for the she-beast to attack."

Katie carefully worded her questions, realizing that not only was Tanis physically frail, she was emotionally frail too. "The she-beast—are you referring to Shelly McDonald?"

She nodded.

"Did everyone call her that?"

"Yes. Because she was," she replied, looking directly at Katie. Diverting her attention to Cisco, she continued, "She was horrible. She was moody, taking things out on us and making us do things that were wrong, especially when the police officer visited. But her anger was mostly fixated on me."

"Why was that?"

"Because I complained the least and I was quiet. It made her mad that I kept quiet, unlike the others who resisted, threw fits, and called her names." She paused. "The others were different. Heather was the cheerleader, she kept it positive and smiled through it all. And you never knew what Terry would come up with, such a drama queen." Tanis smiled, as if remembering better times.

"And Karen?"

Tanis's expression turned sour. "Karen was a dark person, but it was an inward kind of dark."

A slight breeze blew through the tiny apartment and one of the wind chimes jangled. The sunlight seemed to sparkle through some of the trinkets and ornaments.

"What was it like with Candace? The discipline?" Katie looked to McGaven who had been listening intently and seemed to have a melancholy expression on his face—a look of sadness as if recalling a memory.

Cisco sat close to Tanis, reveling in all the attention he received, but it was also as if his sixth sense knew that Tanis needed some comfort and love. Dogs were like that—and Cisco was no different. He quietly panted, ears straight ahead as the pets kept coming.

Tanis looked up. "Oh, no. It wasn't like that for Candace. She was special."

"Special. How?" Katie gently pushed.

"Well, she was beautiful. Everyone loved her and wanted to be her friend. She was one of those people that you noticed, know what I mean?"

Katie nodded.

"She stood up for people. She didn't take crap from anyone. Life was too short."

"You two were close?"

"Yes."

"She watched over you?"

"Oh yes. Things changed for me when she came to stay at Elm."

Katie smiled. "I had a friend like that. Who looked out for me. We were inseparable."

Tanis looked up. "Really? What happened to her?"

"She... passed away."

"Oh, I'm sorry."

"Tanis..."

The young woman stopped petting Cisco for a moment. "You want to know about that night? The last time I saw Candace?"

"Yes, I do. Can you tell me?"

"I told that police officer who took the missing persons report everything I knew. He was always at Elm. And I never lied."

Katie searched her phone photos and stopped on one showing Deputy Hugh Keller, which was from his academy photo. "Is this the police officer that came to Elm all the time?"

"Yes."

"I would like to hear what happened from you. Can you tell me?" Katie kept her tone low as if talking to a child.

Tanis took a deep breath and observed Katie. She remained quiet, studying Katie's face for a moment before speaking. "There's a sadness about you, Detective. You feel torn. Part of you is here and part of you is still there. Don't worry, it will be okay."

Katie blinked in surprise, completely taken off guard. Like Tanis had looked right into her soul and really seen her. She felt her pulse jump and her voice caught in her throat. Taking a deep breath, she said, "Did you plan on escaping before that night?"

Tanis smiled and went back to petting Cisco. "We talked about it for a while. We talked about our dreams and what we would do when we left Elm. We both wanted to get married and have children, live in a big house with a maid, and… always live near each other so our children could play together…"

This time, Katie looked away.

"Then one night Candace woke me up and said it was time to go. We had already packed our small suitcases with what we could and hid them outside. There was no time to change. We were both in our nightgowns."

"What was Candace's mood?"

"She was her usual upbeat self, ready for an adventure."

"What happened? Why didn't you go with her as planned?"

Tanis readjusted her seat and smoothed her skirt. "You don't understand, Detective. If I would have left, then one of the other girls would have to take my place for the discipline. I couldn't let that happen. I only had a few more months before I was legally able to leave."

"I see." Katie had to strain to hear Tanis. At times she spoke so quietly that both she and McGaven had to lean forward to better hear her.

"I'm not sure that you do. Oh, I think you understand a lot about good friends, teamwork, and doing everything within your power to make sure that they're okay—that you are all okay. But…"

Katie felt the ping of prickly energy shooting down her limbs. The mention and memory of her army team evoked so many emotions that it was difficult to process them all at once.

"The girls at Elm, we were like a team. And I was the one that was most able to take the discipline. I knew it wasn't forever. Just like it was Candace's place to protect us from…" She couldn't finish. Her voice went hoarse and tears welled up in her eyes.

Katie swallowed hard, knowing what she was going to say, but she had to hear it from Tanis.

"Candace protected the rest of the girls from what?"

"From whatever he wanted… and whatever the she-beast wanted…"

"Tanis?" she said, and waited for the young woman to look at her.

Finally Tanis met her gaze.

"What did they make Candace do?"

"Awful things."

"I know this is uncomfortable… but…"

Tanis blurted out. "They made her have sex with them. And they told her if she didn't that they would do to us what they did to her. She protected us, just as I did from the physical abuse and so-called discipline." She began to cry. Cisco snuggled close to console her.

It took everything inside Katie not to hug her and tell her that things would get better. But she had to remain professional and keep herself removed emotionally in order to work the investigation to the best of her ability. It was the hardest thing she ever had to do in police work.

"Tanis, are you aware that there was a body found at Elm Hill Mansion on Monday?"

"Um," she said. "No."

"They found a body that they thought was Candace, but it wasn't." Katie waited for her reaction.

Tanis took a deep breath to steady her emotions. "It wasn't Candace?"

"No, it wasn't."

"You said they thought it was her, but it wasn't... I don't understand."

"We've just recently learned that Candace had a twin sister, Carol." Katie thought there would be a reaction from Tanis, but there was none. "Tanis, did you know that Candace had a twin?"

"Yes."

"You did?"

"That's how Candace was able to sneak out all the time. Her sister was homeless for a lot of years and didn't want to be put in the system and possibly lose contact with her sister."

"So you're saying that Candace and Carol would switch at Elm Hill and no one knew it."

"No, not even the other girls."

"Do you think Mrs. McDonald knew?"

"No way. Trust me, she never knew. She would have freaked and someone would have had hell to pay. Most likely, me."

"What was Candace doing when they switched places?"

"She was setting things up for when we escaped."

"Who did she come in contact with?"

"I'm not sure... the only name I knew was Ray. He was going to take us away from there. That's why Carol wasn't there. It was all planned out."

"Did you ever see Candace or Carol again after Candace escaped?"

Tanis pulled her legs close to her body, wrapping her arms around them. "I saw her leave that night. It seems like yesterday..."

Katie felt compassion for the young frail woman and the emotional distress she was under.

"I... never... saw either of them again."

"Tanis, this is important. Do you know who Ray was, or his last name, or anything about him that would help us?"

Shaking her head, she said, "I don't know. I just knew his name was Ray and he was older."

CHAPTER TWENTY-TWO
Thursday 0715 hours

The early morning golden light had barely broken through above the hills around Pine Valley and the temperature was only just touching fifty-two degrees. It had rained overnight, leaving the trail and the forest area filled with a beautiful aroma.

Katie had been able to get to bed at a decent hour and was ready for the early morning to spend some extra bonding and training time with Cisco before work. She had already booked the time with Sergeant Hardy. Dressed in blue jeans, long-sleeved blouse, dark brown jacket, and brown boots, she prepared for the drill. She even wore her gun and badge for the exercise.

Katie knew it was as difficult for Cisco to retire from the army and just relax and be a civilian as it was for her. His days had always been filled with searching for IEDs (improvised explosive devices) and pieces of detonators. Depending upon their mission and special orders received, they searched for specific devices or did sweeps to clear buildings and key areas for other military teams. The least she could do to help him adjust was work him through training and simulations every so often, to help satisfy the high drive of his breed.

Standing amongst towering pine trees with his ears perked and amber eyes forward, Cisco's shiny black coat glistened in the light. His muscles tensed. His back. His legs. He waited with all the patience of an expertly trained dog for Katie's commands. With the anticipated excitement, the dog began to lightly pant—it was like a relief valve.

"We're set," came a voice over her walkie-talkie.

Katie pressed the speak button. "Roger that." She unclipped the six-foot leather leash and snapped on the trailing lead which was about twenty-five feet.

As soon as the lead clicked into Cisco's harness, he began to bark furiously, wagging his tail. It was difficult for him to stay still, but he had to wait.

There was a piece of a torn black shirt lying across the trail. Katie guided Cisco toward it to make sure he had a good whiff before moving ahead. "*Find*," she said.

Cisco was ready to go and began to take Katie down the narrow path, deviating only twice from the track but returning again. She kept him on a short leash.

Cisco's sniffs were the only sounds in the forest. All the wildlife was strangely quiet as they waited for the potential predator to move or reveal himself. False clues of clothing worn by another person had been planted around the area to challenge the dog's concentration on the specific track. Cisco sniffed the air in their direction, but didn't leave his track. He moved quickly and systematically, head down, tail down: focused.

It amazed Katie watching Cisco work. She remembered the first time she saw him in the kennel. Loud incessant barking. Unruly behavior, jumping and growling if anyone got too close to the kennel door. Clearly, he did not want to be there. The training sergeant said no one wanted to work with him and he had even bit one of the recruits. But there was something about the dog that attracted Katie to him. There was a misunderstood quality about Cisco. Maybe black dogs were passed over in the military, just like black dogs in animal shelters. That didn't deter Katie. She was intrigued and asked to see him. After the first walk in the training yard, she knew that they were going to be a team to be reckoned with. His endless energy, focus, and athletic ability were unlike any dog she had ever worked with. At first, he challenged her authority with barking and nipping. But after a while, all he wanted was to hear commands from her.

Katie watched Cisco work with pride, giving him enough lead, following him around obstacles of trees and off-trail bushes. She wasn't sure where the decoy was hiding, but that made the experience a little bit more authentic for both the handler and dog. Cisco stopped, head raised, lightly sniffing the open air in the slight breeze that was coming toward him. Katie stood quietly and let the dog do what he was trained to do.

Another a few seconds passed, then Cisco took off through a tangle of low-lying bushes. Katie, running to keep up, thought that maybe Cisco had been confused by the breeze and perhaps some of the deep forest smells, but knew that wasn't likely.

Pulling her toward a large pine tree, Cisco began barking. As Katie stepped toward the area, she saw the decoy dressed in a full training bite suit stand up with his hands in the air, making aggressive gestures toward them.

"Put your hands behind your head and turn around!" she commanded.

The decoy began walking towards her with a large stick in his hand.

"Drop the weapon now!"

He made simulated stabbing gestures.

"Drop the weapon now!" Katie leaned down and unhooked Cisco's lead and he instantly ran and then leapt in the air, catching the decoy's shoulder and dragging him to the ground. "Stay down!" The decoy pretended to struggle. "Stay down!" she repeated.

The heavily protected decoy stopped moving.

"Cisco, *aus*!"

The dog immediately let go of the decoy and padded back to Katie.

"Good boy," she said, patting him on the side and giving him his favorite yellow ball.

"Great work," said Sergeant Blake Hardy as he emerged from a safe distance with another K9 officer.

"Thanks," Katie said, smiling and a little breathless. Even though it had been a simulation, it still pumped the adrenalin.

"You okay, Rick?" said Hardy.

"Oh yeah," he said, getting to his feet. "Nice work. I thought he was going to flip me on my head for a split second."

Everyone laughed.

"Cisco is great to show everyone else how it should be done," said the sergeant.

"Thank you, Sergeant, for letting us participate. Cisco has been a bit antsy with my schedule lately."

"I heard that you're working two homicides," said Hardy.

"Yeah," she said, feeling uncomfortable talking about a current investigation with other officers.

"I've heard good things about your work—glad you decided to stay on here at the sheriff's department."

"Thank you. That means a lot." She hadn't spoken about work with him before, but he seemed genuine. Glancing at her watch, "I better get back so that I'm not late for work."

"See you soon," he said.

The decoy and other officer said their quick goodbyes.

Katie hurried back the way they came and made it to the parking lot where her work sedan waited. Loading up Cisco and climbing behind the wheel, she quickly checked her cell phone for texts and messages. There was a text from John in forensics: *Have some updates for you—anytime today.*

Katie drove out of the parking lot, leaving behind the K9 patrol cars and a couple of SUVs as the training continued. She was so focused on the road and the cases she didn't see the anonymous hiker wearing dark running pants and hoodie watching her drive away.

CHAPTER TWENTY-THREE
Thursday 1015 hours

Katie rushed into the forensic lab eager to talk to John. Just before she reached the main exam laboratory, she turned to see McGaven heading back in to their office.

"Hey, you want to join me?" she called after him.

"You have it under control. I'm going to keep organizing searches—taking a closer look at the county workers at Elm Hill."

"Oh, okay. I'll update you when I get back."

"Sounds good," he said and kept walking down the long hallway to the last office on the right.

Katie heard the door open and shut. It was easy to hear just about anything in the forensics lab due to the extreme quiet. The soft hum of the recirculated air was the only thing audible most of the time.

"Are you coming in, or are you going to just stand there?" said John. It was difficult to say if he was in a good mood or not.

"Oh," she uttered and then entered the lab. Katie noticed that the work areas had been reorganized to create room to spread out evidence.

"I take it you've been keeping busy," he said.

"Yes, two homicides."

"That's quite a work load for the cold-case unit."

"It seems to work out that way—at least for us." Katie always had a difficult time holding John's gaze. She wasn't sure if it was the fact that he was an ex-Navy Seal and seemed to command that type of attention, or if there were some attraction towards him. Either way, she pushed it aside and dismissed it.

"What do you want to hear first?" he asked, cracking a smile.

Katie moved closer to him, near the computer area. She noticed that all the computers had even larger monitors, which made it easier to see evidence in closer detail. "Let's start with the Harlan case."

John flicked through some files until he came to a large photo of the right index fingernail. The cotton candy pink was difficult to ignore. "You were correct, the fingernail belongs to the right index finger and there are good chunks of DNA which we will compare when we have Carol Harlan's DNA." He looked at Katie for a moment. "What's bothering you?"

Katie sighed. "So many things…"

John chuckled. "Well, let's start from the beginning then."

"Can you tell if the nail was torn because of a struggle or if it was intentionally removed?"

"It was ripped with force, judging by the bits of cuticle still attached. You don't like that it was just sitting in the dirt beside her—like someone put it there?"

"Yes. It doesn't make sense—seems a little contrived. Do you have photos of the victim's hands?"

He switched to another file and did a split screen where you could see the victim's hands and the torn fingernail.

"See, look at the condition of the other nails. They are broken and dirty with an older version of polish, but the nail by itself looks like it was newly painted."

"Maybe the killer took the nail at a different time and saved it, but there are signs of the flexor and extensor tendons, which would indicate that it was torn forcefully, leaving behind these pieces."

"Maybe."

"Here's victim number two." He brought up close-up photographs of Mary's hands. The condition of the nails and hands were similar to Carol Harlan except she didn't have nail polish and they looked as if she chewed them.

"The condition looks similar."

"The dirt under the nails is consistent. But there's no way to determine exactly where the dirt is from in this county because most of the soil is made up of clay, sand and other organic matter. If you get up to the higher elevations, then you might be able to tell due to the organic matter. Like yellow or red soil has more oxidized <u>ferric iron oxides</u> and brown or black soil has more water or oxygen content."

"Hmmm."

"You're thinking again."

"I've seen both crime scenes in person, but when I view them on the computer certain things pop up to me."

"Like?"

"I'm noticing now that both of them have clean hair. Doesn't that seem a little strange to you?"

"I haven't thought much about it, but it does seem unlikely that they would have clean hair. But it does answer the question of why I found traces on their skin of what would be consistent as shampoo."

"What about the nail polish?" she said, going through the evidence in her mind.

"From what we know so far, it's just cheap polish that you can purchase anywhere, the super stores, drugs stores, maybe some beauty supplies outlets. It is a distinct color of pink so that would cut out some of your search. But it belonged to the victim."

"Were the rope or twine the same?"

"No."

Katie felt defeated. "A different type of rope?"

"Yes and no."

"Now you sound like Dr. Dean."

"It was the same *type* of heavy cotton twine, but different thicknesses. One was quarter inch and the other was three eighths of the same. Now, if I had something to compare them to—something from a suspect's house—that would be a different story."

"I see," said Katie, jotting down a few notes to jog her memory. "Nothing I can run with. It could mean the same person, or not."

"I will send you the report."

"I know, but writing it makes me remember it more concisely at the moment. More visual."

"How are you doing?" he asked, turning his undivided attention on her.

"Me? I'm fine." She thought that was a question out of the blue.

"I know how hard it was for you with your aunt's death and your uncle taking the brunt of the investigation." He paused. "I haven't seen much of you and well…"

"John, I've appreciated your friendship and everything you've done to help me during that time. You and McGaven have been priceless to me."

He raised his eyebrows. "Priceless, huh."

Katie laughed rather nervously, and said, "You know what I mean. I don't know how else to describe it. We all have stressful jobs and understand the nature of this business, but when personal things happen it's nice to know who your real friends are."

"I agree."

Katie smiled.

"I didn't know if you noticed or not, but your Harlan victim had a patch of hair removed."

"Yes, I saw that. What do you mean, though? Like ripped out?"

"It appears that way."

Katie thought about it. "Maybe the killer took it as a keepsake or trophy?"

"Could be," he said.

"Okay, now for the $64,000 question," she said.

"The carvings on their backs." He moved to another computer and with impressive speed brought up several files. One graph showed sharp spikes up and down while the other showed percentages of chemicals—both natural and manmade.

Katie watched with extreme interest.

"Okay, we were able to get enough to test what the ink was made of and to determine it wasn't premade or a common type of ink tattoo, or otherwise; it was actually a concoction that was homemade with a few unexpected ingredients."

Katie was completely intrigued and waited patiently.

"We tested in a couple of places from both victims. It revealed that sometimes the ink was stronger and then weaker in its mixture." Clicking to another open window, "Here's the list of the main ingredients: part linseed and soybean oil, mixed with pigments of black henna and oxide to obtain a rust color, with raw materials of equal portions of benzene, ethylene, and propylene."

"Isn't that similar to what's in standard writing ink?"

"Some of it with the manmade oils and various pigments, which makes different hues and adds a type of preservative to keep the colors."

"What if he used an old-fashioned pen—the kind that you dip into a small jar of ink."

"It's possible."

"A nib that's flat with sloped sides that holds the ink—similar to a quill," she said.

John changed photos and stopped on three photos of the victims' carved backs stained with ink. Each photo was taken from a different distance. The close-up one he magnified on the screen. "You can see that there are varying levels of depth—but the writing style is consistent with both victims. You can see the tail on the *g*s and *e*s. This was done freehand and it's quite competent, but it still leaves little craters here and there, based on pressure and hesitation. It would be impossible to keep the pressure exactly the same, free-handed. I would have to say it was written by the same person."

Katie leaned in and studied the photos. It was amazing to see details through twenty-four to fifty magnification. Each stroke resembled a peak or valley with a streaked dark substance running through it. It made her think of the crime-scene locations with the trails and views of stunning landscapes. "It's difficult to imagine anything else making that cut. Would a thick knife or ice pick give that same result?"

"That I cannot give a conclusion on and there's no way of testing for accuracy."

"Dr. Dean said that the Harlan victim was written on post mortem."

"Now we're getting into more of the psychological aspect of the evidence—and that, detective, is your territory."

Smiling, she said, "Well, it never hurts to ask, does it?"

"Oh, by the way." John interrupted her many contemplations.

"Am I forgetting something?" she said.

"An interesting tidbit."

"From the killer?" she said, hoping that was the case.

"The letters were all written in a standard style of calligraphy—a bit crude but a good effort—like when someone buys a beginner calligraphy set."

CHAPTER TWENTY-FOUR
Thursday 1925 hours

Rain tapped on the roof of the car, keeping a distinct tempo as Katie sat waiting for McGaven to arrive before going into The Well to talk with Hugh Keller, ex-deputy sheriff, who was now a managing bartender at the dive bar. She wondered when he had last had contact with Shelly McDonald.

Katie's nerves buzzed with a strange energy. She glanced at her watch again, willing it to tell her something else: McGaven was running late. He had to attend a patrol meeting since he was still active on patrol one to two shifts a week.

Katie took the opportunity to read back through the police reports for Elm Hill Mansion. Deputies from the sheriff's department were dispatched seventeen times in a six-month period. From the reports, it was mostly screaming arguments with some pushing and shoving, but nothing that led to any arrests. Most of the problems stemmed from Mrs. McDonald and Candace. Sometimes it involved Heather Lawson or Terry Slaughter. Some of the statements were worrisome, with accusations of sexual assault, excessive discipline, and outside people being brought in for sexual favors. Shockingly, no one was arrested or prosecuted for any of the alleged abuse.

You don't understand, Detective. If I would have left, then one of the other girls would have to take my place for the discipline.

…Just like it was Candace's place to protect us from…

The conversation with Tanis had left Katie drained mentally and physically. There was something about the young woman that stirred every emotion inside her. Maybe it brought up memories of losing her childhood friend at camp when she twelve. Her instincts told her that Tanis had told the truth as she experienced it—the genuineness of her recollections was undeniable.

Katie didn't want to think about the abuse and violence that was rife at Elm Hill Mansion. McGaven had forwarded her the official report from the county, detailing the reason to close the foster house was that the house was too unstable and posed a safety risk due to its age and there wasn't enough money to fix everything. The allegations of abuse had been investigated, but didn't reveal anything substantial. It was left open.

Her cell phone alerted to a text from Chad: *Hey, haven't heard from you. Love you.*

She stared at the words and smiled. She had forgotten to call him earlier when she was rushing around at her house and feeding Cisco, but he would have to wait a little longer.

As Katie flipped through reports and background pages, she could see why no one wanted to live at Elm Hill or remodel it, until some investors saw the potential—caring more about the location and land than the history. She had to admit it was one of the most beautiful settings in the area.

She looked across the parking lot. There were four more cars than fifteen minutes ago. It seemed that Thursday nights were pretty busy here, but Katie thought that some of the patrons weren't the run of the mill: the last three men were all carrying some type of satchel with them, which seemed odd for a Thursday night beer.

Katie thought she had better check out what was going on at the bar sooner rather than later, so she changed from her blouse into a hoodie. She already had on a pair of jeans and wanted to blend in – it was also easier to conceal her gun with a bulkier top. She pulled the rubber band out of her hair to be more casual, and look less like a cop, and then opened the car door. The light mist dotted her face and clothes. Taking a last moment to decide to wait or not, she jumped out of the car, slammed the door and jogged to the entrance of The Well.

The building had previously been some type of bait store—at least that was what she had heard. The front door was made from old wood, whittled over time by the weather and overzealous drinkers. Katie heard loud music from inside, causing the door to slightly rattle. She pulled it open and was straightaway hit with cigarette and cigar smoke, putrid and thick. As she entered, the cloud of smoke burned her eyes.

There were two men seated at the bar with two bar stools between them. A party of three was in the corner and there were two more men at a table on the right. It struck Katie as odd that there weren't any women—not even a barmaid.

She walked up to the bar. The two men sucking down their bourbons and whiskeys didn't look directly at her. She took an available seat. No sign of Hugh Keller. There was no one behind the counter, but she could hear some rustling in the back room where the cases of booze were stored.

Katie waited patiently. She had the upper hand—at least for now—Keller didn't know who she was. The only photo she had seen of him was his police academy photograph. Katie had a few flutters of anxiety, but her disgust and anger at the former deputy sheriff really made her stomach turn.

A man emerged from the storeroom carrying a case of whiskey. Katie couldn't quite see his face at first as he turned and began unloading the bottles. His short dark hair was streaked with grey, he was medium build, around six feet tall, and his arms looked as if he bench-pressed every day.

As Katie shifted on her bar stool, she noticed that one of the men sitting next to her was staring at her. His face crinkled from years in the sun and long hair pulled back in a limp ponytail made him a caricature member from a biker gang. She coolly returned his gaze until the man finally cracked a smile, revealing large yellowed teeth, and turned his gaze back to his half-empty glass. He was either completely entertained by her, or might have pegged Katie for a cop and he knew what was going to happen next.

Keller turned around and saw Katie sitting there waiting patiently. His sunken dark eyes and bushy mustache didn't change the general overall appearance of his rookie police photo—he was older and rougher-looking. But it was him. There was no doubt.

Katie forced a smile but felt her stomach turn sour and her fists clench.

"Well, darling, did you get the wrong address?" Keller said, eyeing up Katie.

"No."

"What are you doing here? Shouldn't you be at some trendy little sports bar?"

"Shouldn't you be getting me a drink right about now?" she said, holding his stare.

There were a few low moans from some of the men.

"I see we have a tough one here tonight," he said. Then looking around with exaggeration, he said, "Are you really here alone?"

"Do you see anyone else?"

"Honey, I don't think this bar is for you."

"What, are you afraid of women? I would have hated to have been the one that put you in your place."

Keller's demeanor changed. His back straightened, his smile disappeared, and he moved toward the glasses. "What do you want?"

"To drink?"

"Yeah, to drink. What do you want?"

"Oh, I want something, Hugh Keller, but it's not a drink." Katie could feel her anger rise inside her from its usual steady simmer when she dealt with really bad people—at home, or on the battlefield. She kept her mannerisms calm and her wits focused, still not knowing how this was going to play out. She wondered if McGaven had pulled into the parking lot yet.

"Do I know you?" he asked, not making any effort to be cordial anymore. He leaned toward her across the bar. "Who are you?"

"I'm so glad you asked," she said, and reached under her hoodie to retrieve her badge. She stood up facing him and said, "Detective Katie Scott from the Pine Valley Sheriff's Department."

Keller slowly stood up straight. For a moment Katie thought he was going to run, but she watched his hands in case he reached for some type of weapon.

"I have a few questions for you," she said, putting her badge away.

Keller began to laugh—maniacal, over-exaggerated. It was obviously for the patrons' benefit, to show that he was in control of the situation.

"What? Did I not make myself clear?" she said. "I would suggest that we speak in your office unless you want your customers to hear what I have to say. It isn't pretty."

"Okay, I thought it was cute at first, but now, you had just better walk on out of here—cop."

"Not likely."

Katie heard a couple of chairs scrape back from the table to her left.

"Listen, sweetheart, turn your nice little ass around and walk out of here."

"You are Hugh Keller, right?" she pushed.

"Whatever you want to know is just too bad. Walk away."

Katie smiled and almost laughed. She had been trained by some amazing army instructors in boot camp. They had been extra hard on her because she was a woman, but she learned quickly how to defend herself under many different conditions. She wasn't intimidated.

"I'm not leaving until you answer a few questions."

"You're done here," he said, and came around the bar.

"You can either answer a couple of questions here—or, my personal favorite would be to go to the sheriff's department and answer the same questions in my house."

Keller pushed up his sleeves and motioned to his two patrons to sit down. Katie didn't move from her position.

"Here or there? Your choice."

"The department must sure be proud of you."

"You'll have to ask them."

"Wait a minute. You said your name is Detective Scott?"

"Did I stutter?" She knew that she was walking a fine line, but she wanted him to react so that she could have him held in jail for a few days—it would soften him up to answer her questions about the Elm Hill Mansion and Candace Harlan. He was playing directly into her hands.

"You're not related to Sheriff Scott, are you?"

"Yes, I am."

"He doesn't have any kids."

"No."

"But he had a niece, I think, that was in the army or something. Is that you?"

"That's me. Now, are you going to answer my questions here or at the department? It's a simple question."

Keller laughed. "What, you think that you can't be touched because you're related to the sheriff? No one in here will say anything. You're way out of your league, sweetheart."

He stepped forward as Katie took two steps to the side. She anticipated his move and kept eye contact.

"Don't make this harder than it needs to be," he said.

"I was just thinking the same thing."

He lunged for her just as she gave him an uppercut punch to the stomach. It wasn't full force, but hurt him nonetheless. Keller doubled over, gasping for breath—the wind had been temporarily knocked out of him. She listened to him wheeze for about a minute. Katie didn't want to pull her weapon until absolutely necessary, but he wasn't going quietly.

Keller regained his composure and when he looked at her he was seething with rage.

Katie blinked but kept her eye on him—readying herself to pull her weapon to keep things under control until backup arrived.

Before she could outmaneuver Keller again, taking away her full concentration of the room, one of the wooden chairs sailed across the bar and struck Katie's lower back. Her body slammed down onto the floor and she lay there, staring upward at Keller approaching fast. Not taking the time to acknowledge the shooting pain she felt down her back and legs, she rolled twice to get out of Keller's reach, but ending up looking up at a large man with an extremely long beard gazing down at her.

If there ever was a time to use her combat fighting skills—it was now.

Katie concentrated on her breathing and being in the moment, which slowed everything down around her—the voices, the movement, the background sounds. At least that was what it appeared to do for her. It was a technique that she had learned from one of the people who trained her to work harder, faster, and stronger if she was going to survive the army.

The long beard of the patron almost touched her face as he stared down at her. His mistake. The repulsive gray and white hairs almost touched her, so she took the opportunity to kick him in the groin where he dropped next to her, moaning and groaning in a fetal position.

Katie scrabbled to get to a standing position—that's when she felt a surge of pain radiating through her back.

Keller lunged at her like a bear. He ran directly for her, grabbing her in a tight hug and lifting her up like she weighed less than a bottle of whiskey. Pushing her onto the bar, she didn't struggle; instead, she was able to bring her arms and fists together, breaking his grip. She rolled, jumped down behind the bar and skirted to the inventory room. It seemed her best choice even though she had never been in the room and wasn't sure if there was a back door to the place.

There had been a recent delivery and the stacked bottles of booze provided an excellent cover for her. Katie tucked behind them, pulled her gun, and readied herself. She searched for a way out, finding a sliding wooden door leading to the back of the parking lot.

"Scott!" Keller yelled.

Steadying her grip on the gun, she stepped out from behind the stacked boxes.

"Stay right there!" she commanded.

Keller laughed. "What are you going to do?"

Katie readied the gun. "Take one more step and you'll find out."

Even though Keller thought he was a tough guy, he was smart enough not to tempt fate.

Two more men burst through the door behind Keller.

"Stay back!"

The men stopped instantly when they saw the gun she had targeted on Keller.

"You know, Keller, we could have done this the easy way and answered a few questions, but no, you have to go commando and, guess what? You're going to jail."

Katie heard commotion from the bar area.

"Katie!" a voice yelled.

McGaven pushed his way past the men at the door with his weapon trained out in front. "What's going on?" he demanded. Glancing at Katie, he said, "You okay?"

"Fine," she said, gritting her teeth. "Nothing I couldn't handle."

"Alright, everybody, back into the bar," McGaven said. "Now!" Turning back around, "Well, well," he said to Keller. "We meet again. I knew you would crawl out from under a rock someday."

"McGaven," Keller grumbled.

McGaven lowered his weapon and put handcuffs on Keller.

"What am I being arrested for?"

"Simple assault, assault on a police officer, impeding a murder investigation, and oh, I'm sure there will be a whole host of other charges."

Katie lowered her gun and returned it to the holster underneath her sweatshirt. Her heightened pulse began to stabilize.

"The Well, 267 Second Avenue, one for pick up… ten-four…" McGaven instructed to dispatch from his cell phone. To Hugh Keller, "Sit down here and wait quietly." Keller obliged but kept a bitter expression. McGaven steered Katie through the storeroom and then outside just near the back door.

"You okay?" he said quietly.

"Yeah, I'm fine."

McGaven touched her face where there was a minor cut. "You're bleeding."

"I don't have time to bleed, we have two homicides to solve," she said with some humor.

"It's not funny. Did you not hear what the sheriff told you, everyone, during that meeting? You're essentially on probation."

"Hey, if I have to receive a few black spots in my file for stepping out of line to get a killer off the street, I'll do it every time." She stared hard at McGaven and then softened. "I'm sorry. You're the last person I should be snapping at, but I didn't do anything out of line here. I defended myself. This guy is full of rage and has a serious lack of impulse control."

"I know. Why didn't you wait for me?"

"I did. I thought I would do some intel first… until you got here."

"So what happened?"

"I walked in, got his attention, identified myself, and then he came after me. Some weird wizard-looking guy threw a chair at me and knocked me down. I did what I had to do. Kneed the guy, fought off Keller. He slammed me on the bar—I got away from him and managed to get back here. Got the drop on him at gunpoint." She shrugged her shoulders. "Don't look at me like that—I've been through more firefights in Afghanistan that make this scuffle look like a paper cut."

McGaven sighed.

Two patrol cars zoomed into the bar parking lot.

"I read all the reports from the Elm Hill Mansion and the background on Hugh Keller. It made me nuts. I knew he was someone that hated authority but, when he had it, abused it to his personal gain."

"I know," McGaven said softly.

"I knew that he wasn't going to cooperate and answer our questions here. Why would he? The best way to talk to him and get his undivided attention is on our terms—at the sheriff's department."

The rain poured. Large drops hammered the blacktop and small rivulets streamed down the sides. McGaven and Katie took cover underneath a roof overhang.

"Look, I love this job and working with you. I just don't..." he tried to explain.

"I will be careful next time."

McGaven gently squeezed her shoulder.

"Let's move forward," she said.

"You need a good night's sleep and we'll begin early tomorrow. Okay?"

"But what about—"

"I'll handle this and make sure he gets booked in tonight. We'll talk with him tomorrow."

"But—"

"I said I'll take care of it and write the report of the incident. I'm not going to accept anything else. Go home, Katie, and cool off, get a good night's sleep."

Katie felt her back ache and now the side of her face stung. She wasn't in any mood to argue and she could tell that McGaven was upset with her—more than her lack of safety. Sleep was important and she needed it desperately—so she left the bar.

As she sat in the sedan, overwhelming emotions coursed through her body. It was odd that she wanted to physically hurt Hugh Keller and at the same time she wanted to break down and cry.

Gripping the steering wheel with what energy she had left, she watched a deputy escort Keller to the police car. As they walked by in front of her vehicle, Keller made eye contact and a slight lift of his chin to indicate that they would meet again.

Katie didn't know if it was the rain that had saturated her clothes or the look on Keller's face that made her shiver more. She knew that Keller had information that they desperately needed on the murders of Carol Harlan and Mary Rodriguez.

CHAPTER TWENTY-FIVE
Thursday 2115 hours

Katie eased the car up her driveway and cut the engine. She had exerted so much energy that she was left with a drained body and a tired mind. She had completely forgotten about her online session with Dr. Carver and was riddled with guilt. The doctor had emailed her and suggested talking again in the same week—she had agreed.

With a quick text to the doctor, she wrote: *Sorry about the online no show, investigation went long today. I'll reschedule soon.*

It was official, despite the good night's sleep, exhaustion had set in and Katie thought she could barely make it out of her car and to the front door without having to take a break. The rain had stopped and only droplets remained on the trees, bushes, and driveway. There was a constant drip from the gutters cascading the excess water from her farmhouse roof.

She grabbed her briefcase and exited the vehicle with low energy. Unlocking her front door, she was instantly greeted by Cisco. His tail wagging and high-pitch whining as he circled her was the best greeting ever; it gave her a lift in spirit.

Quickly changing into her pajamas, she only had the energy to heat up a bowl of leftover chicken soup. She wasn't hungry, but knew that she would still feel tired in the morning if she hadn't eaten anything the night before.

After going to bed, Katie couldn't sleep for tossing and turning about the day's events and the confrontation with Hugh Keller.

Could he be the killer?

It was possible, but she knew in her gut that it was highly unlikely. As much as she would have liked for it to be him and the cases solved—and closed—there was much more to the cases and she just had to begin putting the pieces together.

Looking at her clock on the nightstand, it had barely been an hour since she had climbed into bed. She pushed Cisco to the side and got up. The dog wasn't going to move from his warm spot.

Katie's mind couldn't stop spinning with the investigations. She also still felt guilty after missing her session with Dr. Carver.

Pulling on her sweatpants and shirt, she decided to go where she felt the most relaxed and where she could actually think about things: the porch swing in the backyard. It didn't matter what time of year—it was still her private place, just like when she was a kid. No matter what problem she was wrestling with, things had a way of working out when she sat there.

She grabbed a blanket from the couch and went outside. The cool clean air helped to clear her head and lungs. The acreage was quiet—no sound of the wildlife, no breeze. It was comforting to sit wrapped in a warm blanket and just be part of the silence.

A cracking noise around the side of her house broke the relaxing quiet. Katie sat up straight, listening to hear it again or to figure out its origin.

It was most likely an animal like a raccoon or skunk milling around after the rains. But, there was something human about the sound. She stood up, peeling away the blanket, still straining to hear.

As with her investigations, Katie always followed through with everything that presented itself, leaving nothing to chance. So her tenaciousness made her check out the unusual noise while most would likely dismiss it.

As she quietly crept around to the other side of her house, she felt the soreness in her back grip, with pain slowing her stride some. With each step, pain radiated downward, stiffening her lower lumbar and causing her to slow even more.

She had the sense that someone was near. "Who's there?" she said, knowing she would feel a bit silly if a raccoon skittered past.

"Katie?" came a voice.

She moved faster and saw Chad standing in the darkness. "Chad, what the hell are you doing?"

"Are you okay?"

"You didn't have to come out and check on me. You could've just called," she said, and realized her mistake immediately.

Chad walked into the light; he wasn't dressed in his official fireman's uniform but now in his jeans and sweater. "I tried that. I also tried calling McGaven but he wasn't answering his cell."

"He probably wouldn't be. We've had so many leads to run down and tonight we had to meet a possible suspect at The Well."

"The Well?"

"Yeah, nice place. Remind me to never go there again."

Chad stood close to Katie. "What happened to your face?" He gently touched it.

"Just a bit of a scuffle."

He didn't look convinced by her explanation. "I'm sorry to come out here and scare you, but I was going to leave a note. And I wanted to see if you were here."

"I'm sorry... come sit down with me." She tried not to walk stiffly or show her pain, but it didn't get past him.

"You had more than a scuffle," he said, watching her walk.

They sat on her favorite swing together.

"Here," he said and began to massage her shoulders and feel down her back. "You didn't take a hot shower, did you?"

"No. I was so tired I just wanted to go to bed. But... my mind wouldn't shut off."

He chuckled. "Know that one. Haven't had that problem in a while, but the new house is causing a few minor panics."

"What? How?" she said.

"Oh, it's just buyer's remorse. Wondering if I made a mistake. Will I make money on the flip? Will it be a money pit? The usual stuff."

"Glad it isn't anything serious." She took a deep breath as the pain became intermittent. "Ouch... still a bit sore."

"You know, you need a hot shower and a good massage." He leaned in and kissed her neck.

Katie missed him so much and wished they were away somewhere where there weren't killers or demands from work. She turned and returned his affections. "Can you stay?" She didn't want to talk to him about anything that was bothering her. Her emotions were fragile and she was afraid that she would start crying and not be able to stop when she did.

"Yes. I'm not on again until 2 p.m. tomorrow."

They went inside. His company was exactly what she needed to end the loop of suspects and evidence running through Katie's mind. She took a hot shower and received the best body massage she ever had, then made love to Chad into the small hours until she fell into a deep sleep.

CHAPTER TWENTY-SIX

Friday 0730 hours

Katie was meeting McGaven at the medical examiner's office to view the body of Mary Rodriguez and to find out the particulars of cause and manner of death. Dr. Dean had called to make an appointment. She thought that she knew what the outcome was going to be, but there were always details you could miss with a naked eye.

She pulled into the sheriff's department and parked the sedan. As she got out of the vehicle, she noticed how much better she felt after Chad's magic hands worked her sore muscles. She had slept better than she had in months. He was still sleeping next to Cisco when she left the house. Not having the heart to wake him, she left him a note.

Pushing through the main doors of the medical examiner's office, she hurried to find Dr. Dean. It didn't take long to locate him with his brightly colored Hawaiian shirt with large orange and pink flowers. She wondered if he ever wore anything else.

McGaven was waiting for her, but didn't look in Katie's direction right away.

"Hi, Dr. Dean. I hope I'm not late," she said entering the room.

The doctor looked up from his files, his reading glasses sloped toward the end of his nose, "Not at all, Detective. It's nice to see you."

She turned to McGaven, giving a quick smile and nod in greeting. He returned the silent hello with a casual nod. It was unclear if he was still upset with her—but she would tread lightly with him until he completely let their disagreement go.

"Well," the doctor said. "It's always interesting working your cases, Detective and Deputy."

"Do we have an official ID?"

Looking at the file, he said, "Yes, from fingerprints compared from an arrest report. She has been identified as Mary Rodriguez."

"Did she suffer injuries similar to Carol Harlan?" she asked.

"Yes… and no."

Here we go again…

Dr. Dean began, "Manner of death was strangulation caused by what appears to be a ligature. A thin rope or twine like what had been left on her wrist. There's no doubt it was murder, but what bothers me is that the message carved into her back was done *before* death, unlike in the Harlan case." He moved closer to the exam table where the body was covered with a sheet. Pulling the sheet back, Mary Rodriguez was a shocking sight to behold. The autopsy had already begun so the chest cavity was cut open and the organs had been removed. Katie tried not to look at the gaping hollow where the ribs were exposed and spread wide. She waited until Dean moved the body by rolling it onto its side. Glancing at McGaven, his expression of horror mimicked what Katie felt. She moved next to the examiner to partially obscure her partner's view of the body.

"These cuts were done when the victim was alive—there's no purple coloring as the blood would have settled there after death. In fact, this lettering is days, if not weeks old."

"Can you ascertain what type of knife or cutting tool was used? Was it similar to what was used in the Harlan case?" she asked.

"It was something thin and flat with rounded sides."

"Could it be some type of writing instrument?"

"It's possible—more like a tool of some sort with sharp and dull areas to make jagged and smooth cuts." He pointed to the lettering in "raccoglitore" and how jagged it was, especially when a curve was made on the *c*s and *o*s. "There are hesitations, too."

Katie thought for a moment about the cutting letters and the use of strangulation with twine.

"Could the twine or thin rope have been from someone in a trade, like a contractor or builder? Or even subcontractors like electricians or plumbers?" she asked.

"Good point. It could've been from something that an electrician might have in their toolbox. You'll have to check with John about all the possibilities. I'm sure he'll be able to sort that out for you, if he hasn't already." The doctor glanced at McGaven who was quiet and pale. He picked up a wrapped cough drop and tossed it to McGaven. "The menthol will help with nausea and the unpleasant smell of cadavers."

"Thank you," he said, and immediately unwrapped the lozenge and popped it into his mouth.

Katie kept her focus on the victim's injuries. "Was there anything in her system? Drugs? It must've been painful to have words carved on her back while she was still alive."

"Detective, you never disappoint. There were no street drugs in her system, except the heavy painkiller similar to morphine called oxycodone, and it was in light and consistent doses." He pulled up the body's right arm and there was a darker blue-purple spot on the back of her bicep. "She had some type of patch inserted here where small amounts of drugs absorbed into her system throughout the day."

"Can you tell if it was self-inflicted, or done by a doctor?"

"No way of knowing unless you were able to contact her physician to find out what treatments she was having—if any."

"What would she have that for?"

"Lots of things. Some patients have these patches inserted for anything from arthritis to migraines to recovering from difficult surgeries to cancer treatments. These are used for pain management, with mostly good results."

"I see."

"I can tell you that she had been dead about six hours before she was discovered."

Katie was already trying to figure out how to track down Mary's doctor.

"One more thing," he said. "She had an abortion no more than a month ago."

CHAPTER TWENTY-SEVEN

Friday 1445 hours

"I don't have to answer anything, but my attorney advised me that it would be best to cooperate with the investigation," Hugh Keller stated smugly as he sat in his orange jumpsuit with his arms crossed. In the daylight, he appeared older than thirty-eight and he still reeked of stale alcohol.

Katie and McGaven had been contacted by the sergeant of the jail that Hugh Keller was available to be questioned, but had refused to be transported to the interview room in the detective division. He wanted to be released as soon as possible and kept constantly complaining about his civil rights and wrongful arrest—that he had been set up.

Katie and McGaven sat with him in a small jail meeting room that smelt of sweat and was barely big enough for all three of them to fit in.

"Well, I have to say that's the most intelligent thing you have said since we've met," said Katie.

"You're not as smart as you think you are," he said, leaning back slightly so that he could look down his nose at her.

"All you had to do was cooperate with me at the bar and answer a few questions and you wouldn't be in this predicament now," she said with little voice inflection.

He snubbed her and looked away.

"How long did you work for the Pine Valley Sheriff's Department?"

"About six years."

"In that time, were you ever called to the Elm Hill Mansion?" she asked.

"A few times."

Katie pulled a piece of paper from a file folder. Reading, she said, "Would you believe, according the records of the sheriff's dispatch, there were seventeen calls for service in six months?"

"It seems high—but that is probably about right."

"And on every call, you were the responding officer."

"If you say so."

"Were you dating Shelly McDonald?"

"Who?"

"Shelly McDonald. She managed the Elm Hill Mansion and oversaw the day-to-day care of the teenage girls. Ringing any bells?"

"Went out a few times. Nothing serious. I have needs, you know." He looked Katie up and down.

"Did you know the six girls who resided at Elm Hill Mansion before it was shut down?" she said, ignoring his crude behavior.

"Only from the calls."

"Where were you Tuesday night?"

"Working."

"All night?"

"Yeah," he sneered.

"Can anyone vouch for you?"

"Don't need it because I was working…"

"Did they refer to you as the 'Hunter' or 'Gatherer'?"

"What?" he said, looking at Katie completely confused.

"What were some of the problems at Elm Hill?"

"Fighting, running away, sneaking out in the middle of the night, stuff like that."

"Did you know Candace Harlan?"

"Doesn't ring a bell."

"Mr. Keller, this can go easy or I can be your worst nightmare. Start answering my questions and don't give me the runaround."

He stopped and stared at Katie, then, leaning forward, he said, "You really want to play rough with me, Detective?"

"I don't play, Mr. Keller. I want answers."

McGaven shifted his position to remind Keller that he was in the room.

"Then why don't you ask me what you really want to know. Not just this bullshit line of questioning."

"Very well, Mr. Keller. How well did you know Candace Harlan? And how many times did you have sex with her?"

The room was silent. Katie knew she had hit a nerve, but wasn't proud of how she had to speak on the same level as Keller to get an answer.

"Answer the question, Keller," said McGaven. His voice cut through the stillness of the room.

Keller fidgeted in his chair and was clearly deciding what he should or shouldn't say. He finally said, "Yes, I knew Candace Harlan, as well as the other girls, but I can't remember their names off the top of my head. It was always the same when I would arrive. Girls screaming about no privacy and how Shelly mistreated them. There was no proof, no bruises, no blood. They were a pain in the ass if you ask me."

Katie leaned closer to Keller and said, "And did you or did you not have sex with Candace Harlan?"

"I don't know what you want from me."

"The truth."

"Truth? That's funny. You only want to put my head on the block so you can close your investigation. I got news for you, sweetheart, I didn't kill anyone."

Katie gritted her teeth and said, "That's not what I asked." Staring him square in the eye, she asked, "So, abuse and rape of an underage girl, that's more your speed?"

He lunged forward. Katie didn't flinch.

"Are we getting close to the truth now?" she said.

"You have no idea what you're talking about," he said, falling back into his chair and looking away.

Katie asked the question again, but he was done talking.

"That how you're going to play it? You have some wonderful things coming your way," she said as she stood up and left the small meeting room followed closely by McGaven.

After the door closed behind them, McGaven said, "Do you think that was the best way to handle things?"

"You really think he was going to answer any of my questions?" she asked. "I wanted to see his reactions, and I got what we needed."

McGaven thought about what she said but didn't say anything.

A correctional officer approached them, "Hey, just to let you guys know. Keller is getting out—his bail has been made."

Another officer approached, entered the room and escorted Keller to begin the paperwork process.

Katie was disappointed, but she had bought them some time. She still didn't believe that Keller was the killer—but she had been fooled before. As Hugh Keller passed by he locked eyes with Katie, licked his lips, and blew her a kiss.

All Katie could do was watch him leave.

CHAPTER TWENTY-EIGHT

Friday 1805 hours

Katie didn't want to go home, but she also didn't want to be alone. She stood on Chad's porch in the rain waiting for him—she had forgotten that he was working his twenty-four-hour shift. After calling him at work, he had sensed her stress, so he had someone cover part of his shift and was on his way to his house to meet her.

As the rain poured harder, all Katie could do was wait. She stood pressed against his front door as the water drenched her clothes and matted down her hair. The last two days had run endless loops of recall through her mind until the memories took on a more sinister tone. She didn't know if it were side effects from post-traumatic stress, her denial of dealing with certain experiences, or just the fact that she was juggling too many things, but the trauma kept coming.

Her behavior had taken an unprofessional turn—going into the bar alone had been reckless and out of character for her. The last thing she wanted was to compromise the investigation. Too many innocent lives depended on her catching this killer.

Shivering in the rain, Katie could smell fresh paint and adhesives that Chad must have used to fix something recently. She saw a few new potted plants on the walkway and realized that he was really working hard to fix up the cottage.

Headlights blinded her as Chad drove his large Jeep up the driveway with the windshield wipers on high. The lights quickly dimmed. The engine stopped. She watched Chad's outline as he jumped out of the vehicle.

"Katie," he said and rushed to her. "You okay?"

For some reason, just that simple question made her break down. She rarely cried, but with therapy and this case, so many emotions were building up inside her like a pressure-cooker.

"Oh, hey. It's okay," he said and held her close to him. Managing to unlock the door, he steered her inside and shut the door.

Lightning lit up the nearby skyline and thunder rolled in the distance five seconds later.

Katie knew that Chad had never seen her like this before, except when they were kids when she had lost her parents in the accident. His concern almost overwhelmed her. She stopped crying but it was difficult for her to maintain her composure. She was now embarrassed and uncertain why she had burdened Chad with her problems.

He hugged her tight and kissed her cheek. Not really knowing what else to do, he held her as they stood at the entrance until her shivering subsided.

"I'm sorry," she whispered. "I didn't want to interrupt your work."

"It's okay. Everyone has personal issues they need to attend to at times. So don't worry. Okay?" he said.

Katie looked at him with tears still in her eyes.

"Okay?" he said again.

She nodded.

"You are absolutely soaked. You've got to get out of those wet clothes. Go into the bedroom and in the top drawer on the left there are some hoodies and sweatpants."

"Okay," she said.

"I'll make us something hot." He left for the kitchen.

Katie went to the bedroom and found the warm clothes neatly folded in the top drawer. She shed her badge and gun, leaving them on top of the dresser. The cold from the rain-soaked garments was beginning to invade her bones, causing uncontrollable trembling. Quickly peeling off her clothes, she pulled on the dry ones. Taking a towel from the bathroom and letting her hair down, she sat on the bed and began drying her hair. She felt better almost immediately.

Breathe…

On a small shelf between the dresser and nightstand, there were several old photographs. One was of his parents, she had always liked them; his mom was laughing, probably about something funny his dad had said. There were frequent barbecues and fun times at their house when she was a child, especially during the summer.

Another photo was of her and Chad—they must be about twelve years old. Katie didn't remember the photo being taken, but they were in a tree house they had built that summer. Chad still looked the same; cute, happy, and with a mischievous look in his eye. Katie had decided that she wanted to cut her hair short because it always got in the way, and she wore shorts, a T-shirt, and sneakers without socks. Both of them smiled broadly at whoever took the photo.

There were more photos of family and friends, then one of him when he graduated with his EMT license along with a group photo of his firehouse #15.

Katie smiled as she thought how amazing and wonderful it had been to be a part of Chad's life for so much of it.

Wandering about the room to spread the warmth around her body, she noticed a small notebook on the nightstand. She didn't know what possessed her to pick it up, but she slowly opened it and flipped through the pages. Neatly folded newspaper articles and printed reports from the Internet about all the cases she had solved were tucked into the pages. There was an article in the *Military Times* from when she had completed training with Cisco.

It was touching that he had a scrapbook of her accomplishments. It made her realize how much Chad was a part of her life.

They had lost touch when she had enlisted in the army, but he never stopped being there for her. She was so lucky, truly blessed, but didn't really know it until that moment.

Katie looked out the bedroom door and could hear Chad moving around in the kitchen. She put the small scrapbook back on the nightstand. After laying out her wet clothes in the bathroom to dry, she returned to the living room.

Walking into the kitchen, the smell of warm spices filled the air. "What smells so good?" she said.

"It's a blend of spicy tea leaves I made."

"Wow, look at you. You buy a cottage and now are an herbalist and a chef."

"Well, I confess. I learned this from Rob at work. His family is from India and he's an amazing cook as well."

He handed her a steaming mug.

"Thank you," she said, carefully sipping the liquid. "Oh, wow, that's delicious."

"Knew you'd like it," he said, smiling. "You look good in those." He referred to the navy blue sweatshirt with the firehouse's emblem on it she now sported.

Katie smiled back but then suddenly realized, "I have to take care of Cisco."

"All taken care of," he said.

"What? No, I need to get home."

"Don't worry. It's all taken care of."

"How?"

"I called McGaven and he and Denise were happy to go over and spend some time with Cisco. He knew where you hid a key. I think he said they were going to watch some action movies—Cisco's favorite."

"He did that?"

"Why are you so surprised?"

"I've been… difficult to work with recently and I thought he was mad at me," she said.

"If he was, I couldn't tell."

Katie looked down and was upset that she'd allowed things to be left the way they were at the office. "I... I don't..."

Chad confronted her. "It's okay. You need to relax and tell me what's going on." He steered her to the living room where they sat down.

Katie was overwhelmed and burdened with some of the most intense things, but she didn't want to whine or dump her problems on anyone. But now, she found herself sitting in front of someone she loved, who was waiting for her to let it all out.

He sat patiently and sipped his tea.

She didn't know how she did it, but the words came tumbling out as she rattled on about *everything*. Her work, the cases, her house, her grief over losing her aunt, the confrontation with Hugh Keller, unrest with McGaven, her work conduct, getting written up for her last case, and everything in between.

Once she finished her monologue she watched for Chad's reaction. He had listened, nodding every once in a while, sometimes he kept her gaze, other times he looked away to give her space to talk, but in the end he was still her best friend and lover.

There was a moment of silence. It wasn't the uncomfortable kind, but it felt like something was missing and hanging precariously in the balance.

Chad moved closer to Katie and he gently kissed her. "I had no idea that you've been balancing all of this. I'm sorry that I can't help to carry some of your burden. But I'm here. I'm always here."

"I'm sorry, I had no right to dump everything out on you."

"You didn't. You needed to get that off your chest and I'm glad you did."

Katie looked down. "It actually sounds worse than it is... it's just... today I think I hit my limit."

"You can't go around carrying this kind of weight. I'm surprised you didn't break sooner. You need a good night's sleep. Stay here and rest."

"But I don't—"

"Let it go, Katie... Tomorrow you'll feel rested and we can tackle all these things, one... at... a... time. Let it go tonight..."

CHAPTER TWENTY-NINE

I stirred the chocolate cake mix until everything had been combined according to the instructions on the box. I wanted to do something nice for my mother, since she hadn't beaten me in almost a month.

She had even begun to straighten up the house and take garbage out of the rooms. She smiled when I came home from school. It was like a miracle had happened.

I looked at the cake box and made sure I added the eggs, oil, and milk. It was going to be a wonderful cake. There was even ice cream in the freezer too. It was going to be a celebration.

I heard the front door open and my excitement grew.

The door slammed.

I jerked my arm as I was stirring the bowl.

Looking up, I saw my mother. Her face was pale, more than normal, and she looked sweaty even though it wasn't hot outside.

"What's wrong, Ma?"

"What do you think you're doing?" she screamed.

"I… I'm making you a birthday cake like we talked about."

"I don't want any stinking birthday cake. I want my stuff. Don't you understand?" She showed me the inside of her arms which were dotted with horrible purple needle marks.

"What stuff, Ma? I can help you find it."

"You can't help with nuthin'."

She snatched the bowl out of my hands and threw it on the floor. It bounced and the batter splatted out, making a dark mess.

I started to cry.

"You were always such a baby and will always be a baby…" She grabbed her packet of cigarettes and forcefully slammed them against her fist until one came free. With a shaky hand, she raised the cigarette to her lips and slowly pressed the lighter. She couldn't light it. Rage spilled over and she threw a plate against the wall. She finally got the cigarette lit, and that's when she tripped on the rug and fell onto a huge pile of newspapers and magazines piled against the wall.

"Ma, you okay?" I managed to say.

"You little shit, you did this!"

I went to her to try and help her up when I noticed a small fire had ignited. I stopped dead.

"Help me up!" she screeched.

I stood completely still, frozen like a statue.

The flame flickered and grew slowly at first—then exponentially, reaching all around with fiery tentacles.

"You did this! Help! Help me you worthless piece of…"

I stood and watched the flames spread until, what felt like seconds later, the entire room was a burning inferno. The heat was overwhelming. Everything in the room was lapped up by the fire. The walls melted. The drapes blackened.

Mom stopped screaming and rolled into a ball.

I slowly left the room and went to my bedroom and closed the door…

CHAPTER THIRTY
Saturday 0910 hours

Katie ran a hard three miles up the Battle Ridge Trail with Cisco at her side. She'd had another great night's sleep of solid restfulness and felt better about her decision of opening up to Chad. Their relationship had improved from that moment and made her realize that she had been holding on too tight, keeping everything inside.

She was going to meet McGaven at the Twin Rifle Trail around 9 a.m. Wanting to smooth things over with him, she thought that the best thing to do was go for a run. She was a few minutes late, but knew that McGaven wouldn't mind.

Katie laughed at Cisco's springy footwork when he saw a squirrel run past and climb up a tree. The area was mostly deserted because of the cooler weather and fewer tourists visiting the area.

She slowed her pace to a light jog as she neared the entrance to the Twin Rifle Trail. She saw McGaven immediately. He was stretching and loosening up for the run as he waited for her.

Cisco ran on ahead and greeted McGaven, jumping around him.

"Hey, didn't expect to see you, buddy," he said, petting the dog.

Katie walked up to McGaven. "Hi," she said.

"Hey."

"Thanks for taking care of Cisco last night."

"Anytime."

"I want to get this out of the way, okay," she said.

"What's that?"

"Look," she said. "Things have been piling up on me and I'm not the best at decompressing or letting things go. And—"

"Wait," he said. "You don't have to—"

"Yes, I do," she interrupted. "That's not how partners treat each other—or friends, or anyone for that matter. I took liberties and willfully antagonized Keller. And I know it's not only me that takes the heat from this, it's you too. I'm skating on some thin ice, so…"

"Katie, I know. With everything you've been through…"

"Let's just put it behind us, okay?" she said.

"Deal," he said and held his hand out.

She reached to shake it and he pulled her to him in a bear hug.

Laughing, she said, "Okay, okay. Ready to get started?"

"Let's go."

They began jogging slowly to warm up.

"You look good," she said. "I think you're slimming down."

"Ah, flattery with get you everywhere."

They finished their picturesque three-mile circuit through the trees and came back to the beginning.

"That was great," she said. "You're doing well."

"Yeah, I'm feeling better too. It's trying to find the balance between sitting at a desk and not."

"I guess I never thought about that because I move around so much." Katie began her cool-down stretches. She felt fantastic after a good cry, a good night's sleep, and a morning run in one of her favorite places.

McGaven slowly stretched his calves and quads. "I actually feel pretty good. I can get out of bed in the morning and not groan now."

"Do you have some time today?" she asked.

"Sure, a little bit. Why?"

"I know it's Saturday, but I wanted to go and take a look at Elm Hill Mansion. There's little chance anyone is around and I wanted to get a better look now I know its history."

Cisco barked twice. His tongue was hanging out and he was having fun running around Katie and McGaven.

"A look, huh?"

"Yeah, what would it hurt?"

"Sure, I'll meet you both over there and *we* can have a look around." He smiled.

"Absolutely. C'mon, Cisco," she said, moving toward her car as the dog padded along behind her.

"Hey, when are you going to buy a new car?" he called after her.

"When I get some time. What's wrong with the police sedan?"

He laughed, finishing up his stretches.

Katie was exhilarated as she drove to Elm Hill Mansion.

The gate was open, so she slowly drove up the driveway which had been covered with white, large-stoned gravel. She didn't remember it being that way when the crime-scene investigation was going on. As she reached the top, she pulled over to the farthest side, parked, and cut the engine.

Cisco whined but made himself comfortable, turning several times and then lying down. Katie decided to keep him in the car. He'd had quite the workout and would snooze while she and McGaven took a look around.

Katie stood in front of the car surveying the property. It was one of those types of property that was more beautiful every time you visited. The investors knew a good piece of land would make a fortune with three luxury-spec houses. It was now officially an ongoing crime scene, but they would be wrapping things up soon.

Clouds littered the sky and the wind was mild but cool. Katie zipped up her sweatshirt and pulled up her hood to keep the cold air out and her neck warm.

The three large metal storage containers on the left side of the property had now all been shut. They intrigued her, so she would check them out before they left—giving them a once-over to complete the search. There was no reason to search or document them as part of the crime scene, but it wouldn't hurt to take a look.

There was one bulldozer and another large piece of equipment still sitting where it had been left. The other oversized work vehicles must've been picked up for other jobs. The yellow tape cordoning off the area to the public had been removed.

Katie slowly walked along the large flat stones that led to the main entrance of the mansion, looking up at the missing decorative pieces around the windows and doors and remembering what the house had looked like after it was finished by the Von Slovnicks. The porch they had stood in front of for the photo was almost non-existent now.

Recalling all the historical information from the county archives, she didn't remember seeing or hearing about why the previous owners wanted to donate this house for the girls and the county.

Where they just being charitable? Philanthropists? Or, was it something more personal?

Sara and Jonathan McKinzie lived there twenty years before donating the house, but there was no other record; no real estate, no other charitable contributions, no photographs of them. McGaven hadn't found anything about them—yet.

Katie heard a car coming up the long drive, gravel crunching under the tires.

Cisco gave a couple of warning barks, but settled back down again after he knew it was McGaven.

Katie watched him park his large truck next to the police sedan and get out. He gazed around the area before jogging up to greet her.

"Glad you could make it," she said.

"We should check out those containers."

"I thought the same thing. Maybe we were hasty?"

"Thinking we should have searched them on our first visit?"

"Maybe. But we can't officially now." She turned and headed toward the house.

Keeping up with Katie's pace, he said, "If we find something, that's a big *if*, it can still be used to guide the investigation, just not in a court of law. Right?"

"That's true."

"So what's the plan?"

"Get inside the house, if we can."

"You want to look at the staircase, am I right?"

"Of course." She steered them around the right side of the house to the storm door she'd seen on her first visit.

"Where are you going?"

"I think there's an easier entrance from the basement."

When they reached the door to the basement, Katie stepped inside and looked around.

"It's creepy in here," said McGaven.

"You can say that again, but... don't please."

They reached the wooden stairs and headed up, into the house—taking each step gently in case the old wood splintered or gave way under their weight.

Katie reached the top where there was a big door; she pushed but it wouldn't budge. She shoved harder—the same result.

"Need some help?" he said, smiling.

She pushed again, resulting in a splintering sound. "I think it's stuck, not locked."

"Here," McGaven said. Stretching up to his full height, he pushed. The door budged an inch. He shoved. The door opened with such a force it slammed open and then shut again.

Pushing it open again, Katie began to move forward into the old house.

McGaven took her arm. "You packing?"

"Of course. You?"

"Yep." He let go of her arm. "Keep alert," he said softly.

She nodded and stepped onto the threshold which creaked and groaned beneath her feet. She stopped. Then continued into what appeared to be the kitchen.

Most of the appliances, refrigerator, and built-in shelves had been removed. There were a few open places in the floor where she could see down underneath the house. They were on the first floor where there was a living room, parlor, and a big open area that fitted the fireplace.

Katie remembered the building plans and made her way to where the stairs were located.

"What are we looking for?" McGaven asked.

"I'm not sure." Slowly moving through the hall, making sure that there weren't any obvious safety issues or booby traps, she saw a floor-to-ceiling bookcase. It seemed like an odd place to have one. The shelves were empty and the overall condition was better than most of the house.

Katie ran her hand along one of the shelves—it was smooth and solid. She repeated it on a different shelf with the same result.

McGaven was lagging behind.

Judging the distance between the stairs and the back of the built-in bookshelf, Katie estimated it to be three and half feet. Staying focused, she searched for anything that wasn't supposed to be on the bookcase. A weird scratch, hole, button, lock, and then… she found a slide mechanism beneath her fingers underneath the second shelf.

"Gav," she said. "I think I found something interesting." She slid the apparatus which made a dull clunk followed by an echoing sound within the wall.

A breeze drifted in and instantly the smell of the outdoors lingered for a moment. It gave her a chill.

"What is that?" he said.

"I think it's a secret…" She pulled the bookcase toward her and the entire wall moved with a loud creak. "Entrance or room," she finished.

"Like in an old mystery novel," he said.

"Something like that." Looking at the staircase around the corner which was quite narrow, she said, "I think it was used for people to sneak between the first and second floors without anyone knowing."

"But, it's close to the stairs. Why?"

"I mean, in the middle of the night. The stairs are open and make a lot of noise when people walk up and down, but this staircase is enclosed and would be fairly quiet." She began to go up the secret staircase.

"Wait."

"What?"

"This house was condemned, right?"

"Yeah."

"How do you know if those stairs are safe?"

"They're still standing," she said, and began to climb.

McGaven let out a sigh as he reluctantly followed.

Katie strained her eyes to be able to see the outline of the stairs. There was no handrail and the darkness was unsettling, made you feel like you were floating in a deep abyss. She used her cell phone's flashlight application and slowly moved forward. Finally, she arrived at the top where there was a thin door with a simple piece of stained wood that turned one way to lock it and the other to unlock. When Katie opened the door, she found herself in a hallway just across from a large bedroom.

"I don't know why I'm following you," said McGaven with a look of relief once on the second floor.

"Because you always have your partner's back." She looked around at the other rooms and realized that the room across from the secret passage was separated from the rest of the other bedrooms, buffering it from noise. "This would make sense, if what Tanis Jones told us were true about Candace having sex with Keller. The other girls might not have known or heard anything."

"So this is just a special entrance for their sexual encounters."

"Looks like a possibility. But…"

"I know that look."

"I'm sure there's more to this house and the foster home than we know. We need to talk to Tanis again."

"And pressure Shelly. Maybe talking with the DA, we can dangle early release for more information?"

Turning to McGaven, she said, "Maybe."

"Seen enough? I don't think there's anything here that will blow this case wide open."

Katie took another look around the second floor and agreed. "There's nothing here."

"Maybe another secret room?"

"I thought of that. I don't think another room, but you don't build a secret staircase unless you've got something to hide. Why would the Slovnicks build this? What's the significance?"

"What do you mean?"

"I don't know for sure…"

"I agree we need to talk to Tanis again."

"Let's go." She headed toward the regular staircase.

"What? Not back down the dizzying stairs made for little people?"

She laughed. "I still want to check out the metal storage containers before we leave."

"I'm right behind you."

Katie walked out the front door of the mansion and the cool air was a welcoming change from the musty house. She thought about what the secret passage might have been used for and how they managed to keep it such a secret—or did they?

"We need to see all the reports from the social services, or at least everything they have," she said.

"I keep playing phone tag with the social worker, Jerry Weaver."

"Maybe we need to set up an appointment? Might want to see if he can send us copies or drop them off?"

"I was going to, but wanted to actually speak to the guy and get his impression about this place."

They jogged down the hill and over to the large metal containers. Two of the containers were secured with double locks. The third one was closed but there wasn't a lock.

Katie took a look around them, trying to find a name of a company that supplied them, but there didn't seem to be any branding. "Strange," she said.

McGaven walked over to her.

"There doesn't seem to be a name or anything."

"Maybe it's on the inside."

"Wouldn't they want to advertise?" she said.

He looked around up high, low, and around the doors.

Katie pulled open the door. The inside of the storage container had corrugated walls with twelve-inch-square vented areas along both sides as well as the end. It was about twenty-six feet long and seven and half feet tall. Stacked inside she could see a pair of vintage doors and mantel from the fireplace. "There's stuff in here, but it wasn't locked," she said and took a couple of steps inside, still looking for the name of the company.

McGaven walked in and said, "You know, we could ask the construction company."

"I know, but I just wanted to see it. There should be identifying numbers too. All these types of containers have numbers—like license plates or VIN numbers."

"These are nice pieces from the house that I'm sure people will want to buy for their remodels." He referred to heavy, craftsman-style interior doors with carvings and carved glass doorknobs. Each door had to have weighed 200 pounds. There were also crown molding pieces in every length, and piles of intricately carved gingerbread bric-a-brac from the windows.

"What are you thinking?" he asked, looking at Katie curiously.

Katie was still searching the interior for some type of identification. She didn't know exactly why but it bothered her. Then she saw at the bottom, behind one of the old interior doors with carved glass knobs, there was some information printed on the lower wall. She switched her cell phone to the flashlight mode and read: *ETL Express, Moving & Storage LLC.*

"ETL," she whispered.

"What?" McGaven asked. He looked to see what she was talking about. "There's the name, ETL Express. How does that help?"

"Oh my, wait a minute." She frantically searched her cell phone photos where she had taken a photo of the piece of paper that was folded in her locker at the police department. She hadn't bothered to tell McGaven about it because it could have been nothing. "I didn't think it meant anything, but I still kept it and took a photo of it. So glad I did... I actually forgot all about it."

"What are you talking about?"

"This," she said, and turned her phone for McGaven to see.

He said out loud, "ETL Express. Where did you get this?"

"I found it folded at the bottom of my locker."

"At the department?"

She nodded. "Yes."

"Why didn't you say anything?" he asked. "Did anyone see anything? I know the security cameras are at the parking lot and the main door, but not the interior."

"No. Nothing. I checked when I had the chance. First, I thought it was something and then I thought it was probably nothing. I didn't think about it until now."

"It seems strange that these are related, but you can't dismiss it either."

Katie's phone rang.

"I better get this," she said, seeing it was Chad. "Hi."

Chad said, "You doing okay?"

"Just fine, Gav and I are at the Elm Hill Mansion checking out some storage containers—"

McGaven urgently said, "Hey!"

Cisco barked rapidly in the distance.

Katie looked over to see the silhouette of a man standing at the entrance of the container, dressed all in black with a hoodie over his head. His face was obscured. "Wait!" she yelled as she dropped her cell.

Both McGaven and Katie rushed the door just as it was closed, secured, and some type of lock was engaged.

"Katie!" Chad yelled down the cell phone.

"Open the door!" Katie screamed, hammering her fists. "We're police officers, let us out now!"

McGaven joined in, kicking and punching the metal door—to no avail.

With no windows, it was now completely dark inside.

Out of breath, Katie said to McGaven, "Now what?"

"Your phone."

Katie stumbled around and found her phone. She picked it up, "Chad? Are you there?"

Static crackled and then there were three loud beeps—then nothing.

"Shit!" She frantically kept trying to call him back but couldn't make a connection. "It's this container that's interfering." She moved around, trying to get a signal. "Nothing."

"Me neither," said McGaven moving his cell phone around. "What do you think Chad heard?"

"I'm not sure."

The sound of a large earthmover started up in the distance and the smell of diesel fuel drifted through the air vents. Katie heard the construction machine shift and began moving—it became louder as it approached them. The floor beneath their feet vibrated.

"What the hell?" McGaven said.

"You don't think—" was all she managed to say before the bulldozer slammed into the side of the container causing it to lurch, throwing Katie and McGaven to the floor.

CHAPTER THIRTY-ONE

Saturday 1105 hours

The second hit was harder than the first—a deafening ringing throughout the metal container that rattled through Katie's body as she was slammed against the corrugated wall. Pain spread throughout her body. She tried to gulp and cough to catch her breath, but the rumble of the giant earthmover brought back horrific memories from the battlefield. Things she never wanted to remember. Images of blood, casualties and broken bodies flooded her mind. She could actually smell gunfire and feel the intense heat of the afternoon on her face. The traumas that she had so carefully hidden away in the recesses of her mind broke free and swarmed her.

Realizing her cell had once again dislodged with the impact, she scrambled around for it in the pitch darkness, found it and stashed it deeply in her pocket. Pushing a door out of her way she managed to stand and call out for her partner.

"Gav?"

There was no response.

"Gav?" she called again, more frantic. She heard a noise—movement and a gasp. "Where are you?" she said more quietly, not wanting the person on the outside to hear her.

Reaching down, she moved through the container with her hands out in front of her, not wanting to lose her phone again, until she found McGaven, caught between a heavy piece of lumber and a door.

"Gav," she said, putting her hands on his face—he stirred slightly. He had been knocked unconscious. She felt blood coming from his scalp. "You okay? Can you move at all?"

"No," he muttered.

"Where's the pain?"

"No pain. Just *hard* to breathe..."

Feeling around, Katie discovered that the door had wedged against him and was pressing hard into his chest. "Take it easy. Breathe slowly, evenly if you can. Let me see what I can do, okay?"

Though her hands were shaking uncontrollably, Katie moved around the door trapping McGaven and the dent of the container pushing in toward him. Shifting back and bracing herself, she put her feet up against the door and pushed with everything she had. But it wasn't enough. Using her hands as her eyes, she found part of a piece of lumber to use like a crowbar.

It took her a moment to get it ready. The sound of the earth-mover roared up again—prowling, hunting, and eager to do some damage.

"Gav, we have to brace for another hit."

"Okay," he barely said.

Katie wedged the wood as best she could and pulled down hard, putting all of her 125 pounds against it. She let out a yell of anger trying to shift it away from her partner. It moved a little... then a little more... then enough to free McGaven.

The diesel beast revved and was bearing down on the container.

"C'mon," she said.

McGaven wiggled free. He grabbed Katie to maintain balance and headed for the door where there was the least number of stored items.

The third hit battered them hard. The ringing through the container was almost unbearable.

McGaven tried to use his weight and size to protect Katie, but they crashed against the side like floppy rag dolls.

Light trickled in, illuminating the metal container a little. They saw that there was a hole the size of a dinner plate where McGaven had been pinned. The strike would have crushed him if he had still been there. Now the metal was torn and folded from the impact.

The bulldozer seemed to be having trouble backing up as part of it was caught on the side of the container. Revving dangerously high, bumping up and down, screeching and groaning, it finally broke free.

Katie could hear Cisco barking, loud and nonstop from the car. He knew that Katie was in trouble and needed help. He was probably doing everything a dog could do to get to her. The back window had been left down about six inches. She wondered if he could get out.

"Cisco," she shouted with torment in her voice. "What if he tries to bulldoze the cars?"

"Wait, where's your back-door release?"

"I… I don't have it on me," she said. "I didn't think I needed it. No… Cisco…" She kept back the tears.

"Where's your gun?" said McGaven.

"I have a snub nose Colt right here." She showed him her concealed holster on her side.

"Five shots?"

"Yeah," she said.

"Try to shoot the lock."

"That's not…" She abruptly didn't finish because there was no time for negativity. Instead, she got into position.

McGaven covered his ears and gave her a nod.

She aimed at an angle that hopefully wouldn't ricochet the bullet and hit one of them. Hearing the diesel engine and Cisco barking, she focused, stood back to the side, and squeezed the trigger. The .38 bullet hammered at the area, but nothing changed.

People and events flashed through her mind: Cisco, her uncle, her parents, her dad barbecuing, hiking with Chad, and being sworn in at the sheriff's department as a new detective.

"Again," McGaven said, turning away from the impact.

Katie repeated the same action twice, hitting the same area, mutilating the metal. "I only have two shots left," she said.

"Use them!"

Katie squeezed the trigger and fired twice. "Nothing. It didn't break free."

"I have my gun, but it came free when I was hit by the door. I have to find it…"

Katie tried to calm her breathing; she knew that her adrenalin wasn't helping her focus or the situation. It caused her to tremble and her vision became slightly blurred.

They heard the sound of the construction equipment start up and rev again—this time at a different pitch.

"Why does it sound different?" she said.

"That's because it's a forklift," he said and began to move to find a place where they could brace themselves.

"What?" Katie said not completely understanding.

"Lifting equipment, so he can push us…"

"… off the side of the property," she finished the sentence. They were going to be tipped into the pit where Candace Harlan's body was discovered.

"Hang on!" was the last thing that Katie heard McGaven shout.

They braced for the impact.

The equipment hit them, but it wasn't as severe as the previous ones.

Katie loosened her grip and looked at McGaven; he had the same expression of wonderment.

Then it happened…

They felt the metal container move beneath their feet. The moment of stillness just before the fateful drop on the roller coaster. The storage unit shifted slowly, rattling everything inside including Katie's bones.

"We have to find your gun!" she said and began urgently looking anywhere where it could have landed.

McGaven copied her, but had to stop and catch his breath.

"You okay?" she said nervously, looking over to where she could just make out his outline.

"I'm okay…" he panted and began to search again.

The container seemed to sit idle for a moment.

"Stop," she demanded McGaven. "Stay still and breathe slowly. I'm going to find the gun." She looked back and he began to help her. "I mean it, stay still!" she ordered.

The equipment outside powered up again and the container began to move slowly towards the edge, like a slow sinking ship. It wouldn't be long before they plunged to their fate over the edge of the pit.

Katie knew their time was running out.

The metal container began to move faster. Then she felt the drop as her body was thrown into a free fall and the container tumbled.

CHAPTER THIRTY-TWO

Saturday 1345 hours

A faint buzzing brought Katie back to a wakeful state—she didn't know how long she had been knocked out. Moving her head slightly, she groaned. She still felt dizzy and nauseous from the drop and not being able to see anything but—darkness—again. Her lips were dry and it was difficult to find her voice.

Finally she said, "Gav, you okay?" Her voice a hoarse whisper.

Swallowing several times, she said again, "Gav, you okay?"

Booming sounds reverberated all around.

"Katie?" said McGaven. His voice was clear and calm.

Relief filled her heart. Closing her eyes for a moment, she said a silent prayer of thanks.

"I'm okay," he said. "You okay?"

"I… think so." Katie went to move and realized that her right leg was stuck underneath something. It didn't hurt but she couldn't get it free. "I'm stuck."

"Let me try to get to you," he said, moving slowly and carefully, pushing bits of wood and metal out of the way.

Katie tried to stand but was unable.

Banging resounded all around them—like several hammers trying to pound the container.

"What is that?" she said with her hands over her ears.

"Someone is trying to get to us."

"Is that the good guys or bad?" She tried to make light of it, but the truth was she was scared. Pushing to stay focused, she kept her mind at how to get out of their predicament.

"I'm putting my money on the good guys," he said, bringing Katie's mind into the present. "But we'll make prep as if it's the bad guys."

"Like what?" Katie didn't really want to know but she needed to hear his voice to keep calm. The darkness was unsettling, making her cold and jumpy.

"You know," he said above the scraping sound of him moving something out of the way. "Good news, I found my gun. It actually hit me during the tumble. Normally, I would make a joke but I'll just leave it as is…"

Katie smiled.

"Keep talking," he said. "Let me get to you."

A huge bang rammed the side, shaking the entire metal container. Then it stopped, followed by a strange hissing sound. Muffled voices. Then more hissing.

Katie then saw the flickering light of an oxyacetylene torch, used to cut open heavy metal. Someone was there to help.

"Katie?" McGaven said.

"How'd they get here so fast?"

"Maybe Chad?"

"You're right."

"Hey! We're in here!" she yelled.

"We're right here. Help!" McGaven followed Katie's example. "Help!"

There was no reply from outside.

McGaven reached out to touch Katie and she startled beneath his hand. "Sorry," he said.

The flashing orange-and-white lights had stopped.

"Take my hand," he said. "Show me where your foot is stuck."

Katie moved his hand to what appeared to be a block of wood.

"Okay," he began. "I think this is part of the mantel that broke in half."

"Can you move it?"

"I'm not sure," he said and his voice sounded funny, weak and wheezy.

"You okay?"

"Yeah, I'm just a bit dizzy."

Katie had forgotten all about his chest injury. "Gav, just sit still and relax—breathe slowly and conserve your energy. Someone will get to us."

McGaven was quiet.

"Gav? Gav, you okay?"

He didn't respond.

Katie twisted her body and tried to reach him. She was able to contort herself to lean against him. His body was limp under her touch. She felt for his pulse—it was erratic, but still strong. Listening for his breath, it was ragged and uneven. She knew his chest injury must be causing a restriction—it could mean his lungs were filling up with fluid.

"Gav?" she whispered. "I don't know if you can hear me, but we're going to get you out of here." She stifled a cry and kept her focus. It wasn't just about her—if too much time passed McGaven could suffocate from his injuries. She wasn't going to let that happen.

"Help! We need medical attention! Help!"

Almost on cue, there was the sound of a chainsaw along with flickering lights. In the strange light, she could see McGaven slumped to the side and his face looked ashen. The flames became larger and the trail of light burned in a circular shape as it inched closer, so Katie shielded them as best as she could in case of injury. She said a quiet prayer.

McGaven murmured something that Katie couldn't quite hear.

"Don't talk. We're going to be okay," she said, not knowing for sure but she had to believe it.

Her thoughts were interrupted by the ear-piercing scrape of metal on metal. Daylight pierced into the metal container causing Katie to shield her eyes.

"Katie?" said a voice.

"Chad?" She barely spoke.

"She's okay!" yelled Chad back to the others.

"We need medical attention for McGaven immediately!" she managed to yell back.

With a bit more scraping, the end of the metal storage container peeled back like a can of soup and two firefighters Katie didn't know climbed through the opening to assess how they would pull her and McGaven out safely. Relief flooded through Katie's aching body.

"Can you move?" said one of the men to Katie.

"My foot is caught. I'm fine. Please… please take McGaven first. He was pinned earlier by a door pressed against his chest. He had trouble breathing, there's bruising… and…" she explained as she caught her breath. "And there was some blood on his chest…"

The firefighter nodded and made his way to McGaven who was now lucid and awake. He checked his vitals and took a quick look at his chest. Turning back to the other emergency personnel, he said, "We need to get him out ASAP. Possible pulmonary contusion."

"Is he going to be okay?" she said.

"We won't know more until an x-ray is done to find out if his lungs have been compromised."

The seriousness hit Katie hard and her worry turned to despair, as she twisted to move as best as she was able to let them do their work.

It took about fifteen minutes before they were able to get him out of the container.

"Hey," said Chad, trying to act like it wasn't a big deal. But his eyes couldn't hide his fear.

"Hi."

"You doing okay?" He leaned down.

"I'll be better once I'm out of here."

Two of the firefighters tried to move the wood but it was too wedged for them to move it manually.

"Did they catch him?" she asked.

"Who?"

"The guy who locked us in here and decided to bulldoze us."

Chad didn't meet her gaze. "I don't know."

"Yes, you do. He got away, didn't he?"

"They haven't found him—yet," he said. Someone spoke to him from outside, but Katie couldn't quite hear what they said. "Okay," said Chad. "We're going to have to cut you out."

Katie's eyes grew big.

Chad nodded to his co-workers. "Okay, I'm going to be right here with you, Katie. I'm going to cover your face and body, and Rodney here is going to cut the board. Okay?"

She didn't know quite what to say, but nodded in agreement and tried not to squirm.

Chad gave her a reassuring smile then gently laid heavy tarp-like material over her, covering her face as well. He grabbed her hand and squeezed it to help reassure her that everything was going to be alright.

The chainsaw screamed to life. As it approached closer to Katie, the sound deafening, she flinched and squeezed her eyes shut. As the chainsaw made contact, woodchips and dust flew everywhere and the pressure against Katie's leg caused her to cry out. She tried to stay still as she could, though every nerve in her body wanted to pull away from the revolving blade so close to shredding her leg.

The noise stopped abruptly, leaving Katie's ears ringing and unable to hear anything. Chad was talking to her but she couldn't hear him. It was as if she were floating underwater and slowly being pulled up to the surface.

As she reached the daylight, she opened her eyes; everything was blurry at first, and then she saw a crowd of people waiting for her arrival—or so it seemed. It appeared dreamlike, as if the entire universe downshifted into slow motion.

"I'm okay," Katie said, feeling a bit woozy. "Really, I'm fine," she insisted, trying to break free of Chad's grip.

"Take it easy there," he said.

"Where's McGaven?" she said.

"He's doing much better. He's over there being checked out but he wouldn't leave until he knew you were okay." Chad pointed to an open ambulance where McGaven sat inside with an oxygen mask on as one of the paramedics was taking his blood pressure and vitals.

Katie started to walk over to him.

"Katie, wait a minute. You need to be checked out," Chad persisted.

"I'm fine. I need to talk to my partner first."

Some of the people in the crowd watched as she sat down next to McGaven. "Is he going to be okay?" she asked the medical tech.

"He's going to be fine, but he still needs to have his chest x-rayed just to be sure that there aren't any other complications."

She turned to McGaven. "You know this is my fault. I know, I know. I hardly ever admit that I'm wrong."

McGaven shook his head and was about to take off the oxygen mask. "No, it isn't," he said, muffled from the mask.

"Just listen for a moment, okay? I know I've already apologized, but I've got to get this out before I lose my nerve and get my wits back."

McGaven quieted and patiently waited, still breathing fresh oxygen.

Katie glanced at the paramedic who appeared not to be listening—but obviously was. Katie didn't care, she continued, "I know there's been a lot of drama during our time as partners, but I would like to think that there have been great times too. Ever since you were assigned to work with me, I've managed to get us into some… serious predicaments. Saying I'm sorry isn't good enough, but I want you to know that I love working with you. You're the best partner anyone could ever ask for. And, because of my stupid curiosity today, I led us right into a trap inside that metal container. I would never be able to live with myself if anything happened to you because of my overzealousness. I never had a brother or sister… and…" She paused as she saw the paramedic smile. "Excuse me, could you give us a minute?" she said.

"No problem," he said, still smiling, and left them alone. The other officers and emergency personnel left them alone as well. McGaven waited until she finished.

"Like I said, I never had a brother, but if I did, I would hope he would have been just like you. I'm sorry about today. I'm sorry about the previous stuff. And, I'm sorry about being so mushy now. I just wanted you to know."

McGaven took the oxygen mask off and breathed some of the natural air. "Are you done?"

"Yeah."

"Thanks." He looked directly at her and said, "You know it's mutual, right?"

"Really?"

He pushed her gently on the arm.

She smiled and said, "Thanks. That means a lot, Gav."

He hugged her tight and whispered in her ear, "Never stop caring like you do. And never stop pushing the investigations. I have your back—always."

Katie was overwhelmed as she returned the hug, quickly wiping the tears from her face.

"Katie," said Sheriff Scott as he approached quickly.

She stood up. "I'm fine, Uncle Wayne. Really, we're fine."

The sheriff took Katie and held her tight. "I was so worried when I got the call from dispatch. What were you guys doing here?"

"We had gone for a run today and then decided, well, *I* decided, we needed to check out the house after seeing the blueprints in the archives. And then on our way out, we checked out the one container that didn't have a lock."

"It was a trap?" the sheriff said, motioning to a couple of the deputies.

"I don't know… maybe an opportunity?" she said.

"I want this property locked down—tight. Everything searched again. Fingerprints taken on the containers, construction equipment, and anything else. Call John and have him go over everything. There must be something that will give us some answers." Sheriff Scott reluctantly left Katie's side and surveyed the property, giving more orders.

"Go get checked out, okay?" she said to McGaven.

"I will."

She slowly walked to Chad who had been patiently waiting for her with Cisco at his side. "Hi. Thank you for saving us." She petted Cisco who had some bandages on his legs.

"Just my job," he said, trying to force a smile, but it was clear that he was concerned and relieved all at once.

She bent down to examine the dog. "Is Cisco okay?"

"He's fine, just some minor cuts trying to get out of the vehicle."

Katie hugged the dog tight—she realized how close she could have been to losing her partner and dog.

"Looks like you were all lucky."

"McGaven is going to get checked out at the hospital."

"And you?" he said.

"I will go too."

"Are you?"

"Yes, I promise."

Sheriff Scott had already made his rounds and came back to Katie and Chad. He said, "That crazy bastard is still out there. Chad, I want you to stay with Katie until all this is over. Understood?"

"Absolutely, sir. You have my word."

"I'm not a little girl. I'm a police officer, remember? And I have Cisco too."

"I would feel better. Is that too much to ask?"

"Of course not," she said as all the heavy feelings of juggling everything alone came tumbling back.

CHAPTER THIRTY-THREE

Monday 0745 hours

Katie drove Chad's extra Jeep to the sheriff's department, her mind whirring with fresh ideas. Chad hadn't let her lift a finger to do anything for the entire Sunday as he fussed around her doing all the cooking and cleaning, sternly instructing her to rest. Even her uncle checked in twice to make sure that she was following explicit orders—his and the doctor's. So thinking was all she could do under the circumstances.

Katie had to admit that she did feel rested, even with a few more bruises than usual, but she felt recharged and ready to tackle all the evidence and leads on these cases. She had jotted down a few notes over the past day and wanted to get started immediately.

McGaven had called her Saturday evening and told her that he was fine—no serious damage to his lungs or organs—just bruising. He was supposed to rest for a few days and he didn't say for sure if he would be in on Monday morning.

Katie parked and made her way to the office, running scenarios of the case through her mind as always. She had some follow-up questions for Tanis Jones and wanted to talk to her as soon as possible, and she also wanted to get someone tracking Keller's movements.

Opening the door to the cold-case office, she was surprised to see McGaven sitting, as usual, at his laptop keying in search parameters.

"Hi," she said, amazed that he had decided to come to work.

"Hey, partner," he said not looking up from the computer.

"I thought you'd be taking a few days off."

"For what?"

"To rest."

"Nah, I'd just be sitting at home thinking about stuff here. So at least I'm sitting here at work being productive."

"Okay, great." She put her things down and retrieved her notebook. "Have we heard anything from forensics taken from the bulldozer and container?"

"No. But I don't think they'll be much—at least according to John. I ran into him this morning."

"Oh," said Katie disappointed. She had thought they would have found something—anything—fingerprints—*anything* of interest.

"I've been trying to find the other girls from the foster home and it's been frustrating. Terry Slaughter has had so many aliases it's next to impossible to track. And Heather Lawson moved to Kansas, but there's no information found: death certificate, job, social security, owning anything. Nothing."

"If she's alive, it's clear that she's staying off the radar. Perhaps she's homeless."

"No arrest records either."

"Hmm… she might have decided that she didn't like Kansas and moved to another state."

"I'm checking now. But it will take some time."

"What do we know about her?" she asked.

"Not much."

"I want to talk to Tanis Jones again—maybe she might have some answers?"

McGaven turned in his chair and grimaced.

"What's wrong? You okay?"

"Yeah, just sore. The doc said I would be hurting for about a week to ten days."

Katie sat down in her chair and rolled next to McGaven. "You sure you don't want to go home and rest?"

"Katie, I'm fine. I'm just not going to be running for a while though."

"Okay," she said and stood up, studying her whiteboard. "What do we have now?"

McGaven swiveled in his chair and began skimming the lists. "Well… we have new information about the Elm Hill Mansion."

"Yes, we do… Now, more than ever, Elm Hill sits at the center of the two homicides." Katie paused, thinking that there was something blinding that she wasn't seeing about the mansion. "What about the employees at Elm Hill? Anything?"

"Okay, I was able to track down Margaret Adler, the house-keeper, she's since retired and is residing at Bella Vista—old folks' home. Elmer Rydesdale, maintenance and groundskeeper, is still working and I have an address for him. And, finally the tutor, Tatiana Wolf, only worked there for a few weeks before she transferred to Boston for a teaching position."

"Ms. Wolf will probably not be too much help, but let's call her and see what she says—perhaps there's a reason for her leaving that we need to know about." Katie stood up and studied the county map. "Okay, Bella Vista is close. Where's Elmer Rydesdale located?"

Reading his notes, McGaven said, "Over in Crowley Creek, about twenty minutes from here."

"I think we need to get a better idea of what was going on at Elm Hill before it shut down. What better way than talking to ex-employees?"

"No doubt. You just have to know how to ignore the personal BS and get to the root of the matter."

Katie laughed. "I'm still waiting to hear back from Dr. Samantha Rajal, Mary Rodriguez's doctor, and see what she has to say about the abortion and the drugs she was taking." She leaned back in her chair. "Oh, anything new on 'hunter-gatherer'?"

"Let's see." McGaven keyed up several chat rooms and social media sites. "Not much. You know there are people who transcribe every time a certain phrase is used in movies, TV, and even radio shows. I checked that. If I have to read more about what someone thinks of a book, I'm going home."

Katie leaned in to read his computer. "It can't be that bad."

"Oh, you have no idea. I cannot find anything about the books— or any bookstore who carries them. The only thing I can find out from these chat areas is that there's an old bookstore over on the south end. It's a mystery shop for only 'invited' people. There's no sign or indication on the building that there's any type of business there."

"What do you mean?" Katie said.

"Well, it's where people dress up as some character from books and mingle. But the owner, a Donald L. Holmes, supposedly has the most extensive book collection, especially anything written from 1940 through the 1960s."

"Are you kidding me?"

"I just report the facts."

"And his last name is Holmes?" Katie rolled her eyes.

"Actually, I checked his background, and yes, his name really is Donald Lee Holmes."

"Okay, let's get on the phone, divide up calls, and see what we can do today. It's still early and we can cover a lot of ground if we get started now—sound good? You up to it?"

Picking up his cell phone, McGaven said with enthusiasm, "I'm on it."

Later that morning, Katie turned the sedan down a narrow lane without a sign and continued along a driveway that seemed more like a walking path than anything fit for a car. She slowed her speed. The instructions were to take a left at the broken fence and then proceed until there were four trees in a circle.

Crowley Creek was a small town of 200 acres that ran along the edge of the county. It technically wasn't a town, but it had a population of sixteen people incorporating two families, along with a gas station, feed store, and a small grocery and supply store that also doubled as the post office.

Katie stopped the car to look out the window at the cluster of trees. "What do you think? Does that look like four pine trees in a circle?" She wasn't so sure.

McGaven craned his neck and took a moment before answering, "I think so…"

"You spoke to Mr. Rydesdale," she said.

"I did. He was difficult to understand because he seemed so excited to talk to us, but at least he was willing to talk."

Katie exhaled loudly. "Well, let's keep going. You can't see anything in between all these trees."

The sedan inched forward, squeezing by several more trees, and then it opened to a beautiful valley. A dozen acres of expertly landscaped garden with rows of vegetables, flowers, and patches of meadow greeted them. A large yellow 1920s farmhouse with white trim sat to the north end of the property, and several trucks were parked in front.

"Wow," she said, looking around. Finding a place to park, she sat for a moment admiring the area.

"Wow is right. I've never seen anything like this except—maybe in a movie."

Katie and McGaven got out of the car and continued to marvel at the area.

"Hi," came a voice behind them. A woman in her forties with auburn hair and a large floppy green hat greeted them. She was dressed in dark jeans and a lightweight long-sleeved blouse. "Are you the detectives?" she said.

"Hi," said Katie. "Yes, I'm Detective Scott and this is Deputy McGaven."

"Pleased to meet you both," she said. "I'm Sandy, Elmer's daughter. Elmer will meet you on the porch. In the meantime, you can enjoy a glass of sweet tea."

"That would be lovely," said Katie, glancing at McGaven. They obediently followed the woman along the carefully manicured path to the house.

"Take a seat and he'll be with you shortly," she said and disappeared into the house.

Katie raised her eyebrows and then took a seat.

McGaven walked to the railing. "It's really beautiful here. Makes me want to buy some land."

"I could see you as a farmer," Katie joked.

"No, really. I would love having land around here somewhere. My own land."

The screen door opened and an older man in his seventies stepped out carrying a tray with three glasses of sweet tea. He was thin, tanned, and moved like a much younger man. "Hello, Detectives."

"Mr. Rydesdale?" asked Katie.

"Please, you can call me Elmer," he said and offered Katie and McGaven each a glass. "After I heard about that woman's body found at Elm Hill, I figured it was only a matter of time before the police came around here."

"You worked there when it was a foster home?"

"Yes," he said, taking a sip of tea. "About four years." His excitement showing as he began to talk faster again.

"Why? May I ask? You have such a wonderful place here."

"Well," he began, "we were going through some rough times and our farm wasn't producing enough for the market. I took the job temporarily to make ends meet."

Katie understood and nodded. "Did you enjoy it?"

"Not particularly. Don't get me wrong, I was thankful for the opportunity. But, it was always a problem."

"What do you mean?"

"Well, there was a lot of drama with those girls."

"Can you be more specific?" said Katie, taking another sip of the tea, which was delicious.

"They were always arguing, yelling, and plenty of door-slamming. Seemed like I was always fixing a door, replacing a window, sweeping up broken dishes and such."

"I see. Did you happen to hear what the arguments were all about?"

"I tried to stay clear most of the time, but the best I could conclude would be the girls thought they were being treated unfairly, too much discipline, I'd imagine." He took a seat in one of the wicker chairs with bright yellow cushions. His face had many lines from being outdoors in the sun for so many years, but most of them were from smiling and laughing.

"Did you witness any of these disciplines?"

"Can't say I did. A lot happened behind closed doors."

"Did you ever see men coming to the house?"

"Just police officers occasionally. My day usually ended by 6 p.m., so I couldn't tell you if anyone visited after that."

"Did you know any of the girls? One you spoke to the most?"

"I spoke with Candace, she was a lovely girl. She was polite and always asked how I was doing. The others were just in passing, with the exception of maybe that quiet skinny one... what was her name..."

"Tanis?"

"Yes, that was the one. She would bring me bottles of water on the hot days and sometimes sodas. Nice girl," he said remembering. "I spent most of my time outside tending to the flowers and lawn areas, which, I understand, have all gone away since the house has been abandoned." He looked down sadly. "It's a shame that they couldn't find someone who wanted to remodel the house and bring it back to its glory."

"I agree," said Katie. "I never saw it when it was all together, but it must've been stunning."

"Yes… yes it was…"

"I won't take up much more of your time, Elmer. We're trying to get a picture of what was going on at the house. One more question…"

"Of course," he said.

"In your four years there, was there ever an incident, something you saw or heard, that would make you think that someone would want to do harm to any of the girls?"

"You mean someone that would want to hurt or kill them?" he said, taking a moment. "Detective, I can't say I know what motivates people to violence, but I didn't see or hear anything that would push someone to that extreme."

"Thank you, Mr. Rydesdale… Elmer," she said, correcting herself. "I appreciate your time and this fantastic tea." Katie was disappointed. She wasn't sure what he would be able to tell her. Noticing his scar on the back of his left hand and how he couldn't use it well, she wondered if he'd had an accident at his farm or at Elm Hill. She asked, "Do you remember anyone else regularly coming to the house? Workers? Friends? Anyone? Emergency first-responders for anything?"

Elmer thought about it a moment. "I had two laborers that helped with tree trimming and all in the spring and fall. They seemed to be interested in the girls, but I suspect it was because they were interested in all pretty girls."

"Did either of the workers take a special interest in any of the girls in particular? Especially Candace? We know a man named Ray helped her escape, does that name ring any bells?" she asked.

"No, I don't think so. I forget their names, but they normally worked in other areas at the county—I think sanitation and maintenance."

McGaven made notes and finished his iced tea.

Standing up, Katie said, "Thank you, Elmer. I think that's all I need right now. If you happen to think of anything else, please don't hesitate to call us." She handed him a business card.

Katie and McGaven were quiet as she carefully maneuvered the police sedan back down the tight driveway. Driving slowly, Katie thought about the conversation with Elmer. It didn't bring about anything new, but it did confirm what they had been hearing with the fighting and the discontent at Elm Hill.

"What do you think?" McGaven asked.

"I think I want another glass of that iced tea," she said half smiling.

"I know," he said.

"You feeling okay?"

"Yeah, I'm fine. Why?"

"Just asking."

"If I'm getting tired or not feeling well, I'll let you know. You don't have to keep asking me."

"Okay."

Once Katie hit the main road, she sped away as fast as she dared on the way to Bella Vista to visit Margaret Adler. She might have more information, having been on the inside of Elm Hill.

"I think we need to speak to Mrs. McDonald again," said Katie. "We need to press her more."

"I agree. I'll call the prison and set up a time tomorrow." He called the number and left a message with his and Katie's name, department, and name of prisoner he wanted to talk to. "I hate that," he said after ending the call. "They'll have to call me back."

Katie felt frustrated: she wanted answers and wasn't getting any. "I spoke with Ms. Wolf, the tutor, and she won't be any help. She didn't see or talk to anyone except Mrs. McDonald and two of the girls who needed math tutoring during her three-week employment. Nothing seemed out of the ordinary and she definitely didn't see any kind of abuse."

"End of that road with her then," he said. "We'll just keep digging."

Returning to the main area of town, she took a right that led to a business development. There was a big sign: *Bella Vista, Premiere Assisted Living*. She pulled into the parking lot. The area was a landscaper's dream with every kind of blooming flower and varied shades of greenery. It was a two-story building that stretched along the lot with patios and breezeways in between. There were a few people enjoying the weather sitting on benches and in chairs. It was quite cheerful.

"Okay," said Katie. "Let's go see what Mrs. Adler has to say."

Katie and McGaven walked up the meandering white cement pathway to the front doors. Once inside, it was set up like a spacious living room. There wasn't a front desk, but an office to the left. An older dark-haired woman sat at a desk working on the computer. There were no signs of where to go—just numbers on doors and at hallways.

"Hello?" said Katie catching the woman's attention.

"Yes?" she said.

"I called earlier about speaking with Mrs. Margaret Adler."

"Oh, yes, of course. Detective Scott, right?"

"Yes, and this is Deputy McGaven." Katie smiled.

"Oh my," she said, looking up at McGaven. "You're probably the tallest police officer I've ever seen."

"I think he's the tallest I've seen too," Katie chimed in, having a bit of fun at McGaven's expense.

"Okay," the woman said. "Margaret is out on the porch reading. Just follow through the main area until you see the sliding doors."

"How will we know Margaret?" Katie asked.

"Oh," the woman said and giggled. "You'll know. Have a nice visit."

Katie looked at McGaven and shrugged. "Okay." They continued through the large living room where people were playing cards, working on puzzles, and a few reading books in the corner.

They came to the sliding doors which opened onto a large deck area where there were maple trees and low blooming bushes. Two men were chatting, and two women reading paperback novels.

"What do you think?" asked Katie.

"I don't know. Just ask, I suppose."

Both were feeling conspicuous, but no one paid them any attention.

Katie walked up to a woman fitting Margaret Adler's build and what she thought she would look like. "Excuse me," she said. "Are you Margaret Adler?"

The woman politely shook her head no.

"You looking for me?" said a voice behind her. A robust woman with fire-red hair, clearly dyed, and a colorful floral top, had appeared, riding a scooter. "I'm Margaret Adler. Judging by your suit, not to mention your gun and badge, you must be Detective Scott."

"Yes," said Katie. "Yes, I am. And this is—"

"Deputy McGaven," Adler finished her sentence and smiled up at him.

McGaven nodded his head in introduction.

"Can we talk?" said Katie.

"Of course. Follow me," she instructed and took off at full speed to another area of the patio.

Katie and McGaven almost had to jog to keep up with the woman—each feeling their bruises as they hurried.

Mrs. Adler settled in a nice spot between some of the landscaping and where there were two Adirondack chairs for Katie and McGaven.

Taking a seat, Katie jumped right in and began asking questions about Elm Hill. "Mrs. Adler, how long were you employed at Elm Hill?"

"Four years, three weeks, and sixteen days."

"Okay," said Katie and she lightly laughed. "I guess I'm just going to come right out and ask."

"Please do. I have no secrets." She waited patiently for the questions.

"Did you like your job there?"

"Sometimes. The girls were nice, just misunderstood and defensive because of their situations. But mostly, many days were filled with hassles and long hours. The county wouldn't pay for overtime unless it was over forty hours during the week. So that made for some long days."

"I see. Did you witness anything unusual?"

"C'mon, Detective. Just spit it out. This isn't a court of law, you know—just a couple of gals talking." She smiled broadly, showing her perfect false teeth.

"Okay. Was there anything going on at Elm Hill that had to do with abuse?"

"From what I saw, yes."

"Can you elaborate?"

"I witnessed on several occasion Shelly McDonald using physical force on the girls—especially the quiet one… Tanis. She would slap her, punch her in the stomach, and I heard her beating her with something—I assume some type of switch or stick."

That made Katie sad and mad that the woman used violence on the girls. "Did you report this to the police or social worker?"

"I would tell them everything I had seen when I was asked—I didn't offer. Just wanted to keep my nose clean and keep my job."

"Were there any men visiting Elm Hill—especially at night?"

"Interesting you should ask that… Normally I would say no, except for the police officers being called. Well, it was the muscular one. Can't remember his name—I never spoke to him but just once." She stopped and studied Katie and McGaven. It was unclear why, but she continued, "On one of the late nights I was finishing stocking the fridge with pre-made meals, when I saw two men accompanied by Shelly go upstairs. They parked their car outside, but I never saw them leave. When I left, the car was gone. That's all I know."

Katie leaned forward, "Mrs. Adler, I get the feeling that there's something that you're not telling us."

"Well, I don't know if it makes a difference or not. Or if it's important or not, but it's bothered me to this day."

"Go ahead."

"I used to hear crying, a woman crying. At first I thought it was a ghost because I could never find out who it was. I would search, but never found her. Until one day. That's when I saw it. The wall was partially open… and there was a secret staircase. It suddenly made sense to me about all the crying and other strange things… I would see one of the girls or someone visiting… and then I wouldn't. There was a secret passageway that no one would admit to. Seemed strange to me."

Katie was surprised that she knew about it. "Did you tell anyone about this secret staircase?"

"No, but I did make mention of it to Candace once. She just laughed and said that all old houses had their weird secrets."

"Anything else?" asked Katie.

"I was never an eyewitness to anything except what I told you… but I knew in my gut and common sense I carry, there was something bad going on and those girls were the victims. I hoped that the county would do something about it but, as it turned out, they just closed the house."

"Think she was telling the truth?" McGaven asked as they made their way back to the car.

"Definitely. It really doesn't push the cases forward, but again, it confirms what we already know, which means we're on the right track."

McGaven's cell phone rang. "McGaven," he said. "Yes. When? I see." He slowly ended the call.

"What's up?" Katie knew something was terribly wrong. "Gav?"

"That was the prison. Shelly McDonald committed suicide two hours ago."

CHAPTER THIRTY-FOUR

Monday 1400 hours

Katie was still reeling over the news. "Gav, what have you been able to find out about McDonald's death?"

"There was nothing suspicious and she hadn't been suicidal at all during her incarceration, but she took her life when she was on kitchen duty. Apparently, she sliced her carotid artery. I'm still waiting for any final information."

"She must've known more than what she was telling us—and something we said upset her enough to make her take her own life."

"Maybe. She might have been hiding some issues too."

Katie sighed. "It's possible." She still wasn't convinced.

"We'll know more later."

"I think Hugh Keller is looking like our main suspect at the moment," said Katie adamantly, even though she wasn't completely convinced. There was more to his story, she thought, as she studied her notes back at the office.

"Aren't there books written about guys like that?" McGaven concluded.

"Absolutely. I couldn't say if he's a textbook 'psychopath' but he sure ticks the boxes of several traits: lack of remorse, lack of guilt, lack of impulse control, shallow, superficial, and such. His alibi sticks, but it's still sketchy. He could have left and come back."

"Sounds like a dozen guys I trained with at the academy."

Katie laughed. "Yep, the military too." She perused her notes and began writing. Looking at her list again, she said, "When can we get into that bookstore?"

"I'm going to call back Mr. Holmes tomorrow to see if we can take a look at those books. I tried the library, the Internet, and other mystery stores and can't get a copy. If these books were so important to the killer—and that's a BIG if—it was a small print-run of the series."

"You know, these girls were like family and they seemed to have distinct positions—like a hierarchy," she said.

"What do you mean?"

"It's like they each had a part. It's small but there's a pattern for a special group. All distinct. All serve a purpose. Could this be what the killer is attracted to? These girls, this family, their strengths and weaknesses. Is it something he wanted? Or hated?" Katie said as she wrote it out for viewing.

Candace Harlan—*leader, everyone looked up to, respected (best friends with Tanis)*
Mary Rodriguez—*the loudest, and would fight for her sisters. Enforcer?*
Tanis Jones—*quiet, least combative, but took the punishment for all the girls (best friends with Candace)*
Heather Lawson—*the cheerleader, always positive, wanted to be part of the group.*
Terry Slaughter—*lots of aliases. Not sure of her identity—she didn't open up as much as the other girls, but was involved in some of the fights with Shelly McDonald that required the police.*
Karen Beck—*deceased. Most likely to commit suicide and she did. Depression? Other mental illness? Not much information.*

"Interesting clarification."

"And where does Carol Harlan fit in?"

"And, why did someone attack us and basically try to kill us?"

Katie turned to McGaven. "Do you think they were trying to kill us—or scare us?"

"It seemed pretty serious to me."

"Yes, but they could have killed us in the house. Shot us. Ambushed us."

"Locking us in that metal storage was an ambush," he said.

"Ambush, or opportunity?"

McGaven remained quiet as he studied the board.

"What's the status of Jerry..."

"Jerry Weaver."

"Yes."

"I put another call in to him and sent him an email."

"We haven't received copies of any of the reports on the girls yet?"

"Nope."

"So we're back to square one, even after the event on Saturday," McGaven said with doubt in his voice.

"Remember, Gav, even when there is no evidence found at a crime scene, it's still evidence."

He smiled.

"My big question is—who is the guy in the black hoodie who keeps showing up?"

"Do you think he's followed you before?"

"I don't know—I actually don't think so," she said slowly. "He seems to hang out at the places of interest for the investigations. The mansion and the new neighborhood when we looked for Amy Striker."

"Why?"

"That is the question."

"What about that piece of paper in your locker?"

"I don't know," she said slowly. "It doesn't make sense. I've been thinking about it a lot. What does this company have to do with the Harlan sisters or Mary Rodriguez? Was it a message for us to go to that container? To bring what to our attention? The house? The crime scene? Or just scare the crap out of us? Like a warning?"

"It could just mean nothing—something to throw us off the trail," he said. "It could be just as simple as that."

"I still think that if we find Candace Harlan—everything will fall neatly into place. Well, maybe not neatly, but it will set this investigation on a straighter path."

"Do you really think that one: she's alive; and two: we would be able to find her if she doesn't want to be found?"

Pacing around the small office, Katie said with conviction, "Both homicides of Carol Harlan and Mary Rodriguez stem from the Harlan sisters—something about them or revolving around them. There's a reason, a secret, something we're not seeing." She read the murder board one more time. "And where are you on Sara and Jonathan McKinzie?" She turned to McGaven.

"I've been trying to search for them through other means," said McGaven. "I'm assuming that they have money and do a lot of charity work, so I'm seeing where they've been and that might help us find them."

Katie nodded. It was important to talk to the McKinzies and find out exactly why they donated that mansion to this particular cause.

As Katie exited the police building, she was looking forward to going home and being with Chad and Cisco. Her body was still sore and she really noticed it after she had been sitting at a desk for several hours.

Her cell phone buzzed and the message said: *Jerry Weaver is waiting for you at administration.*

"Oh," she murmured. McGaven had already left ten minutes ago, but she needed to get the reports. She texted her reply: *Be there in five.*

CHAPTER THIRTY-FIVE

Monday 1725 hours

Katie decided to walk to the community entrance in the administrative building of the Pine Valley Sheriff's Department. Since it was after 5 p.m., the receptionist had to unlock the door for anyone needing to get inside. There was usually someone there until 6 p.m.

Katie approached the two large doors and tapped on the glass. A friendly receptionist by the name of Dana unlocked the door for her. "Hi, Detective."

Katie walked inside. "Thanks, Dana." She looked around and didn't see anyone, but there was a briefcase, jacket, and files on one of the chairs. "Where is he?"

"I think the restroom," Dana said, returning through an unmarked door to get to the main reception desk.

Katie glanced at her watch and waited.

She heard a loud rush of water as the men's room door opened. A man adjusting his glasses walked through and hesitated, then quickly tried to tuck his shirt into his pants. There was a large wet spot at the top of his shirt where he had obviously tried to remove a stain, with little luck.

"Mr. Weaver?" said Katie.

He looked up and said, "Yes, you're Detective Scott? Oh, I was expecting a Deputy McGavnor."

"McGaven, Deputy McGaven," she corrected. "And yes, I'm Detective Scott. Nice to meet you."

"Yes, indeed," he said and extended his hand.

Katie immediately noticed that his palm was hot and sweaty. He stared at her for a moment.

"Do you have some paperwork for us?"

"Oh, yes, of course. I'm sorry, it has been the busiest and somewhat worst day today. And it's only Monday. I had to visit sixteen locations—sixteen cases. There just aren't enough hours in a day—and I still have to visit four more." He fumbled through his briefcase for a full minute, and then went to the files, shuffling, sorting, and putting paperwork in the correct order. "You don't want to hear about all that, I'm sure."

Katie watched with mild amusement, wanting to get home. "It's Monday for all of us." She didn't know what else to say.

"Ah, here we go. I made copies of everything I could find about the Elm Hill Foster Home. There might be some pages missing, but I assure you everything you might need is there." He handed Katie a stack of papers clipped with a large metal fastener.

Katie thumbed through them briefly just to make sure it was what McGaven had requested. There were reports, some handwritten, others typed, from the visits to the mansion. "It looks great, Mr. Weaver. You know, you didn't have to drive here personally. You could have scanned them and emailed, or had them couriered."

"Oh, but that's so impersonal. I thought if you had any questions I could answer them for you in person. I apologize for taking this long," he said, dropping paperwork from one of the files. It sprayed the eight-and-a-half-by-eleven sheets across the floor.

"Here, let me help you," said Katie not knowing what else to do.

"Thank you."

They picked up all the pieces of paper and he returned them to the folder.

Katie thought about the house with the secret stairway entrance and said, "Actually, you could answer a couple of things for me."

"Of course."

"Do you remember the mansion well?"

"I deal with many cases, but the Elm Hill Mansion definitely left a lasting impression."

"What was your overall impression of the girls and Mrs. McDonald?"

"Every time I made an appointment, things were tidy and the girls were behaving. I knew it was a show, but I was never able to get what I needed for the reports. At that time, we weren't allowed to do unannounced visits."

"I see. What about the police reports?"

"Now that was different. Every time the police were dispatched, I had to come out and speak with everyone. It became almost routine, and seemed like every week, or every other week—like clockwork."

"Did you notice anything that alerted you to abuse or psychological damage?"

"There was only one girl that I worried about, and tried to get Mrs. McDonald to get her to talk to a counselor."

"Karen Beck?"

"Karen, no. I was talking about Candace… Candace Harlan."

That assessment struck Katie as strange because of everything that she'd heard about her. "I thought that Candace was the strongest of the bunch, the one that the other girls looked up to?"

"Oh, that's true. But what has probably been overlooked by others is that she was a troubled girl who suffered from dramatic changes in mood, grand highs and depressing lows. I suspected that she might be bipolar. I've seen many people who suffer the same."

"Bipolar?" said Katie.

"That was one of my thoughts, but she didn't want to talk to anyone. Me or anyone else. We couldn't make her talk—she'd just go mute if we brought it up."

"What about the other girls?"

"Mmmm," he mumbled, thinking about it. "They were typical teenage girls with the added stresses of being in the foster care system. It's not easy. There's a lot of resentment, abandonment and anger issues that get thrown into the mix. Sometimes it's difficult to separate everything to get to the main issue."

"I see," said Katie. "My partner and I will go over these reports and if there are any questions, we'll call you."

Jerry Weaver put the loose files back in his briefcase and then he made notes on what looked like a sign-in sheet. "Okay, then. It was nice meeting you, Detective."

"Likewise."

He picked up his jacket and briefcase and headed for the door.

"Dana," she said, alerting her to let the social worker out. To Weaver, she said, "I have a hypothetical question."

"Okay."

"Do you think, in your opinion, that one of the five girls could be capable of murder?" Her words hung strangely in the air. Almost as if it were taboo to even ask such a question.

"Detective, I've been doing this a while. I've worked with the most passive to the most aggressive children that were capable of committing murder. But with these girls? I just don't see it."

"Okay, thank you, Mr. Weaver. I appreciate your time."

Jerry nodded his goodbye and left.

Katie began to follow him out when she heard someone calling her name. Turning, she saw Undersheriff Dorothy Sullivan coming out the door. She tensed.

"I thought that was you, Katie," she said.

"Hello, Undersheriff."

"Let's have that lunch tomorrow. Are you free?"

"I... yes, I think that would be fine."

"Good. I'll text you around 1 p.m. and then we can meet at a restaurant?"

"That would work."

"Great. I'm so excited to have some time to talk with you. Sheriff Scott has talked about you so much that I feel like I already know you."

"I hope not too much."

Laughing a bit too long, she said, "All flattering, I assure you." Turning to leave, she added, "I'll talk to you tomorrow."

CHAPTER THIRTY-SIX

Monday 1945 hours

Katie walked through the front door and was immediately greeted by Cisco running in his usual circles, filled with doggie glee. "Hey, I missed you too." She inhaled deeply and said, "What's that amazing smell?"

"Thought you'd never ask," said Chad, in the kitchen. He met Katie in the living room and kissed her, then kissed her again. "You feeling okay?"

"You don't need to keep asking me. I'm fine…" She kissed him once more to prove it.

"You look a bit tired, that's all."

"Gav and I spent most of the day running all over the county interviewing people, but not getting any further." She let out a sigh louder than she had anticipated.

"Dinner will be ready in ten."

"Great. I'll go change."

Katie went to her bedroom, followed closely by Cisco. She kicked her boots off and slipped out of her work clothes, opting for a more comfortable ensemble of loose pajamas and a hoodie.

Suddenly, there was a crash—as Cisco bounced around the bedroom he had obviously knocked something over. She startled and then berated herself that she needed to relax and to stop being so jumpy. She looked to see what he had done and found that on a small table near the window, one of the framed photographs had tipped over. It was the one of her parents during a summer barbecue; they were laughing together and clearly were in love. She stared at the photo for a moment, remembering what summers were like living in this house as a teenager. Fighting back the tears, she missed them terribly and would give just about anything to have one more day with them.

She sat down on the bed still holding the photo. Cisco jumped up next to her, pushing his nose against her arm. "You would have loved them," she whispered. She thought about her parents all the time, but when she felt that she was taking on the world it seemed that she clung to their memory even more.

"Hey," said Chad at the doorway watching her closely. "You hungry?"

Looking up, she smiled. "You bet, I'm starved. I skipped lunch today."

"Well, c'mon then."

Katie returned the photo to the table and followed Chad back to the kitchen.

"Wow, you cooked all this?" she said, sitting down at the counter.

Moving with a chef's expert speed, he said, "Don't forget, there are some of the best cooks around at the firehouse and I've been paying attention these days."

There were perfectly cooked filets wrapped in bacon with a special mushroom sauce, baked potatoes and green beans.

Chad slid over a glass of wine.

"You read my mind. I usually save wine for the weekends, but this hits the spot after today."

Katie made herself comfortable on the couch as Cisco chose a chair to curl up in. After a wonderful meal and two glasses of wine, she was finally able to unwind, leaving the job and all the loose ends of the investigations at work.

Chad draped a blanket over her and then snuggled up against her, trying to find a movie channel with something entertaining to watch that wasn't about the police or fire department.

"I get the feeling that you're trying to loosen me up to take advantage of me," she said.

"That's *always* the plan."

She laughed. "You know you don't need to take care of me, right?"

"Of course. But isn't that what people who love each other do?"

"Well…"

"Well, what?"

"I just don't want you to see me as a needy type."

"What?" he said, looking at her. "Needy? That wouldn't be the word I'd use to describe you."

"You know what I mean."

"No, I guess I don't."

"I don't want you to have to take care of me every time I have a bad day. It's give and take."

"There's no keeping score here."

"I know. It's just…"

"How long have we known one another?"

"A long time."

"Then why are you worrying about whether or not I should take care of you?"

Katie pulled up the blanket, suddenly feeling a chill. It was more of a reaction from anxious energy and not the temperature in the room. "Things seem heavy, burdensome in my life right now and I don't want to bring you down or make you feel less appreciated… because…"

"You love me?" he finished, giving her that wide-eyed playful expression that she grew up with—she always found it difficult to resist.

"Of course. More than you know."

"This is nice, right? And don't you want every day to be like this—together?"

"Yes," she began, and knew where he was going with his narrative. "It's wonderful, but we both have fairly hectic schedules right now." Katie knew that the next logical step would be more of a commitment, but there was no way she could make such a huge decision like that right now.

CHAPTER THIRTY-SEVEN

Tuesday 0810 hours

The early morning rain caused Katie to run a little bit late. She hurried from the car to the sheriff's building trying to stay as dry as possible. Her thoughts weren't far from Chad. He didn't ask her to marry him, but he was hinting at something. His restlessness about their relationship was showing and even though Katie had no doubt that he loved her, he wasn't going to wait forever.

What do I say?

Once inside the building, she shook off the raindrops, wiped her feet, hurried down the corridor and was about to run her security pass card when the door burst open and McGaven charged out.

"What's going on?" she said, taken aback that her partner almost knocked her off her feet.

"Saw you on the security cameras," he said, almost breathless. "Just got a call from the sheriff and Detective Hamilton; patrol brought Bob Bramble in last night."

"The contractor?" she said, accessing her memory for the day of the crime scene at Elm Hill.

"Yep. You'll never guess what for?"

"Murder?"

"No, it was a routine traffic stop and they found something interesting in his car."

"Just tell me," she said, teetering on her last nerve.

"They found three things: a roll of twine, a large bag of old-fashioned ink pens, and... a lock of brown human hair with a pink ribbon attached. And a small amount of cocaine."

Katie's jaw hit the floor.

"When the deputy asked him what all this was, he said something casual about the twine and pens for his daughter's art project, but he finally confessed that he took the lock of brown hair at the Harlan crime scene before we got here."

Katie couldn't believe what she was hearing. "What?"

"I know—you heard me."

"Where is he now?"

"He was in jail last night but they are bringing him up to one of the interview rooms for us to talk to him."

"Okay," she said. "What about a search warrant at his house and office?"

"They're already on that, but they left the interrogation up to your discretion."

"Let me put my briefcase away and dry off a bit first."

Katie and McGaven rushed into the detective division to find a commotion underway. Several detectives were speaking loudly to a civilian making the area feel busy and claustrophobic. Jennifer, the office assistant, intercepted them at the door and said, "Detective Hamilton told me to tell you that the suspect is in interview room 4. This is for you," she said, giving Katie a file.

"Thanks, Jen," said McGaven.

Outside the door, Katie skimmed through the reports and photographs of the items seized from Bramble's car. There was also a brief resumé and background check for Bramble.

Katie said, "You want to do it?"

"It's your party," he said.

Opening the door, Katie stepped into the room followed closely by McGaven. She chose to stand while McGaven took a seat uncomfortably close to the prisoner.

Robert John Bramble, age 52, sat quietly in his orange jumpsuit, his eyes darting from Katie to McGaven and back to her again. His wrists were cuffed but kept moving nervously—which was common for many suspects.

Katie slammed down the file folder, making it snap loudly against the table. "Mr. Bramble, how did we get here? You were so helpful at the crime scene, and now you're here in cuffs. What's up?"

He stared at her, his eyes almost black, his skin washed out. He shook his head.

"C'mon, do I need to spell it out for you?" Katie paced the floor to keep him on his toes—to fix his eyes on her.

"I don't know," he said in a whisper.

"I'm sorry, I didn't, *we* didn't quite hear that."

"I don't know what I can tell you. I don't know anything."

"That's a lot of 'don't knows' you have." She paused. "Wait, I'm sorry, but I didn't properly introduce myself and my partner," she said dramatically. "I'm Detective Scott and this is Deputy McGaven."

Bramble stared at her without any reaction.

"And we're investigating the homicides of Carol Harlan and Mary Rodriguez. Did you know that?"

"I don't know them."

"It says in the police report that you're being charged with drug possession, being a possible accomplice to murder, and impeding a murder investigation. What do you think about that?"

"I didn't do anything."

"Do you know Carol Harlan?"

"No."

"Do you know Mary Rodriguez?"

"No, I don't know those women."

Katie was warming up for the real questions she wanted answered. "Have you ever been part of a murder investigation before?"

"No."

"You seemed fairly competent when your crew found the body of Carol Harlan. You knew what to do: stop the work and keep everyone away from the murder scene. That says a lot, don't you think?"

"I've seen enough TV to know that you're not supposed to disturb a crime scene."

"I see."

"I have a daughter about that girl's age."

"You have two daughters," she said. "What do you think they think about what's going on right now?"

The mention of his daughters made him break and cry.

"These young women are murdered. Do you understand that?"

"Please, I don't know those women and I didn't kill anyone."

"Maybe you did, maybe you didn't. It's not up to me to say if you're innocent or guilty. It's up to a jury. What do you think they'll say?"

He sat and stared at Katie as if to discern why she was being so mean to him. Leaning back, trying to push himself out of the way—as if he could disappear.

"This brings me to the big question. Can you explain why you had a lock of woman's hair with a pink bow in your car?"

"I…"

"Did you take evidence from the crime scene at Elm Hill? When we get back the DNA report—who do you think we will find the hair belongs to?"

"You don't understand—"

"Did you take evidence from a murder scene?"

"It's just—"

"*Tell me*, did you take evidence from a crime scene?" Katie paused. She saw in her peripheral that McGaven had scooted forward a couple of inches, making it extremely uncomfortable for Bramble.

"I have a problem," he said.

"A fetish? A perversion? What would you like to call it?"

"I can't help myself. I take pretty things from women."

Katie was taken aback, not expecting that answer. It didn't initially occur to her that he was more creep than serial killer.

"Explain to me. How does that work? What triggers you? What goes through your mind?"

"It's…"

"I'm listening."

"It's hard for anyone to understand."

"Try me." She knew that he was embarrassed because she was a woman but he would have to deal with it.

"I can't help it. I've had this problem since I was young. I love girls. It makes me want something of theirs. Anything," he said, trying to compose himself, shifting in his chair. "I collect things. A discarded cup they'd been drinking from, a piece of fabric from their clothes, a barrette, sunglasses, anything connected to them."

Katie took two steadying breaths and lowered her intensity. "Take me through the events from when you found the body until the police arrived."

"Okay. It was a pretty stressful morning. One of my men came to me and said they had found something horrible. I saw it was a woman's body so I moved closer to see her. That's when I saw her naked body… I saw the fingernail but it was too close to some of my men that had gathered around." He paused.

"Go on," she said. "The more you tell us about that day, the better prepared we are to investigate and find the real killer."

"I *wanted* the fingernail. Badly. I ached to have that beautiful pink nail from that once beautiful girl. But I couldn't let my crew see what I do—what I am…" He picked up his hands and banged them on the table. "I turned and saw the lock of hair held by a pink ribbon. It was so pretty…"

"And so you stole it from a crime scene?"

He nodded.

"Did you realize what you were doing?"

"Yes, I knew. I always know. Don't you get it?"

"And the twine and calligraphy pens?"

"I… I… wanted to pretend… to re-create in my mind that it was me that tied her up and wrote on her back… I bought those things after the crime scene—I have a receipt." He wept. "I didn't kill anyone. I can't even kill an insect."

Katie sat down and flipped through the file again. There was a quick background check done on him, showing where he went to school from kindergarten through college.

"Where did you live when you were in high school?"

"Cloverdale. Just over in the next county."

"I see," she said. "Where were your parents? What did they do?"

"I don't know."

"You don't know where they were or what they did?"

"No. I don't know."

"Do you know a Shelly McDonald?"

"No, I don't think so."

"Do you know a Hugh Keller?"

"I don't know anyone named Hugh."

"Who did you live with when you were in high school?" She kept the questions flowing to keep him off guard—sometimes the person being interviewed gave little insights and honest answers when they were fired at them without a break.

He kept shaking his head in defiance.

"You had to have lived with someone. Who?"

"I never knew my parents. I lived in several foster homes my entire life—no one ever wanted me. I cursed every single one of the homes I was forced to live in—every single one."

Katie paused. This revelation changed some things, but not everything. It didn't mean that he was that much more likely to be the killer—it put a further twist in the investigation.

"How did you feel about the other kids in foster care?"

"Just like anywhere else. Some were okay but there were always those that you steered clear of."

"Did you ever meet girls that were in foster care?"

"No. But we met up with girls a lot."

"How did you feel about them?" Katie gently pushed. She glanced at McGaven and he remained stoic, eyes fixed on Bramble.

"I'm sorry, what do you mean?" he said.

"It's a simple question. How did you feel about the girls you met up with?"

"I don't know. We were just excited to be out with the opposite sex."

"Any girl in particular you liked the most?"

"I can't remember. It was a long time ago." He intentionally turned his body away from Katie, trying to focus on something else.

"Try," said Katie. Her tone had a sharp bite to it, causing Bramble to look at her.

"Okay I liked her."

"What happened?"

"Nothing. I tried to get into her pants, she wouldn't go for it, and then nothing."

"What did you do when she refused you after flirting with you?"

McGaven turned his head slightly toward Katie as if to warn her to stay on track.

Bramble pressed his lips tightly almost to the point they turned pale. It was clear by his body language, tense shoulders, shallow breathing, fidgeting hands, that he did not like the question. Something triggered him, but he fought against it.

"Mr. Bramble, did you hate her, didn't care, wanted to get even, what?"

"I…"

"C'mon, it must've made you mad?"

"Didn't…"

"Did she make fun of you?"

"Kill…"

"How did she make you feel? I can tell you are still angry about it today."

Bramble stood up and yelled, "I didn't kill anyone!"

"Take it easy," said McGaven.

"I like fantasy! That's all it is—fantasy! I'm sorry… Is that good enough?"

"Sit down, Mr. Bramble," McGaven ordered.

"What's wrong with you, lady? I told you that I didn't kill anyone."

"Just sit down," McGaven repeated as he guided the man to sit back down in the chair.

"I'm sorry… I'm sorry…" he repeated sarcastically.

"Sorry about what? Sorry that you took evidence in a homicide investigation, or sorry that you got caught?" said Katie.

"NO!" He banged his hands on the table and pushed himself back as far as he could away from Katie.

Katie didn't blink. "Thank you, Mr. Bramble, we'll be in touch." She picked up the file and left the room.

After McGaven had let the detective division know that they were through with Mr. Bramble for the time being, he caught up with Katie.

Katie saw his expression. "I know…"

"That was…" he began.

"Look, I had to push him or…"

"Brilliant," he finished.

"What?" She was shocked that he had apparently approved of her tactics.

"You heard me. That was brilliantly done."

"I'm so glad to hear you say that, but it didn't really give us anything. We have to wait and see what is found at his home and business after the search." She paused at the forensics door, turning to McGaven and making sure that no one was within earshot. "How long would you wait before asking your significant other to marry you?"

"Wait a minute. You've switched gears on me here."

"I know. Just curious. How long?"

"I don't know. It depends on the situation. What's going on in their lives. Katie, there's no set timeline for the right time to ask someone to marry you."

"Okay," she said.

"Wait," he said and stopped her. "Did something happen that I don't know about? Did your firefighter…"

"No. Well, maybe… well, actually, no. I'm just curious, that's all." She swiped her badge and pushed the door open, abruptly ending the potentially embarrassing conversation.

Katie and McGaven returned to the office, trying to piece together what they had from the social worker and from Bramble's interview.

Katie's cell phone buzzed and she looked at the text: *Katie, I can meet you at Gypsy's Diner at 2pm, Dottie.*

"Oh no," she said in a low tone.

"What? News?"

"I forgot that I said I would have lunch with the undersheriff today."

McGaven made an unhappy face. "Good luck with that."

"She cornered me yesterday. What was I supposed to say?"

"Well, it's better to get it out of the way."

"Why do you say that?"

"It seems to me that she wants something—or…?"

"Or what?"

McGaven swiveled his office chair. "Look, it's none of my business."

"We're way past that."

"I'm just saying that it seems like she might be fishing for something or giving you a warning, considering her new position and all…"

Katie nodded. The thought made her cringe, but the sooner she found out what this transplant from Fresno Police Department wanted, the better. "I'll keep that in mind."

She sent a text back: *Looking forward to it. I'll see you there.*

CHAPTER THIRTY-EIGHT
Tuesday 1350 hours

Gypsy's Diner was a new restaurant Katie hadn't had a chance to check out yet. The interior was decorated in black and white with pink highlights and silver accents in a 1950s-type diner atmosphere. There was no jukebox, but pop hits from every decade were piped in from speakers embedded in the walls.

Glancing at her watch, Katie saw that it was nearly 2 p.m. She didn't see the undersheriff yet, so she decided to get a booth and wait for her. It was then that she noticed that all the staff were dressed as celebrities from the past eighty years. With everything going on in her professional and personal life, Katie thought this lunch distraction might be what she needed. She began perusing the menu, deciding on what she wanted.

Just as Katie began to relax, she saw Undersheriff Dorothy Sullivan enter the restaurant. She was dressed in a pricy suit and her blonde hair seemed to be more on the platinum side than yesterday. The undersheriff smiled brightly to the waitress, dressed as Marilyn Monroe, and then was directed to where Katie was sitting. She made her way through the restaurant and around tables of patrons before seating herself across from Katie.

"Hi. I'm so glad that you could make it," she said with an overly friendly smile.

"My pleasure," said Katie forcing a smile.

The undersheriff took her jacket off and made herself comfortable.

The Marilyn lookalike appeared and asked, "What can I get you two ladies to drink?"

"Iced tea," said Katie.

"Sounds good," said Dottie.

The server left.

"Well…" began Dottie.

Katie felt a heaviness of dread, but maybe she should have more female friends. The fact was she was more comfortable around men than women after so many years in the military and the police department.

"It's been quite the transition coming from Fresno PD but I was up for the challenge when it was offered to me. I've been following the interesting cases of the Pine Valley Sheriff's Department."

Katie nodded politely.

"And of course, I know all about you."

Katie tried not to gulp.

"When you came back to town after being released from the army and you found yourself in the middle of a missing persons case; and you find her grave after everyone had searched for her for almost five years, and you were trapped, and, well, I don't need to tell you about it—you were there."

Katie wasn't sure how she was supposed to handle this conversation, so she nodded and agreed, keeping a smile on her face. With perfect timing, the iced teas were delivered. "What would you like to eat?" the server asked.

"Oh, I'll have the Gypsy Burger with fries please," the undersheriff said.

"Sounds great, I'll have the same," replied Katie. "Thank you."

The blonde bombshell server took the menus and left to put in the orders.

"Your uncle told me that you two love getting together every month to have burgers and milkshakes," she said.

"Yes, it's been a tradition for us since I was young." It pinched Katie a bit that her uncle told a new employee about their personal life, but she knew that there was more to this "girls' lunch" than it appeared.

"That's really nice," she said, "and special."

"We're family. We only have each other left." After losing her aunt in such a traumatic and tragic manner, she took their relationship very seriously.

"Well, he's lucky to have you." After sipping her iced tea, Dottie said, "Life is so very precious."

"So," Katie said. "Tell me about you. Are you married? Children?"

"Oh, no. I'm divorced for four years now. No children, I'm afraid to say."

Katie politely nodded. "What made you want to move to such a rural area?"

"I've been here before and just fell in love with the area, and I needed the change from the city, high crime, and pollution."

"It is amazing here. I never realized how much until I was gone for a while and then came back…"

"Oh, that's right. You did two tours in the army?"

"Yes."

"That must've been something."

"Yes, it was definitely something," she said.

"I don't know how you do it," she said, sipping her drink delicately through the straw. "You've seen more than most seasoned cops will in a lifetime."

"I don't know about that. Depends upon where they are working."

Their huge burger plates were delivered.

"Wow," said Katie, staring at the burger with all the trimmings and twice-fried French fries.

The undersheriff goggled too. "WOW."

Both women laughed and began to figure out how they were going to eat the burgers with the least amount of mess.

They engaged in light conversation as they ate, but Katie still sensed that Dottie had other intentions.

With her burger half eaten, Katie finally said, "I get the sense that you have something specific you wanted to talk to me about." She watched her superior contemplate how she was going to say whatever she had to say to her. Dottie didn't make eye contact and seemed to be rehearsing the right words before she confronted Katie.

"You're very perceptive. I've read just about all your reports and you've solved every case to date." As Katie listened she took a small bite of burger and fidgeted with a French fry. "All the outcomes of your cases are fantastic. You couldn't ask for anything better—case closure, high arrest rates, and families getting the answers they long for. You see, one of the reasons that I was hired is that I'm, what you would say, a cleaner, a good housekeeper, which means I make sure everything is running smoothly and that there aren't any… rogue or potentially misplaced events or employees. I want, and strive for, a clean and perfect record. To create a police department that can be used as a model for other departments."

Katie raised an eyebrow as she fought the urge to confront her—but calmly kept her wits.

"I hope that you understand what I'm trying to say."

"Of course. You make sure that the department runs efficiently and under the guidance of strict rules and regulations. The way it's supposed to be," she said. "You run a tight ship." Katie didn't hide the slight sarcasm in the last comment.

Dottie smiled and gave Katie a scrutinizing look. "Yes, you could say that."

Katie decided to put everything on the table. "So where does all this put me?"

"Interesting way of putting it."

"Look, let me make this easy for you. I do my job. No one has to tell me to do my job. I do it. In fact, I make sure it gets done. It's not easy and sometimes I have to make decisions on the spot that not everyone agrees with." Katie watched the undersheriff's face but saw no reaction, so she continued as she wanted to get everything out and get back to work. "I've made mistakes, but I take full responsibility for them and they're all written up in my file. I don't ask for special treatment, and I certainly don't get it. You know that—you were there in the meeting."

"I understand that, and I commend your passion, but you have to see it from my perspective. I'm here to ensure that this department is exemplary, and by that I mean that everyone obeys the rules, is safe, and is there to assist the public."

"So you are talking about image?"

"Well, yes and no, but image is important. The public needs to feel comfortable with how we are doing our job and interacting with the community."

Katie leaned back. She could see that there was no winning this conversation because they were at the department for two totally different reasons: politics and catching criminals.

"Look, I know you're a very capable detective, but it's not just you as one person. The department is a team. It's all about the team."

"So, what's the bottom line?"

Dottie didn't respond at first, but finally said, "You know that the sheriff has you on probation…"

Katie was surprised and angry. "I see," she said, keeping her anger under wraps.

"I knew you would," said the undersheriff. "I know that you wouldn't want to let your department or your uncle down." She smiled and went back to enjoying her food.

It was easy reading between the lines: if she stepped out of line one more time, Dottie would fire her. Katie couldn't finish her burger, everything tasted spoiled.

CHAPTER THIRTY-NINE

Tuesday 1545 hours

Katie was still fuming but it was becoming less and less intense as she concentrated on the investigation. She just got off the phone with the Pine Valley Medical Center and Dr. Samantha Rajal would be available to meet with them in an hour.

"Okay," she said. "We have a fifteen-minute window to talk to Mary Rodriguez's doctor."

"Sounds good," McGaven said. "And... if you're up for it tonight, I was able to get the mystery bookshop owner Mr. Holmes to let us in to view his collection. What do you think about that?"

"We're on a roll. I hope someone can give us something substantial." She looked at McGaven; he appeared more tired than usual with a hint of dark around his eyes and his skin a bit sallow. "Are you sure you're up for it? I can go to both places alone and give you an update before going home."

"Nope."

"Are you sure? You look tired. I would go home if I could..."

McGaven put his pen down and looked straight at her. "Katie, I'm fine. Yeah, I'm a bit tired, but you're not holding the fort alone. I can handle a few interviews."

Katie and McGaven hurried towards the medical center main entrance. The four-story building was large and bland. The interior smelt of cleaning agents and the walls were bare. It appeared to have no identity whatsoever, but it was bustling with people—medical personnel and patients.

Katie searched the list on the wall and saw that Dr. Samantha Rajal, general practitioner, was on the second floor so they made for the stairs.

Katie pushed open the door and saw that the waiting room was empty and the front desk was absent of a receptionist. She waited a moment. "Hello?" she finally said, looking around to see if anyone was there.

After a few minutes, a striking woman with long, dark hair opened the door and said, "Detective Scott?"

"Yes, and this is Deputy McGaven."

"Nice to meet you both. Please come in to my office."

Katie and McGaven followed the doctor down a long corridor and into a nice office with windows across the back overlooking the hills and trees of the county.

Katie noticed Mary's file on the doctor's desk.

After everyone sat down, Dr. Rajal spoke first. "I know that you're here to ask about Mary Rodriguez. I'll try to answer your questions."

A red flag went up when Katie heard the word "try".

"Mary Rodriguez's body was discovered last Tuesday at Stately Park," she said.

"Yes, I saw the news. It's terrible."

"During the autopsy, our medical examiner noticed that she had inserts for pain medication. Was she being treated for something?"

"Yes, she had chronic fatigue syndrome and suffered acute body pain. In patients like Mary, taking pills isn't always the best practice, so I prescribed the intravenous pain medication for her. And it was helping."

"How long have you been her doctor?"

"About two years."

Katie wasn't sure how to word her next question. "Did Mary have any trouble mentally? I realize you're her general practitioner, but did you refer her to anyone else such as a specialist or psychologist?"

"No, no one like that," she said, but it was clear that she was withholding information.

"Dr. Rajal, Mary was brutally murdered and it's our job to find the killer. Anything that you can tell us would be helpful."

The doctor sighed. "The only place that I referred her to was a clinic for an abortion. And from that, I don't know anything else. I don't know if she had the procedure because I didn't see her after that."

"I see," said Katie. That was going to be her next question. "In your opinion, during her last visits here to your office, did you notice if she seemed anxious or upset about something? Did she seem different to you?"

"No," she said. "If anything, she seemed happier than normal."

"Really? Did she say why?"

"I think she'd met someone. She said something like, 'I didn't realize that there were still kind, wonderful men in the world.'"

"Did she say who or where she met him?"

The doctor stopped to think about it for a moment. "I think she said his name was Ray. She didn't mention a last name."

Katie stopped cold. Her heart pounded. Ray was the name of the man that Candace had escaped the foster home with. "Are you sure she said his name was Ray?" she barely said.

"Yes, but then that was it. I never saw her again after that visit."

Katie took a deep breath, glancing at McGaven who had the same curious look. "Did she happen to say if the baby was his?"

"I'm sorry," the doctor said, shaking her head. "No, she didn't say who the father was. I only know that she was in a relationship with a man named Ray."

CHAPTER FORTY

"Can you hear me? Can you hear me?" came a strong authoritative voice from very far away. It was as if I were in a box and they were outside trying to get in. Curious.

Again, they said, *"Can you hear me?"* It was the voice of caring concern, something so foreign to me.

The next moment I felt like I was flying through space, soaring through the water, or floating on a cloud. I breathed deeply... in and out... in and out... hearing my own breathing in my ears. It was strangely soothing. Peaceful. But strange.

Voices were all around me. At first I thought I had been kidnapped or taken by aliens. I opened my eyes and stared up at a face with kind eyes, inside a helmet, looking down with complete focus at me.

I suddenly realized I was looking at a firefighter in full uniform, and that I lay on a gurney being wheeled toward an ambulance. Snapped back into reality, tuned in to the sounds and chaos, just like an old-fashioned radio coming on.

Lifting my head, I saw several firemen fighting a blaze. I felt the heat. Flames leapt out the windows and doors with a crackling display of what once had been my home. The only home I had ever known. It was gone. Forever.

Her voice came back louder than ever.

"You think you're so smart, but you're not!" screamed my mother. *"You're a loser. A failure. You'll never amount to anything. You make me sick..."*

I looked to the right to a black bag on another gurney being wheeled to another location. It was her. I knew it was her. What was left of her. I didn't care. And it was the last time I ever had to see her again.

CHAPTER FORTY-ONE
Tuesday 1945 hours

McGaven drove to the bookshop. He was familiar with the area from patrol and seemed to be excited about the fact that they were going somewhere shrouded in so much secrecy. It was the only place where they'd tracked down the Hunter-Gatherer book series from the 1940s—no one else, including the Internet, libraries, and specialized rare bookstores, had copies that they could find. It was still unclear if the killer had read them or was engaging in murder because of them, but it was the only lead on the message carved into the girls' backs that they had.

Katie laughed to herself.

"What?" he said, glancing at her in the passenger seat.

"You."

"What do you mean?"

"You seem so excited about this visit," she said.

"Ever since I was a kid, I've loved mysteries and magic and all that stuff. It's like getting to play out one of my kid dreams."

"Okay, I get it," she said.

"You think I'm weird."

"No, not at all. I just hope you're not disappointed."

"We'll see. We shall see."

He accelerated as they raced toward the downtown area. They knew the building was next to 6317 Sycamore Street. McGaven stopped the car and stared at a large brick building with few windows. "Where's the entrance?"

"Here." Katie pointed. "Park there."

McGaven parked the car and they both jumped out and began searching the outside of the building—walking back and forth looking for a number or a name.

Nothing.

"The alley?" Katie said, and moved quickly around the building where there was a narrow path with two large dumpsters. She stopped and studied them. Something didn't seem right and her instincts spiked, almost feeling that they were being watched. Studying the side of the building, she saw a plain wooden door. "This is it."

McGaven stood next to her. "I see it too. You must be great at jigsaw puzzles to see that."

They moved cautiously to the door. It looked as if there weren't any handle, hinges, or other hardware.

Katie glanced at McGaven. "Here goes," she said, and knocked three times.

They waited.

To their surprise, the door slid left and disappeared into the wall. No one was there and there weren't any further instructions.

Katie stepped forward as McGaven put his hand on her arm. "Wait."

She did as instructed, the hair prickling on her neck. "What do you want to do?" she whispered.

McGaven stepped forward first, keeping Katie back. He ran his hands up the side of the opening and across the top, double checking everything and then moving forward with caution.

Katie followed, alert. It wouldn't be the first time that unsuspecting and unprepared police officers walked into a trap. Once inside, the door closed behind them and they were left in darkness.

"Mr. Holmes," said Katie, a little nervously. "Are you here?"

The light went on and the place lit up like a carnival ride. They were in a large room filled with furniture and fixtures, art and rugs from the 1800s, but arranged like a set on a stage. Katie looked around; there were no windows but lights and lamps had been placed all around to bring the room to life. She seemed to recollect something in the news a while back about this bookstore, but at the time, it didn't mean much to her.

"Detectives!" came a voice with a slight British accent. "The game is afoot." He laughed. "I'm sorry, I couldn't help myself." A tall thin man with dark hair, goatee, and smoking a cigarette, entered the room wearing a long vintage burgundy coat with silk pants and some type of slippers.

"Mr. Holmes," said Katie. She felt silly saying that out loud in the surroundings, but it was his real name.

"Yes, I am."

"I'm Detective Scott and this is Deputy McGaven."

"Pleased to meet you both. I have to say when I received a call from Deputy McGaven I was quite intrigued." Noticing Katie and McGaven's response to the place, he said, gesturing to the lavish setting, "Oh please, this is all for show, the public loves it."

"Mr. Holmes, we understand that you have the set of books entitled 'Hunter-Gatherer' from the 1940s."

"Yes."

"What is the name of the author?"

"Why, Ray Roland, of course."

"I see," said Katie, stunned that the author's name was Ray. "The existence of these books has come to our attention as part of an ongoing murder investigation and we were hoping to take a look at your copies."

"Well, you're very lucky. I would imagine it would be very difficult, if not impossible to find them. There were printed by a very small vanity press, and only 200 copies were ever published. Most likely many of the sets were probably lost or damaged."

"And you have a set?" said McGaven.

"Yes, and in fairly good condition."

"What's so special about these books?"

"Well, they are written about the journey of the main character, Izzie, and everything he encountered from his perspective. It's part fantasy, part reality, and part the struggles of growing up, I believe. Basically, a story about a child living a terrible life in a family that doesn't love him, so he creates a life that's pure fantasy—in his own mind."

Katie thought about it and how it related to the killer profile on her murder board.

"Detective, I can see this is troubling for you," Holmes said.

"Yes, it is," she said slowly, thinking about all the links with the name Ray, the title of the book, and being an unhappy child.

"Well," he said. "Would you like to see them?"

"Yes, please."

Holmes left Katie and McGaven alone.

"I'm sorry," McGaven whispered.

"For what? We're running down leads. This phrase or description means something to the killer—we need to find out why. There are too many links that makes sense. We're on to something here."

McGaven took a seat on the antique couch and frowned. "Not too comfortable."

"My dear deputy, those weren't made for comfort and not someone of your stature either…" He held a small box. "Here they are." Setting them down on the coffee table, he pulled out the first volume in the six-book series. "Here you go."

Katie took the book and was surprised that it was small and thin with a brown cover and gold lettering for the title and author—it was only forty pages long. It was more like a pamphlet or short story, she thought. The four-by-seven-inch book had yellowing pages, so she was careful handling it as she began to read. She flipped to the front where it said: *Abacus Publishing 1942 copyright*. It also said that the previous year 1941 it had been published in Italian. That made sense about the Italian writing. The killer was beginning to make more sense to her, and seemed to have a thing for the Italian language.

Holmes gave McGaven the second book to look at, which was the same size.

"Wow, it's more like a journal," McGaven stated as he thumbed through the book.

Katie skimmed pages and read paragraphs, gleaning life sentiments and personal growing pains from the author—it was more appealing to teens and the younger generation. The main thing she figured out was that "Hunter-Gatherer" referred to being alienated and left to fend for himself. Hunter-Gatherer had been cited as being alone in this world, surviving mostly by hunting and fishing, and harvesting wild food. The obviously young author used the title as a metaphor for the growing pains of his young life.

"What do you think?" asked McGaven.

"I think we might be reading something that the killer feels is his memoirs."

"You want to see more?" asked Holmes.

"Yes, please."

"Why didn't you say so?" said the host as he approached one of the bookshelves, opened a small box and retrieved a small flash drive. "I have the entire series scanned into computer files."

"That would be fantastic, Mr. Holmes," said Katie. "We'll return it to you when our investigation is over."

Holmes gave Katie the drive and said, "My dear, if you ever want to mingle at one of my mystery parties, you just let me know."

"I will, thank you," she said, slightly embarrassed by the invitation. "I have one more question for you."

"Of course. Anything I can answer that might help."

"Have you ever had anyone else refer to or ask you about Hunter-Gatherer, either at one of your parties, or anywhere else, for that matter?"

He paused. Katie wasn't sure if it was for dramatic effect or not, but he appeared to contemplate the question, searching his mind. "No, not to my knowledge and I've heard a lot of people talk about obscure books in my day, but nothing rings a bell."

Katie gave him the book back and pocketed the flash drive. "Thank you, Mr. Holmes, for taking the time to talk to us and lending us the digital copy."

"My absolute pleasure," he said, and was suddenly gone. Vanished like a magician after entertaining an audience.

Katie and McGaven were finally on the road back to the department. It was beginning to get dark and Katie was exhausted, but her mind wouldn't shut off from all the information they had learned today.

"What the hell does all this mean?" asked McGaven.

Katie noticed that he was looking even more tired as the day went on. "There's definitely some clues and similarities for our killer. We're getting to know more about him, what makes him tick, but no closer to finding him."

"We're getting closer," he said.

"So what we have right now is… A book series about the feelings of what it's like navigating life as a teenager and feeling like you're all alone. Mary Rodriguez had a new boyfriend by the named of Ray – the same name of the person who Candace Harlan left the foster home with. The author of some obscure book series by the name of Ray. Coincidence?" She sighed. "That's what we need to find out."

"Don't forget that two of the county employees that worked at Elm House confirmed the problems, abuse, and unsettling incidents that took place," McGaven added.

"It gives us quite a bit to think about," she said.

CHAPTER FORTY-TWO

Wednesday 0930 hours

Katie had already been working for several hours before McGaven arrived. She couldn't sleep. There was too much information swirling around in her mind—she was beginning to feel the clock ticking down for a new victim. It was like walking around a time bomb.

Every time she closed her eyes, she saw the victims, looking just as she had found them, reaching out to her from their graves, begging for her to find justice for them.

Katie let out a much-needed exhalation—it was more out of frustration than being overwhelmed or uncertain. Again, they were facing a tremendous amount of information; each fact by itself didn't mean much, but piecing certain ones together, it began to form a picture.

It occurred to Katie, as she scanned the freshly updated board as well as the notes in her file, that there had to be a way to push the investigation forward and flesh out evidence—in a way that the department would be in agreement with.

She ran scenarios as she chewed the end of her pen.

Adding questions nagging at her, she wrote:

Who is the unknown man in the black hoodie? Is he following the investigation? Why? Can we trap him?

Who left the piece of paper in my locker directing us to the company
that manufactures the metal storage containers for construction
sites? ETL Express?
Is Tanis or Candace the key to unlocking the secrets at Elm Hill
Mansion?
Who/where are the McKinzies?
Who was the father of the baby that Mary Rodriguez aborted?
Who was her Ray?
Was the killer using the Hunter-Gatherer books as his play book?
Why Italian?

"Morning," said McGaven as he burst into the office.

"You always make such an entrance."

"Sorry I'm late, but I had a quick check-up about my injury," he said. "And if you must know, everything is just fine." He smiled. "What's been going on? I've been thinking…" His voice tailed off as he read the new additions and the questions on the murder board. "Interesting." He continued, "I've been running some reports and put in some favors to find out where the McKinzies are. Basically, what other organizations they are involved in. That's a place to start. I haven't heard anything back yet."

"Some things are making more sense," she said.

"Have you called Tanis Jones?"

"I have, but she hasn't returned my calls. She's a bit skittish, maybe I'll stop by her studio if I don't hear from her soon."

"An idea occurred to me. Black-hoodie guy seems to be watching us and following us around. Right? So I think we need to set an *acceptable* trap."

"Acceptable trap?" she said, and laughed. "I like that. Is that what you're going to put in your report to Ms. Undersheriff?"

"Well? We need to be extra vigilant and extra by-the-book-Betty."

Katie laughed and said, "By-the-book-Betty? I've never heard that. Did you just make that up?"

"Maybe."

She laughed again.

"So, about trapping the unknown black-hoodie guy."

"Go on," she said intrigued. Before McGaven had arrived, she was thinking they should do something similar. She loved the fact they were on the same page.

"I figured you were going to go back to the Mary Rodriguez crime-scene area sometime."

"Yes, I've been thinking about it. I wanted to explore it again, since it was under such difficult conditions."

"Well, why don't we use that as a trap?"

"I like where you're going, but obviously 'they' are keeping a close eye."

McGaven grabbed a piece of paper and drew a basic area of the park and where the body was located. "Okay, I was thinking that we could get surveillance cameras at these points," he said, indicating areas of the trail and the main one heading to the crime-scene area. "It would be actual footage that someone has been following us."

"That's great, but black-hoodie guy will no doubt see us setting up."

"Not if we have someone else do it."

"Okay," she said slowly, not sure who it would be.

"Who do we both know that can set up surveillance without drawing attention?"

"Of course," she said. "John."

"Exactly. What if we have him set up some basic cameras? Even if hoodie guy sees him, it'll look like a birdwatcher or nature lover setting up."

"That might work, and we're keeping it by the book within our department. We have reason to believe that hoodie guy has been following the investigation, spying on us, and he was the one that trapped us, so this would be a way to get proof and hopefully record an identification." She made a couple of notations on the sketch. "But we're going to need these three areas watched so that there's no chance of hoodie guy escaping without an ID."

"We can handle it," he said with confidence.

"You're assuming two things: that the brass are going to let us do this; and that John has time to set up cameras for us."

"Of course he will."

"What makes you say that?"

"I already asked him on the way in."

"Of course. What if our guy is armed? And what if he brings a friend to complicate things?"

"Well, we'll be ready. I've thought about that."

"You sound like you're going to enjoy this too much."

"So what do you think?" McGaven asked intensely, waiting.

"I think it might work."

"Yeah?"

"Yeah," she said. "Let's do it—I'll run it by the 'proper' channels. It shouldn't make anyone upset that we're trying to find a possible witness in two homicide investigations."

"I'll go set it up with John right now," he said, standing up. "We'll be there ahead of you tonight. I'll text you when it's time and hopefully hoodie guy will be watching… and with some good ol'-fashioned police luck… we'll have our guy before the end of the night."

"And hopefully, we will have more answers than questions for a change."

CHAPTER FORTY-THREE

Wednesday 1745 hours

Heavy clouds and thunder brought some heavy rain bursts throughout the afternoon, but it was good that the weather was dismal because it would lessen the chance of running into anyone else at the park just before dark.

Katie went home to take care of Cisco and then came back to work for about an hour, to make sure she had the okay from the proper channels, before McGaven gave her the go-ahead in a text: *Ready to go.*

He and John had made sure that the areas were set with weatherproof cameras and they each had taken their watch positions around the creek.

Katie was soon behind the wheel and slowly leaving the parking lot at the sheriff's department. She was nervous. Mist filled her windshield as she drove along the deserted road heading to Stately Park. It seemed closer to midnight than approaching 6 p.m., and the darkness had an extra sinister quality to it—maybe it was just her imagination.

Checking the rearview and side mirrors occasionally, Katie didn't think that she had been followed but she had a nagging feeling, a strong gut instinct: the unknown hoodie guy had been at some of the other locations too. She'd felt uneasy at the mystery bookstore and even looked around several times when they had arrived at Bella Vista.

Another text came in from McGaven:
What's taking so long… cold feet?
Katie's return text: *Taking it slow.*
McGaven: *Copy that.*

Katie turned into the parking lot at Stately Park and slowed her speed. The rain had left large puddles and two large chuckholes near the entrance to the trails.

"Great," she mumbled to herself, navigating around the water traps. The Jeep bobbed and weaved until she found a spot where she didn't have to exit the vehicle into mud or ankle-deep water. Double checking her weapons, she secured each appropriately and tucked her cell phone into a pocket. Pulling on a lightweight rain jacket, Katie took a little bit more time than necessary making sure she felt comfortable and ready to go.

Opening the Jeep door, she quickly stepped out and then secured the vehicle. There was about an hour left before it got really dark, but the storm began to build with force. She had a flashlight if needed.

The crisp evening air hit her sinuses and cooled her face. The wonderful smells of the forest made Katie relax and want to stay outside in the wilderness for a while. Her boots hit the walking path quietly, no sound emitted from underneath her feet. She wondered where McGaven and John were, but they knew where she was. She almost cracked a smile, but instead, she kept her focus forward and headed to the dumping area next to the creek where Mary Rodriguez was found. She squeezed her eyes shut to block out the image.

As she continued the easy hike the screech from an owl and movement of nesting birds in the trees around her made Katie more intensely aware that she was alone. In her opinion, it was probably the worst night to try and draw out anyone who had been following her. But she wasn't going to stop now. A twig snapped about fifty feet from her but Katie kept her cool demeanor as if she didn't hear a thing and continued walking to the creek bank.

She casually looked from side to side, making her way toward the creek. The rushing stream was louder than it was before and obviously had picked up more water and momentum after the rain. The closer she got to the crime scene, the louder the rising creek became. It was more humid here and the air seemed so heavy you could cut it with a knife. The ground was saturated and slippery beneath her feet.

Weaving around a few pine trees and dodging low-hanging limbs, Katie caught herself before she slipped into the running stream. Mud mixed with rainfall made the trail slippery and uneven. The shoreline where Mary Rodriguez's body was found was now under several inches of water. That struck her.

Did the killer want the body to be completely submerged? To wash away the evidence?

Katie stayed a couple of feet from the edge, but now surveyed the area in a slightly different way. She wondered if the killer knew these areas well. Perhaps it was a place he had hiked many times before.

Prickly bumps went down her arms and neck, making her shiver. Looking up, Katie could see the yellowish orange ball of the sunset between the trees, casting weird morphing shadows all around her.

She thought she would make her way down further, but on second thoughts she turned around to head back up to her Jeep.

Standing four feet from Katie was a dark figure dressed in dark pants and a hoodie covering his face. She blinked twice to see if it was an illusion. The figure stood completely still, like a statue, arms at his sides, looking directly at Katie.

"Who are you?" Katie said forcefully.

No response or movement.

"What do you want?" She carefully reached her hand inside her pocket and touched the handle of her small Beretta. "Why are you following me?" Katie's voice sounded distant, almost getting lost in the increasing wind developing all around them—rain was sure to follow.

The figure moved slightly, shifting his weight to one side.

Katie realized that the guy was getting ready to run, so she decided to make the first move and lunged forward. The figure turned and sprinted upward along the trail back toward the entrance. Katie thought the guy she was chasing was slower and more slight in stature than the last time she saw him. She picked up the pace and was able to grab the back of his sweatshirt and was about to tackle him, when he turned toward her, shoving her backward.

Katie hit the muddy trail and slid back down the rest of the way—first on her back and then slipping around on her left side. No matter how hard she tried, she couldn't stop herself from falling. But she reached out, trying to grab anything—a branch, a bush, the side of a tree trunk—anything. Everything slipped past her clawing hands.

Realizing that the rushing creek was near, Katie continued to flail her arms and legs to stop the momentum. Nothing helped. She screamed, a multiple echo ringing throughout the forest and through the canyons.

The impact of the splash rattled her insides and her jaw clacked her teeth together. Instant cold permeated her entire body. Shuddering, Katie fought the current, not knowing where she would end up or what was in the water.

The water grew shallower, and her speed subsided, and she was able to get her legs underneath her body and stand up. Falling a few more times, Katie finally managed to get control.

Shivering and breathing hard, the adrenalin was flushing throughout her body in a manic manner. Katie looked up and saw movement and heard voices in a heated exchange. Gathering her wits, she climbed onto the creek bank and slowly stood up. Her legs were rubbery and the uneven footing made her view blurry. She heard more voices arguing.

Climbing up toward the building commotion, Katie took careful steps so as not to slip and start the entire falling process again. She crept the rest of the way, not wanting to alert anyone to her presence.

The sound of crashing coming through branches and bushes came directly at her as a dark figure materialized. Waiting for the right moment, Katie pushed her body and was able to block him like a linebacker. The hooded man abruptly stopped and landed hard on his back, letting out a groan.

Katie was soaked, filthy, tired, and felt like she had just jumped from a moving vehicle into a river. She wasted no time and jumped on the hooded man. "Who are you?" she said breathlessly, holding him down.

McGaven came hurtling through the woods. "Katie, you okay?" he said.

"I said, who are you?" she demanded, ignoring McGaven, and tore the hood from the phantom's face in a fit of anger.

She gasped in disbelief. It was like looking at a ghost. She flashed on the first crime scene in every detail—long dark hair, the pink fingernail, and the body dumped at the Elm Hill Mansion. Lying on the ground, staring up at her, wasn't a man at all—the mysterious hooded person that had been following Katie was Candace Harlan.

The rain began to pour.

CHAPTER FORTY-FOUR

Wednesday 2000 hours

McGaven and John managed to help Katie and Candace back up the trail to a waiting police car. Candace was put in the backseat. Three patrol officers had assisted their call. Technically Candace Harlan wasn't wanted for anything specific yet, but she had a lot of explaining to do.

Katie peeled off her raincoat and shirt to replace them with a heavy sweatshirt she had borrowed from McGaven. Then she used her shirt to try to clean the mud from her face. Her jeans were still wet, causing her to shiver, and she hoped that she wouldn't catch a cold. Not having time to go home and change properly, Katie went to the patrol car, opened the passenger door and sat inside for a silent moment, trying to form her questions and keep her anger under control. Candace didn't say a word—she sat quietly in the backseat, obviously detecting the extreme tension in Katie.

"I don't know what I'm angrier about. The fact that you shut the door to a metal container and tried to kill two police officers or the fact you didn't come forward when your sister was murdered. Am I missing anything?"

Candace didn't answer her questions; she sat with her head down and kept quiet.

It was unclear to Katie if Candace was remorseful or trying to play her and the investigation. Either way, Katie was going to get some answers.

"You understand that you're in trouble, right?"

Candace didn't move. Her dark hair was shorter than her sister's, just past shoulder length, and was messy and dirty from the fall. In a better light, it was clear that she resembled her sister almost perfectly. There was no mistaking that they were sisters. She had a gold nose ring and there were subtle remnants of makeup around her eyes, now smeared along with the mud.

"And you understand that you have compromised a murder investigation and things are looking sketchy for you. You do understand, right?" she said, and raised her voice. "I'm not a fan of repeating myself."

"What… what do you want to know?" the young woman finally said.

"Oh, so you *can* speak," Katie said, still remembering being pushed down the hill.

"Yes," she said slowly, as if afraid to say anything at all. Her words slightly trembled as she spoke.

"Good." Katie took a deep breath; she was too angry to suffer from any anxiety right now. As strange as it sounded, anger fueled her drive, pushed unnecessary thoughts and memories away, but in the end it was psychologically draining for her.

Katie heard Candace shift her weight in the backseat.

"Where have you been for the past five years?" she asked.

"Everywhere. I left town not long after I left Elm Hill."

"That's not telling me much."

"LA, Sacramento, Boise, and then Phoenix."

"Who helped you escape the mansion?"

"Ray. We hung out for a while, but he got weird, possessive, and I bailed."

"Last name?"

"Ray Conner."

"How did you meet him?"

"In town."

"Look, Ms. Harlan. I don't know if you realize how much trouble you are in. If I were you, I would strongly suggest cooperating with us." Katie turned her gaze and stared at Candace. She looked defeated, hair wet and hanging in her face, and eyes looking at the floor. "I can help you, but you have to be honest with me." Katie couldn't help but see her twin sister lying in her grave covered with mud and it tamed her anger. Now she felt compassion for the woman.

"I used to go to a coffee place on the corner of Maple and Jensen Streets."

Katie nodded. "I know it."

"I would go there a lot. It was a place where I could be alone and think… and prepare for when I turned eighteen."

"You met Ray there?"

"Yes. I saw him several times. He was cute in his own way… older… but I liked him. After a while, we would share a table and talk about things: my life, his life, and living in this town."

"What did he do?"

"I'm not entirely sure. It had to do with business, accounting, I think. He always had files of reports and spreadsheets in his briefcase."

"How long did you stay with him?"

"About three months."

"Where did you stay?"

"We rented a motel with a kitchen by the week."

"Why not his house?"

"He said it was too small and his roommate was always around. This way we could be alone."

Katie took a few notes, but she was beginning to get an instinct of who "Ray" was and it wasn't a good feeling. "What motel?"

"I don't remember the name. It was over near where the railroad stores their cars and cargo. I do remember that it had a big red dot and it said 'weekly rentals with kitchens'."

"You say you left Ray after three months?"

"Yes."

"Where did you go?"

"Um, I went to Los Angeles. I worked as a waitress and tried to get a modeling job."

"During all this time when you've moved—did you see Ray again?"

There was a pause before she answered, "I thought I saw him in Sacramento, but I was mistaken. It made me think that he might have tracked me down and was following me."

"You never spoke to Ray again?"

"No."

The heater was turned to low in the patrol car and Katie started to feel better—her shivers had stopped. "Were you ever in contact with any of the girls from Elm Hill?"

"I spoke with all of them for a while at first, except..."

"Except who?"

"Tanis," she said.

That revelation surprised Katie. "Why not Tanis? Wasn't she your best friend?"

"Detective, you probably won't understand this... and I mean it from my heart. I wanted to protect Tanis."

"From what?"

"Bad experiences, life, bad people. She had done so much for the rest of us and I wanted to make sure that she was happy and at least had a chance—more than the rest of us."

"Ms. Harlan, are you aware that your sister was murdered? And her body was found last week at Elm Hill Mansion?"

"Yes," she said shakily, holding back the tears.

"When was the last time you saw her?"

"It had been a while. A few months... I don't know..." She sniffled and wiped tears from her eyes.

"Do you know who would have wanted to kill her?"

"It wasn't her. It was me."

"What are you saying? That whoever killed your sister Carol meant to kill you?"

"I got in with some bad people, gambling, escort service, that sort of thing. They don't like it when people want to leave. I've been looking over my shoulder every day since. And then… and then…"

"I see. Where were these bad people?"

"Sacramento."

Katie had first been a patrol officer for two years at Sacramento PD and she was aware of some of these nefarious gangs. She made a few more notes. "Any names?"

"I don't know their real names."

Katie turned around in her seat because she wanted to see Candace's face when she asked the next question. "Why did you try to kill me and my partner?"

"I didn't."

"I saw you, well, not your face, but I saw you standing there and shutting the door to the container."

There was a knock at the window. McGaven stood there waiting as he made a hand gesture for her to come out.

"I'll be right back," said Katie as she got out of the vehicle, immediately regretting it with the cold air piercing her body. Shutting the door quickly, she said, "What's up?"

"I just wanted to let you know that we've looked over the cameras and it was definitely Candace Harlan." Katie saw John walk from the trail carrying cameras.

"Was there anyone else?" she asked.

"Nope, just her."

Katie made a frown and bit her lip.

"What?" he said.

"I'll fill you in on everything later, but for now, check out…" she said and retrieved a piece of paper from her notebook. "Do a check on Ray Conner, early- to mid-thirties. Businessman. Not sure of profession."

"Who's this?"

"This is Candace's Ray—the one she ran away with that night. According to her, she dumped him three months later and took off to LA."

He took the notes. "On it." He looked at Katie with a questioning expression.

"I'm fine, really. I'll see you in the office tomorrow. Don't worry about tonight's report—I'll take care of it."

McGaven's face looked relieved, so he smiled and started walking away. "See you then."

Katie returned the smile. Then she saw John loading up the surveillance equipment and thought for a moment she needed to talk to him, but that would have to wait. He turned and looked at her, his somber expression difficult to read, but he smiled at her with a gentle nod.

Katie opened the patrol passenger door again and slipped back inside to the welcoming heater.

Candace burst out, "I didn't try to kill you and your partner."

"Why were you following me?"

"I… I wanted to make sure that Carol's murder would be solved. And… I've been terrified that whoever killed her is coming after me, so I followed you on the investigation to make sure. I had a car for a while."

"Why did you shut the door on us?" Katie persisted.

"I just wanted to give myself time to get away. I knew one of these times that you would catch me."

"So who was driving the bulldozer? Who was your partner?"

"I don't understand. Partner?"

"Who were you working with?"

"No one."

"So you mean to tell me that 'no one' tried to push the metal container off a cliff with me and my partner in it?"

"I'm telling you no one was helping me. I just put a stick in the lock, I figured you'd be able to escape within minutes, but it gave me enough time to get away."

"So you didn't start the bulldozer?"

"What? I don't know anything about bulldozers. I just wanted to slow you down, not kill you. Why would I want to do that?"

"That's what I'm trying to figure out," Katie said.

Candace leaned forward. "I'm telling you the truth. I didn't lock you in the storage container. I swear, I'm telling the truth."

"Who was there with you?"

"No one, I left as fast as I could."

Another knock tapped at the window. This time, it was the patrol officer wondering how long Katie was going to take. She held up a finger indicating it would be a couple more minutes.

"Who is Amy Striker?" said Katie. "You listed her as your emergency contact at the dentist."

"She's a name I made up from a singer that used to sing at the coffee shop once in a while."

"Why?"

"I didn't want to be traced—besides, I don't have anyone to list as an emergency number."

"What about 1457 Green Street?"

"Oh… I saw a flyer about that new development and all the houses for sale—I dreamed of a place like that and I just used one of the addresses."

Katie thought it was a little too convenient—even though it made sense. "And I suppose you put that piece of paper in my locker?"

"What paper?"

"ETL Express. The name of the storage container company."

"I don't know anything about that... honest. What's going to happen to me?" Candace asked. Her voice strained, like that of a young girl.

"Honestly, I don't know."

"What do you mean? I've told you everything—the truth," she stressed.

"Look, they are going to ask you some questions back at the department regarding the missing persons report, and probably the child protective services as well to clear the case that was opened on you. To clear that allegation—of you going missing." Katie softened her voice; she could see that Candace was scared. "Just be cooperative and you'll be fine. I'm sure we can dismiss the charges of you pushing me down the hill—it was maybe a misunderstanding and you were trying to protect yourself."

"But I won't be fine... There's someone out there that wanted me dead and they killed my sister by mistake. I'm not going to be fine."

"If that's true, you'll be safe at the department. No one is going to let anything happen to you."

"Please, Detective, *please* let me go."

"That's all the questions I have right now. I'll be talking to you soon." Katie knew that there was more Candace wasn't telling, but maybe some time in holding might make her more forthcoming.

"How can I reach you?" she begged.

"Okay," Katie said, looking for her business card and pulling it out of her pocket. "Here's my card, okay?"

Candace took the card. "Thank you, Detective." Her hand shook and the look of fear washed over her face. "I don't know if someone from my recent past killed Carol. But now... I'm not sure of anything... I'm not safe and I don't think anyone is safe from Elm Hill. I know whoever killed Carol won't stop until there's none of us left. I'm going to be the last girl alive."

Katie looked at the wide eyes of the young woman, scared, unsure, but knowing that there was a killer looking to murder her. She wanted to help her, but she couldn't get personally involved or slack in her thinking. "You'll be fine," she said, and stepped out of the car. Turning to see Candace's face, the woman mouthed the words *Please help me.*

Katie turned, gave the patrol officer the thumbs up sign, and returned to the Jeep. She sat in there until everyone had left the parking lot and the last of the headlights disappeared. She turned over the engine and the SUV roared to life. Slowly driving out of the parking lot, Katie digested everything that Candace Harlan had told her. The case was becoming more complex and Katie's gut instincts were turning into trepidation.

Please help me.

CHAPTER FORTY-FIVE

Thursday 0905 hours

"Morning," Katie said as she dropped her briefcase on her desk. "What a night, but I got everything done and submitted. Hopefully we won't be getting a surprise visit from she who shouldn't be named."

McGaven watched her as she went through her routine of clearing the desk for her notes and updating the murder board. "I have an update," he said solemnly.

"What?" she said with concern.

"I received a message from my buddy at the prison about Shelly McDonald."

"She did commit suicide, right?" The thought of McDonald being so distraught over their visit that she took her own life made Katie extremely distressed.

"Yes, unfortunately. But, I wanted to know if anyone had visited her recently besides us."

"And?" Katie knew there was a bombshell about to be dropped, by the look on McGaven's face.

"She had one visitor," he said and paused. "They signed in as Ray Roland."

"Are you kidding me? The name of the author of the 'Hunter-Gatherer' series?" Katie's mind spun with all the reasons why the visitor picked that name. "Would the killer really take the chance of being identified? Or perhaps it's a hoax?"

"I saw the camera footage of this guy as he signed into the prison and he definitely knew how to avoid the cameras."

"Of course."

"And this," he said as he pulled a piece of paper from the printer, "is the best we can see of him."

Katie eagerly took the printout and studied the grainy photograph. It was a man, average height, average build, standing at the entrance, readjusting the clipboard to an awkward angle and signing in. He kept his face at an angle that made it almost impossible to see it clearly. He wore a heavy jacket and baseball cap.

"Damn," she said. "I can't tell if the man is twenty or fifty from this angle."

"I know, he knew what he was doing. Which means he's been to the prison before."

"So, if this is the killer, that means that he knew Shelly McDonald and had a connection to her... and possibly Elm Hill."

"I watched the video several times." He clicked the video file on his computer. "Here."

Katie watched it four times. She exhaled loudly and leaned back in her chair. "Well, by the build of the man, it definitely isn't Hugh Keller. This guy is leaner. We can now tell it's a man, but who? And of course, why was he visiting McDonald?"

"And then shortly afterward, McDonald commits suicide."

Katie stood up and made a couple of notes on the murder board.

"Sorry it wasn't better news," he said.

"Okay," she said, sitting down. "Did you get a chance to read my copy of the interview with Candace Harlan?"

"Yep, and I did you one further."

"Oh?"

"I updated the information on the murder board."

"Great," she said, reading his notes about Candace's relationship with Ray Conner and where she had been the last five years. "I didn't have time last night."

"And… one of my requests has actually paid off."

Katie's eyes lit up. "Oh please, let's have some good news."

"I had set up a search with some of the more prominent charities for various fundraising arenas. Everything from building a new wing on a hospital to feeding the children. And…"

"And?"

"I found Jonathan and Sara McKinzie."

"Fantastic. When can we set up an appointment with them?"

"Well, that's not the way it works."

"What do you mean?" she said.

"These are very private, very wealthy people who only really come out into the public for a rare charity event. I couldn't find their residences, probably because the real estate is under trusts or corporations. With more time, I can probably come up with something more."

"So we can't talk to them?"

"We can, but…" he said hesitating, "it's going to require some creativity."

Katie thought about what McGaven had said. "Are they in California?"

"That's the good news."

"More good news?" She smiled.

"There's an event on Saturday in Sacramento at the Four Seasons."

"This Saturday?"

"Yep, and the McKinzies are the benefactors of the Children's Cancer Research & Medical Care Gala." He read from his notes. "It's an annual event and dinner that takes place in different cities in California, Texas, and New York. The cost is, are you ready for this, $2,500 a plate."

"Wow, not in my budget."

"I think we should go."

"How?"

"We can go in undercover with the caterers and then change and make our way into the event. This would be a police undercover assignment to gather more information for not one, but two of our active homicide investigations."

"I don't know…" she said. "I appreciate what you're trying to do here, but I don't think Dottie is going to go for it. They let us slide on the park surveillance, but… And it's in two days."

"C'mon, Katie, it's worth a try. Just ask. I don't know how we're going to be able to speak with them otherwise. I haven't been able to get a response from their spokesperson, attorney or whoever."

Katie stood up, rereading the murder board, painfully aware of this gaping hole in it. "Okay," she said.

"Yes."

"Don't get all happy yet, the sheriff still has to approve it. Don't forget, this is out of our jurisdiction, so the sheriff will have to smooth it over with Sacramento PD. I'll put the request together."

"You used to be a cop there. That should help. And the fact that the McKinzies could be jetting off to who knows where afterwards. This is the only time that we'll probably get a chance to talk to them."

"Maybe."

McGaven turned back to his computer and seemed to be excited about the prospect of working undercover.

Katie wasn't as convinced, but she would get the paperwork together and speak with her uncle. "Okay, first we have to try to fill in some of these blanks."

"I'm game."

"We need to talk to Tanis again. I'm worried she's not responding. And I need any information about the McKinzies we can get ahead of time, especially around when they owned Elm Hill Mansion. And, we should try and check out Candace Harlan's story and find her ex-boyfriend Ray Conner."

"I'm on it."

"You up for a quick trip to Tanis's place first?" she asked.

"You have to ask?"

CHAPTER FORTY-SIX

Thursday 1115 hours

Before leaving, Katie emailed Sheriff Scott about their proposed undercover assignment to go to the Four Seasons as guests to talk to Mr. and Mrs. McKinzie. She would wait to hear if they received a preliminary approval and then she would write a more in-depth request.

The rain had stopped and the sun shone brightly as they drove back to the small tourist town where Tanis Jones lived. Katie was quiet, lost in thought.

"You know," said McGaven breaking the silence and Katie's train of thought. "You didn't need me to come with you to question Tanis Jones."

"I know. I just thought… that we both needed to be there."

"You're keeping an eye on me, aren't you?"

"No."

"Yes, you are. I know the entire metal container thing scared the crap out of you. It did me, too."

"No."

"Yes, it did."

"Maybe a little."

"I'm fine. The bruises are much better and it doesn't hurt when I laugh. Okay?"

Katie glanced from the road to McGaven and she smiled. "Yep, everything's okay."

"Now, getting video footage of you doing a muddy cannon ball down that path was something else."

"Great. Don't pass that around."

"Don't worry. John and I won't ever share it."

Katie looked at him sternly. "You better not."

He laughed.

Things were better between them and Katie was glad how things had turned out. They now shared a more solid bond of trust and she felt it was a blessing.

"I'm glad we were able to figure out that the folded piece of paper with 'ETL' had been torn from a full piece of paper from another locker," he said.

"Weird coincidence?"

"It was in Deputy McAlaster's locker next to yours, and because she had been doing some research and in haste she had slipped the torn piece in the wrong locker."

The sun flickered through the branches and the landscape was greener and lusher than before. It was as if a new, stronger beginning was launching and anything was possible. Katie hoped that was the case for the homicides.

It took Katie about ten minutes before they arrived at Tanis's apartment and found a parking place. Katie and McGaven exited the vehicle and took a look around. Everything appeared just like it was when they were there last.

"I'm calling lunch at that awesome-smelling bakery after we catch up with Tanis," said McGaven.

"You don't need to twist my arm."

Katie led the way as she walked down the back alley and up the stairs to the studio apartment. The door was closed, so Katie knocked. "Tanis, it's Detective Scott. Are you home?"

There was no answer and no sound from inside.

She waited a moment and then knocked again. Turning to McGaven who was waiting a few steps down, she said, "I guess she's not home."

"Maybe she's at the shop?" suggested McGaven.

"Of course."

They left the apartment and walked to the little souvenir tourist shop. Opening the door, the chime announced their entrance. Mandy, dressed in a tie-dyed purple and yellow dress, came out from behind the counter. When she saw Katie and McGaven, she raised her arms, causing the dizzying bangles on her wrists to clatter. "It took you long enough. Where have you been?"

"What do you mean?" said Katie.

"They said they would send someone out when I called, but no one came," she huffed and then had to sit down.

"Take it easy," Katie said as she helped the older woman to sit down. "Now, tell us what's wrong? Who did you call?"

"The police."

"About what?" she asked.

"Tanis is missing." It was clear that Mandy was distraught. "I knew that something might happen to her based on her past, but I always, always protected her, you have to know that."

"Okay, Mandy, start from the beginning. Take a breath, okay."

She rubbed her arms and took a few breaths before explaining, "Tanis didn't show up for work."

"When was that?" asked Katie.

"Tuesday."

"That was two days ago." Katie's gut instinct turned cold and she knew that it wasn't an accident that Tanis didn't show up for work and wasn't home. "Are you sure?"

"Yes, I'm sure. I called the police right away, but they wouldn't help me at first. I didn't think to call you because I thought I needed to call the local police. I waited another day and called again. They finally took a report and said that they would send someone out, but they didn't."

"Okay, take it easy. Are you sure that Tanis didn't say anything about going somewhere? Or visiting someone? Anything?"

"No, you don't understand. She wouldn't go anywhere without letting me know. I hadn't talked to her for a few days, but that wasn't unusual. But her not showing up for work is not like her."

The breeze from outside blew through and several wind chimes fluttered a tune that was almost eerie, like a warning. "Okay, have you been inside her apartment?"

"I just looked inside to see if she was there but she wasn't."

"You own the apartment?"

"Yes."

"May I have your permission to look inside?"

"Yes, of course." She got up and rummaged in a drawer and retrieved a key ring.

"Thank you. We'll be right back, okay?"

She nodded.

Katie gave a look to McGaven as they left the store and then recovered their search gloves from the car.

When they were at the landing at the studio apartment pulling on their gloves, she said, "I think she's in trouble." Her words hung in the air and didn't need a response from McGaven. She tried the doorknob and it was already open.

She slowly pushed the door open and scanned the room. Everything looked like it did before but there were several pillows thrown on the floor which didn't seem right.

They entered. Katie saw that there were two coffee cups on the table. She motioned to McGaven. "Looks like she had a visitor."

By the impressions on the carpet, he saw that the chairs had been moved. It appeared that she knew her visitor well enough to make tea. The kitchen revealed a half-full teapot and two small plates with crumbs left behind.

"Her personal toiletries are still in the bathroom, toothbrush, hairbrush, and such," said McGaven.

On one of the small tables, there was a crochet purse. Katie picked it up and inside there were a set of keys and her wallet. "Her purse and everything is still here," she said, laying it back on the table. "We need to contact the local PD that Mandy made the report to, and have them search and document this studio. Maybe we might get lucky and get prints off the mugs or plates. There might be cameras across the alley—have the PD pull those as well." She thought about it. "And, we need to get someone to stay with Mandy and make sure she's alright."

"On it," said McGaven as he pulled out his cell phone.

Looking around the studio, Katie realized that her worst fear might have become a reality.

CHAPTER FORTY-SEVEN

Thursday 2115 hours

"You going to be okay?" Chad asked.

"Of course," Katie replied and kissed him again.

They stood at the front door threshold. The cold air rushed inside making her shudder as Chad held her tighter.

"I can stay."

"You need to spend some time at your new place. I'm fine. Look, Cisco even thinks so."

The dog let out a low grumble.

"See?" she said.

"Get a good night's sleep, okay? I don't know what's going on with your cases, but I can see that it's wearing on you."

She nodded. "I'm going to bed in a few minutes."

He kissed her again and headed toward his truck. "Talk to you in the morning."

"Talk to you then," she said and slowly closed the door.

Katie stood for a moment listening to the quietness and then she heard Chad's truck start up, headlights pierced through the blinds, and then he backed down the driveway, the lights slowly dwindling.

She knew that she had missed two sessions with Dr. Carver and that wasn't the way she wanted it to be. Dr. Carver had expressed that she sensed extra tension and anxiousness so she wanted to talk to Katie more than twice a month. Her work, Chad, and all the recent drama had taken up every minute. But still—she felt guilty—that was the way it had to be… for now.

"It's bedtime," she said to Cisco. "C'mon."

The dog jumped off the couch and followed Katie as she turned off the lights and secured the doors.

After going through her evening ritual, Katie tumbled into bed and fell asleep within minutes. Her dreams were tame. No victims begging for help. No crime scenes needing attention. Just sleep.

Rapid knocking at the front door woke Katie out of a deep sleep. At first she thought it was in her dream, but the knocking continued as she groggily became more awake.

Cisco barked and stood in the doorway of her bedroom. His tail low. A guttural growl. His body tense.

She had left her phone in the kitchen and couldn't see her security cameras. The knocking continued. Glancing at her alarm clock, she had only been asleep for forty-five minutes. Pulling on a robe, Katie secured her sash and rummaged in her nightstand drawer until she pulled out a gun. Readying it, she moved quietly through the house, leaving all lights off. She used a hand gesture to Cisco and he shadowed her in silence, blending in with the darkness.

Peeking out the window, Katie didn't see any car and wondered who had so boldly knocked on her door at night. It wasn't Chad because he would have had his truck.

She stood next to her door and turned on the outside light. "Who is it?" she said with authority.

"Candace," came the unexpected reply.

Katie took a moment to comprehend. "What are you doing here?"

"I'm sorry, Detective, but I had no other place to go."

"*Bleib*," she instructed Cisco to stay.

Katie opened the door. Candace stood there in the same clothes she had been wearing during their scuffle in the rain at the park. She had a lightweight beige backpack slung over her right shoulder.

"How did you find where I lived?"

"I... I have been following you."

"Of course," she said with some cynicism. "You have my number. Why didn't you call me?"

"I did. It went to voicemail."

"Oh." Katie remembered that she was charging her phone.

"Is there something wrong?" Katie didn't know what else to say.

"May I come in?" the girl asked.

"I don't think that's a good idea."

"Please can I crash here tonight?"

Katie blinked in surprise, realizing that she probably didn't have anywhere to go.

"Please, just for a little while. I can't get ahold of anyone I know here. They just let me go tonight and it's late."

"They just let you go?"

"Yeah."

"What did they charge you with?"

"Obstruction. Hindering an investigation."

"How did you make bail?"

"It was $5,000 and I was able to give the bail bonds $500—that's all I have."

Katie felt bad as she watched the girl explain what had happened to her. "I can't let you stay here with these investigations underway. But, you can stay tonight due to extenuating circumstances—I'm going to see if I can get you some safe housing. I have to let my bosses know tomorrow that you were here. I don't know if that's going to help or hurt your case. Understand?"

She nodded.

"Come in," she said and opened the door wider.

Candace walked inside and stood about six feet away, politely waiting.

"Have you eaten anything?" Katie asked.

She shook her head.

"I can make you a sandwich," Katie said and walked to the kitchen.

Cisco padded to the new person and gave her a once-over, finally ending up sniffing her shoes.

"Is he friendly?"

"Cisco? Yes, he's friendly. He was a war dog. We did two tours in Afghanistan."

Candace carefully walked past the dog and sat at the counter facing Katie.

"Turkey and Swiss?" Katie asked.

"That's great."

Katie put together a hearty sandwich with turkey, Swiss cheese, mayo, lettuce, and tomato on wheat bread. She put it on a small plate and slid it over to Candace. "You want something to drink?"

"Milk? If you have it."

"I get the feeling that you have something to tell me," she said, pouring a glass of milk.

Candace took two hefty bites and thought as she chewed. "I've had a lot of time to think. And I think that someone is going after us girls—"

Katie put down the milk. "Why do you think that?" she said suspiciously. Still not convinced that the ordeal with the containers at Elm Hill was as innocent as Candace claimed.

"Because."

"Why, Candace?"

"It's no secret that we, all of us girls, aren't perfect."

"And?"

"We've all done things that we're not proud of—but we've had to survive," she said, stuffing more of the sandwich in her mouth.

"Slow down. When was the last time you ate?"

She shrugged. "I dunno."

"What are you going to do?"

"I've been trying to get in contact with a friend. I know she'll let me stay with her."

"Who's your friend?" said Katie.

"Tanis," she said quietly.

Katie sighed and her heart sank.

"What? What's wrong?" Candace stopped eating. "Tell me."

"I went to visit Tanis today."

"Yeah." Her eyes watched Katie carefully.

"According to her landlord and boss, she has been missing since Tuesday, maybe earlier."

"What? No… no… no." Tears welled up in her eyes. "Not Tanis." She stood up and was going to head toward the door. "You have to find her. Please…"

"Take it easy. Sit down." Katie took her arm and steered her to the couch. "First, we don't know if something is wrong. Second, both the city and county police departments are searching for her. Okay?"

Shaking her head, Candace said, "It's not good. The only real friend I ever had and now she's gone. It can't be true."

"We don't know that."

"C'mon, Detective. What does your cop experience tell you?"

Katie didn't answer. The truth was it didn't look good but she wasn't going to add to Candace's already trauma-filled life.

Candace began to cry. "I've lost everyone."

"We don't know that yet." Katie felt helpless to try to make the situation better—she knew, at least her cynicism chimed, it was most likely only a matter of time before they found the body of Tanis dumped somewhere with the eerie message in Italian—*hunter-gatherer*.

"Candace. I need to ask you a couple of questions. And I *need* for you to be honest. Okay?"

She nodded in agreement, wiping the tears from her face.

"Tell me about Ray Conner. What does he look like?"

"Um, he's average, I guess. Brown hair, green eyes, and um…"

"Anything that stands out? Tattoos? Scars?"

"No. He had a couple of moles." She laughed.

"Okay. Was he thin, muscular, pot belly…"

"He was thin, not fat, he was particular about his food. Everything had to be healthy. I got the feeling that he might have been heavy when he was a kid or he didn't have a lot to eat. Something happened that he didn't want to talk about."

"What makes you say that?"

"I'm not sure, just some things he said to me. And some of the things he didn't."

"Is there anything else you're not telling me about him?" Katie had the feeling that she was holding back about Ray. She was scared of him. Didn't want to get him in trouble. Something made her hesitate.

"No, that's all. It's been five years. There's not much to tell."

"Are you sure?"

"Yes, I'm telling you everything I know."

"One more question."

Candace waited.

"Were you in contact with your sister?"

"We were in contact about a week before she died, and before that it had been a year."

"Were you in contact with Tanis?"

"No."

"Then how did you know how to contact her?"

"I was following her on social media and I knew that there would be a safe time to reconnect." She fought back the tears. "I guess I was wrong."

"C'mon," Katie said. She pulled out two towels and gave them to Candace. "You need to take a shower and I'll get you some clothes, okay?"

She nodded and went into the bathroom, followed by Cisco. "Does he always do this?"

"Pretty much," she said and laughed.

While Candace took a shower, Katie rummaged to find some clothes for her: a T-shirt, jeans, a hoodie, clean socks, and a pair of old running shoes. She also took the time to make a phone call to someone she had worked with in the past, Madeline Day, who worked to find housing for battered women—she would be over to pick up Candace within the half hour so that she would be safe for the time being, or until the Elm Hill killer was found.

Candace came out of the shower with her wet hair and scrubbed face.

"Here you go. I think they'll fit," Katie said.

"Thank you." Candace went back inside the bathroom to change.

It wasn't long before there was another knock at the front door. Cisco barked once and then made himself comfortable on the couch.

Katie opened the door, "Hi, Madeline."

"Katie, it's nice to see you," said the striking dark-haired woman.

"Candace," she called.

When the young woman came into the living room she was dressed in Katie's clothes and they seemed to fit.

"Candace," said Katie. "I want you to meet Madeline. She's going to take you to a safe place to stay for a while, okay?"

She hesitated but then nodded. "Please, Detective, please find Tanis."

"You have my card and my personal number. Call me if you need anything, okay?"

"Okay. Thank you, Detective."

"Call me Katie."

She nodded and then followed Madeline out to her car.

Katie watched them leave and wondered what was going to happen next for Candace. She would have a social worker stop by and talk to her to see if they could get her into a program where she could get a job and find her own place to live.

"Well, Cisco, it's back to bed."

She once again fell into bed and was asleep within minutes.

CHAPTER FORTY-EIGHT

Saturday 1715 hours

Katie fidgeted with her black gown for the charity event as she waited impatiently for McGaven to pick her up. She hardly ever wore anything that was dressy, much less this elegant. Her pantyhose hiked up and were bugging her and her strappy heels were already killing her feet. She grimaced. The low neckline made her feel conspicuous but the lady at the store said that it looked great.

It took her almost an hour to sweep up her hair and fight to look like she was some socialite and this party was just another gathering in her glamorous lifestyle. She had make-up that was perfect for such an evening—and it covered her scratches.

In the end, the sheriff's department had been able to finagle a pair of invitations to the event at the Four Seasons, so Katie and McGaven didn't have to sneak in with the caterers. The invitations had been delivered to her house. She was surprised that her uncle and his partners weren't going to fight her on it. She guessed that they figured among themselves she couldn't cause much harm at a fancy gala.

Cisco nudged his nose against her hand.

"I know, but this isn't a K9 mission. I wish I could take you but it's not a charity for rescuing dogs and cats." She laughed because she was talking to Cisco as if he understood.

Katie felt naked, not due to the neckline, but without her gun, which she wasn't going to attempt to bring hidden underneath her dress. There was a metal detector at the main entrance so that wiped that idea out. She didn't predict any trouble.

Headlights appeared, illuminating the front windows, and moved up her driveway. A dark expensive foreign sedan parked. To Katie's surprise, McGaven, dressed in a black tuxedo, exited and walked to the door.

She opened it before he reached the porch. "My, my, who is this handsome guy? *GQ* or what?"

It was the first time she had ever seen McGaven blush with embarrassment and unable to meet her eye. "I don't know about that, but you clean up gorgeous, you know. Wow, look at you. Denise made me promise to take photos."

Katie laughed. "She would, but she better not share on social media. I'll deny it."

McGaven took his phone out. "C'mon. Selfie time."

Katie stood next to him and McGaven snapped a couple of selfie shots of them.

She grabbed her purse and wrap, kissed Cisco, and locked the door behind her.

"Let's go," McGaven said dramatically. He opened the car door for her and then climbed into the driver's seat. "I thought it would be prudent for me to drive."

"No problem here. I feel like a law-enforcement princess."

The drive to Sacramento was just under two hours which was mostly freeway, and Katie had time to process the conversations with Candace—her body language and answers. There were some things she had said that Katie wasn't sure were the truth. There was something about the lack of detail on her boyfriend Ray that didn't make sense.

"So what's causing you to fret?" he asked.

"I wouldn't say *fret*, but I'm just thinking about some things that Candace said."

"Like?"

"Well, she seemed a bit too careless about her ex-boyfriend Ray. He was the one that helped her escape and had everything planned. There was a lot of talk and planning. But she hardly said two words about him." She sighed. "I don't know, something doesn't quite fit. There's something that she's not telling us about him."

"You know, it's been about five years since he was her knight in shining armor. Feelings fade."

"That's true, I guess. But he was such an influence on her; older guy, helping her escape horrible conditions," she said, watching the cars pass going the opposite direction. "So whose car did you borrow?"

"Police impound."

"I really like it."

"Maybe you should get one like it?"

"I've been thinking about what kind of car to buy, but this, as comfortable and nice as it is, just doesn't fit my lifestyle. Plus it's not in my price range."

"Oh, I don't know—you could lease or buy a good used one. I don't think Cisco would mind."

Katie chuckled. "No, you're probably right. He would be fine riding shotgun."

"And besides, if you go camping, Chad has all those off-road vehicles."

"Yeah," she said, staring out the window, watching the daylight turn to dusk.

The traffic picked up in intensity and the crowds increased the closer they got to the city. People drove their vehicles with aggressive tactics, cutting in and out of lanes. It made Katie a bit uneasy, like she was sitting in the middle of a minefield trying to run the gauntlet of unknowns before someone took her out. That seemed like the story of her life.

"You okay?" asked McGaven, glancing at her. "You look a little sad."

"Oh, no, I'm not sad, just thinking about how crowded the city is and I used to patrol some of these areas. Never thought about it then, but now, I can't imagine living here again."

"I love Pine Valley. I never want to live anywhere else."

"So," Katie began. "What's the deal with you and Denise? I mean, the real deal?"

McGaven flushed a bit red again.

"C'mon, tell me."

"We've been getting along so well. We're so in sync it's a little scary. I don't want to lose her. She was so worried at first because of her daughter, Lizzie. But I love them both, you know?"

"That says a lot, Gav. I'm really happy for you."

"Look who I'm talking to. One half of the total power couple."

"What?" She couldn't help but laugh.

"You don't see it? The beautiful detective and the dashing firefighter... I mean c'mon, the perfect couple."

"For a movie. That's what you make it sound like." She leaned back in the comfortable leather seat. "It's been good."

"Yeah? Well, Detective Scott, I'd say we're both lucky."

She smiled back at him. Looking up ahead, she read the exit signs. "I think we're close."

"Yep, the GPS says we're about a mile from the Four Seasons. You nervous?"

"Nervous about doing my job, no. But, I'm a little nervous being with all those fancy rich people."

Less than five minutes later, McGaven drove through the main entrance and followed the signs for parking and stopped at the appropriate area. Two valets opened their doors and escorted them out.

Handing the keys to one of the men, "Thank you," he said.

"Well," Katie said to him. "Let's check it out, Mr. McGaven."

"My pleasure, Ms. Scott." He took her arm and they ascended the wide staircase and passed through the grand entrance.

Katie was mesmerized at how oversized and elegant everything was: the lights, large indoor plants the size of a car, a breathtaking waterfall, and the furniture swathed with red and gold fabric. It was fit for a king and his entire entourage—she was positive that royalty had most likely stayed at this hotel.

"This is incredible," said McGaven.

"Feeling a bit like a fish out of water—that's for sure," she whispered.

"You would never know—you are one of the most beautiful women here. Many people have noticed."

Katie glanced at McGaven, not knowing quite what to say.

There were many couples, each dressed exquisitely and mingling with small groups of people.

They could hear classical music playing as they neared the grand ballroom where two men stood. They were dressed like hotel employees, but Katie knew that they were armed security guards. She figured there would be guards dressed as caterers as well in hopes of blending in. There were too many people of privilege and financial standing to not have this type of affair completely protected.

Katie and McGaven waited behind three other couples that were being checked into the charity event. It was finally their turn.

The man with a digital clipboard asked, "Name, please."

"Mr. and Mrs. Sean McGaven."

The man swiped his finger on the board and then took two seconds first looking at Katie and then at McGaven. "Yes, sir, please go in. Enjoy your evening."

"Thank you," said McGaven.

They moved through the entrance and saw the entire gala gearing up. There were round tables, each with flowers, candles, and a chandelier hung from above. There was a full bar with several bartenders and servers. A large dance floor with a live orchestra was playing as guests were enjoying themselves.

"This isn't something you see every day," said Katie quietly to McGaven.

"No, can't say it is…"

Their plan was to separate for fifteen minutes and meet up to compare notes, and then start over again until they found the McKinzies; they would then decide the best way to corner one or both of them. McGaven had eventually found a couple of photos in newspaper articles from years ago, so they had an idea of what they looked like when they were much younger, before they became so camera-shy. Not wanting to ask too many questions about them to the other guests, they were going to work their way to the couple.

Katie immediately surveyed the entire ballroom and counted nine private security guards—both men and women.

McGaven handed her a flute of champagne.

"Thank you. I counted nine private guards around the perimeter."

"There are two couples over there," he said, indicating with his eyes. "They each had a personal guard."

"This is going to be more difficult than I originally thought," said Katie.

"Let's find the McKinzies first and then figure out what to do next."

Katie nodded as they began to move through the crowd. She noticed that there were many people giving them the once-over.

"Did you see the looks?" she whispered to McGaven.

"Yep," he said and kept his smile.

They meandered around for a while before deciding to go to the dance floor.

"You can dance, right?" Katie asked.

"Both my brothers and I learned from my mom when we were teenagers."

"Bless her."

They began to waltz slowly. It gave them the advantage of seeing most of the people in the room.

"I see them," said Katie in McGaven's ear. "Near the stage. Each has their own personal bodyguard."

"I see them too." He whirled Katie across the dance floor. "Mrs. McKinzie will need to excuse herself for the ladies' room. Right?"

"Great idea," she said.

"I'll see what I can do with Mr. McKinzie."

Both of them exited the dance floor and separated. Each going to their assignment; hopefully one of them would be able to speak with one of the McKinzies.

Katie made a beeline to Sara McKinzie as she was speaking to an older distinguished couple. She was a stunning woman wearing an elegant white dress showing off her still youthful figure, even though she was in her early forties. Her dark hair was partially in an up-twist. There was an unusual strand of pearls in a choker around her neck.

Katie watched her mannerisms and could tell with most certainty that the woman was bored and was trying to figure out the best way to make her excuses to leave the couple. This was Katie's chance. She picked up a glass of water and made her way through the crowd purposely bumping into a few guests as she went, as if she had a bit too much to drink. Smiling and weaving, she made a beeline for Mrs. McKinzie and tripped herself up at the perfect moment to send the water in her glass in a perfect arc that spotted the front of her dress.

"Oh my, I'm so sorry. Here, I have a trick to help you get that out," she said and guided her to the ladies' room. The female security guard zeroed in on them, but Mrs. McKinzie waved her away.

They walked in the ladies' lounge and restroom. It was larger than any restroom Katie had ever seen. Beautifully decorated with several stations where you could sit down and check your makeup. There were changing rooms. Attendants if you needed them.

"Mrs. McKinzie, I'm so sorry, but—"

The woman laughed with an almost musical tone as she took a seat in front of one of the beauty stations. "It's quite all right.

I was trying to figure out how to get away from the Lawsons." She studied Katie for a moment. "You seem familiar. What's your name, dear?"

"I'm Katie Scott."

"Nice to meet you, Ms. Scott."

"Actually, I'm Detective Katie Scott."

"Detective?" she said as her smile faded.

"Mrs. McKinzie, I wanted to speak with you and I know that you don't have to but I was hoping that you would make this exception…"

The older woman watched Katie closely—with curiosity. Her mouth straightened as her right eyebrow lifted. "Well, I find it refreshing when people just say what's on their mind."

With relief, Katie explained, "I'm investigating the death of two young women that were both the last residents at the Elm Hill Mansion."

"That's terrible. I believe I read something about that."

The bodyguard entered the restroom and Mrs. McKinzie waved her away again.

"I have just two questions for you."

"I'll give you five more minutes, so I'd make it quick." She began touching up her makeup and hair.

Several women entered and exited the lounge. No one paid them any attention.

"Why did you and Mr. McKinzie donate the Elm Hill Mansion?" said Katie.

"We didn't want to live there anymore. It was too big and we weren't interested in remodeling. We thought it would feel more remote. After giving it much thought we wanted to have it benefit the community, so we spoke with a couple of local councilmen and asked if there was something the county needed. They gave us some suggestions."

"And you wanted it to be a home for foster girls."

"Why yes."

"What was the real reason, Mrs. McKinzie?" Katie watched the woman closely as she stiffened, indicating she might be hiding something.

"I have a feeling, Detective, that you are very good at your job."

"I try to follow up on every possible lead."

Mrs. McKinzie stopped applying her lipstick and turned to face Katie. "I like you, Detective. And I'm rarely wrong about people. I can count on you for your discretion about this, of course."

"Yes. That goes without saying."

"I love my life. I've been blessed with the right decisions, right pedigree, and with a lot of luck. But… I made one decision that I wish I could take back."

Katie listened intently, trying to second-guess what the woman was going to tell her.

"I was seventeen when I got pregnant. As a silly girl, I thought he loved me and that we would get married and life would be wonderful." She sighed. "But that didn't happen, of course. I was forced by my parents to have the babies, and then give them up for adoption."

"Excuse me, but did you say 'babies'?"

"Yes, I had twins—actually twin girls."

Katie's heart almost stopped.

It couldn't be—could it?

"What happened to them?" Katie managed to say.

"Well, my parents said they were adopted, but years later I found out they went into foster care. The horror of babies going into something like that—I just couldn't bear it. So, I thought that donating Elm Hill Mansion to be a place for these foster girls would be a good thing. Since it was in the vicinity where I had lived and given birth." She reached into her small clutch purse and pulled out an old photograph of the newborn babies. "I know this may seem silly, but the nurse in the delivery room took a photo for me and I've kept it with me all these years."

"I'm so sorry."

"Well, my sin was paid for by me being barren. I could never conceive again. I've made peace with it."

"I know that this is somewhat presumptuous and maybe even far-fetched…"

"Again, spit it out, dear."

"Would your daughters have been twenty-three today?"

"Twenty-four in three months. Why?" Her dark eyes seemed to search Katie's soul for what she was about to suggest.

"And you never knew what happened to them?"

She looked down. "No, but I pray for them almost every day."

"Mrs. McKinzie, the girl that was found murdered at Elm Hill was twenty-three-year-old Carol Harlan, who had a twin sister, Candace Harlan. Both of them were the last girls at Elm Hill."

"I see what you're saying, but what are the odds? You couldn't possibly think…" Her face turned pale as she struggled to finish the sentence.

"I don't know, but would you risk the chance to find out? Here's my card. Call me if you would like to meet Candace Harlan, or possibly have a DNA test done if you think that she might be one of your daughters. I'm sorry for being so blunt but you only gave me five minutes."

Mrs. McKinzie was speechless as her eyes welled up with tears. She expressed gratitude and appreciated the kindness Katie had shown her.

"It was nice meeting you."

Katie got up and left the ladies' lounge. She was taken aback by the thought that was meant to be routine information about the mansion could result in a family reuniting and meeting for the first time.

"Hey," said McGaven as he took her arm and spun Katie to face him, holding her tight. "No such luck with Mr. McKinzie, maybe you might be able to get his attention." He studied Katie's face. "What's wrong?"

"Nothing. It's just… We got what we came for… and more."

CHAPTER FORTY-NINE

Monday 1045 hours

McGaven was in the middle of printing out reports but nothing seemed to be giving him the information he was looking for. Frustrated, he said, "We keep uncovering interesting things, but not something that will get us a step closer to the killer."

"You're sounding like me," Katie said. She had the arduous task of going over everything from the child protective services. She had spent her entire Sunday reading every word of the reports along with everything she had outlined so far. They were complete and detailed but nothing that would set them straight and in the correct direction. "Heard anything about Tanis from Spreckles PD?"

"No," he said sourly.

"You making headway on the electronic version of the Hunter-Gatherer series?" she said.

"No. Everything is blurring together."

"Anything that stands out?"

"No. What about those social worker reports?" he said.

Katie stopped and turned toward McGaven. "Well, for example, with the child protective reports, sometimes when social workers fill out forms, they may have someone else fill them out."

"You mean like an assistant?"

"Yeah, or pre-forms. Where they have the wording all made up or phrases used as a general response."

"Why would they do that?"

"To get the reports turned in on time. Also, if they were being paid off or if they were going to extort someone. It's not that common, but it does happen."

"I'm not finding anything that seems weird about the books. It's just tedious and repetitive about the terrible treatment as a child. How adults aren't willing to understand the juvenile mind."

Katie's cell phone rang and she snapped it up.

"Scott," she said.

"Detective Scott?" said the caller. She didn't recognize the caller ID number.

"Yes, this is Detective Scott."

"Hi, Detective, this is Shane from the county archive department."

"Yes, hi, Shane. What can I do for you?"

"Well, you told me to call you if I found anything that you might find interesting." There was heavy static in the background, making it difficult to hear his words clearly.

"Yes."

"Well, I found these pages from a book that were mixed in with the Elm Hill Mansion file."

"What kind of pages?"

"They appear to be from a journal."

"Oh."

"And on one of the pages it refers to the secret staircase in the house."

"Sounds interesting."

"I have a few errands and I will be right by the Elm Hill Mansion. Can I meet you there to show these to you? I'd like to see the house," he said.

Katie thought about it and then said, "Can you make copies and send them over?"

"I would, but these types of documents are so old that I need to be super-careful with them and they're not allowed out of my keeping. But I can bring them to Elm Hill where you can have a look at them. You could take a couple of photos with your phone."

She looked at McGaven poring over his work and reading endless pages of the manuscript. She also knew that Shane probably wanted to take a tour of the house, and she really owed him one. "Yeah," she said slowly, looking at her watch. "I can be there in twenty minutes."

"Okay, sounds good. See you then."

Katie ended the call.

"What's up?" asked McGaven.

"Shane from the county found some pages from an old book or journal that was mixed in with the Elm Hill Mansion stuff."

"Could be interesting."

"Yes, I'm sure. I'll run over to Elm Hill and check it out." She began packing up some things, putting her cell phone in her pocket and gun in the holster. "I'll be back in about an hour."

"I'll be here," he said, not looking up from the piles of paperwork.

Katie hurried to the Elm Hill property and drove up the driveway. This time it stirred emotions inside her—some fear and some trepidation from her previous experience. She tried not to think about the time ticking away as it usually did during these types of investigations. So many things seemed to be tied back to this property. She thought about the people who built the home in hopes of having a big family—but it ended up being the biggest grief in their lives with the loss of those babies.

The property looked the same, but the gate was open. The large metal container was still on its side down the hillside. The crinkled and torn end was a reminder of her rescue. There were strips of metal bent back, looking like a giant tin can. She knew how close she had been to that container being her tomb.

She shuddered as she walked across the main area where long strands of yellow crime tape lay strewn across the property—now partially covered by mud. The large earthmover and heavy-duty forklift were still in the same position from that day. Looking away from the monstrous machine, almost able to hear the roar of its diesel engines, Katie turned her concentration to the rest of the property but nothing appeared out of place.

She saw another car, a small white compact, and assumed it belonged to Shane. Glancing up at the front door, it was open. Smiling in spite of herself, Katie knew that Shane was curious about the house and wanted a firsthand view—and to get out of the county basement for a change.

Katie stepped inside the foyer. "Shane?" She waited and looked at the remnants of the blue-and-yellow wallpaper which must have been stunning in the day. "Are you here?"

"Yeah," came the reply. "Upstairs."

"Oh, okay," she said as she jogged up the staircase. She was getting a bit more excited about what he had for her to see. It must be quite interesting if he reached out to her like this.

As she rounded the bend in the staircase, she caught a whiff of stagnant air mixed with mold. It was a shame that they were going to demolish the house and not keep it for historical purposes—maybe a museum, or even a bistro. It was too late now.

There was a thud, so she stopped. Her first instinct was that something in the house wasn't sturdy—but her footing was solid and, glancing around, nothing appeared to be falling in on her.

She grabbed the ornate wrought-iron railing and continued upstairs. When she reached the landing, it was vacant. There were several pieces of odd beige paper scattered on the floor.

"Shane?" she said. "Hey, where are you?"

Katie scanned the room suspiciously and slowly bent down and picked up one of the papers. It was a journal entry, dated 1897, in fancy cursive handwriting.

Abigail has now joined her sister Greta in the garden. I don't know why God needed these two children, but they are in better hands now. May my sweet, precious girls rest in peace. I love you forever, Mommy.

"Wow," said Katie. "This is amazing." It appeared to be the journal of Emily Von Slovnick.

Another entry:

We rarely look at one another. I know he doesn't blame me for the stillborns but his eyes never look into mine. I don't know how much longer I can take this...

"How sad," said Katie. She gathered all the papers together, wondering why they were on the floor if they were so valuable, and then decided to take some photos first.

Someone walked up behind her.

"Oh, these are fantastic, Shane, but I don't know if it will help in the investigation," she said and stood up.

"Don't move, Detective," the stern voice ordered.

She turned to see Jerry Weaver, the social worker, pointing a gun at her face. "Drop your weapon."

Katie shook her head to indicate she didn't have one. She was stunned by the change in appearance of the fumbling, goofy social worker she met just days ago. His eyes were steely, hardened, and his movements were deliberate. Hundreds of questions flooded her mind—all while she was trying to keep her wits about her. Her thoughts raced in fast forward.

"Do it," he said. "I know you have a weapon." He walked to a closet. "Let me make this easier for you." He opened the door and inside was Shane, his body doubled over to his side, tied with his hands behind his back, and he appeared to be unconscious. "I will put a bullet in his incompetent brain if you don't relinquish your weapon... Detective," he said with hate-filled venom.

"Okay, take it easy," Katie said. Slowly, she opened her jacket, revealing her Glock in its holster. She unsnapped it. At first, she thought she could overpower Jerry Weaver, but after watching him, she decided it wasn't a good idea.

"Do it, Detective," he said again, never changing the tone to his voice.

She dropped her gun but made sure it was still within fighting distance. "You know it doesn't have to be like this."

"Like what?" he said. "It's going to be what I say it is." He picked up the gun.

"Where's Tanis?"

"Safe."

Shane began to stir and expressed low moans. There was blood seeping from his scalp from where he had been struck.

"Look, let him go. He doesn't know anything about what I know," she said, testing him.

Laughing, he said, "You're not going to analyze me, convince me, change my mind, relate to me, or walk away alive. Is that clear enough for you?"

Trying to ignore the rage that was simmering just below the surface in Jerry, she said, "Oh, I get it. It's very clear to me now. Thanks for clearing that up."

Jerry scaled back his anger slightly and took two steps from Shane and then back to Katie. "Why do you do that?"

"Do what, Jerry?" She knew that she was walking a very thin line with his psychological disturbance, but some things were becoming quite clear.

He stopped moving but the gun was still aimed at Katie's head.

"Go ahead and mock me. You have no idea who I am."

"Why don't you tell me," she said trying to decipher his movements and the intent behind them. "Or maybe I've heard it all before. Bad home life, mommy didn't love me, I'm so misunderstood."

He twitched. She'd touched a nerve.

"So maybe you just decided to make up a world where you are important? You immersed yourself in a fantasy about being in charge, about taking care of yourself and being a hunter-gatherer. But why did it have to be in Italian?"

"Detective, you never know where your inspiration will come from. His words consumed me, it was like he *knew* me. He looked right into my damaged soul and healed it with the romance of the Italian language…" He readjusted his grip on the gun. "You think you know me? You know nothing."

"Oh, I know more than you think. What? You were kicked into a foster home? You somehow relate to these kids? At least you thought you did, but guess what, they didn't relate to you," said Katie watching him closely.

"I know what you're doing. And it's not going to work."

"I must be getting warmer… foster kid… maybe you fell for a girl who didn't return your affections… but she had your heart and then stomped on it… Am I getting warmer?" She taunted him, throwing out wild theories, but they could be very effective.

Jerry used his free hand to rub the side of his head vigorously in a strange, almost mechanical manner.

"I am getting warmer, huh?" she said. Knowing she only had one chance, she was waiting for the perfect, almost imperceptible moment to attack. Her training had taught her that there was always one… To be patient was key…

"Why did you have to kill them? What did any of them do to you?"

"They're all…"

"The same, Jerry? How can that be?"

"They are all the same… they can't… don't understand…" His speech became inconsistent and jerky.

"They don't understand you? Is that it, Jerry?"

"I took care of them when they were dead, not mocking me anymore, no more laughter. I bathed them, washed their hair. I left them just as they came into the world—naked and pure."

"You killed the wrong girl," she said loudly.

"I know… I didn't know for a while… it's just… it was my first mistake."

"No, Jerry your first mistake was feeling sorry for yourself." Thinking quickly, she continued, "You made quite a few mistakes. The fingernail?"

He took a step back, confused. "No, that wasn't a mistake. It was… I didn't…"

Katie thought she might be able to disarm him and that he was going to admit defeat.

Jerry changed mood again, his personality suddenly forceful and condescending. "You think you're special, Detective. But none of you are—just teases."

"All this turmoil and killing because of a bad relationship? You can do better than that. Grow up… We all have problems, Jerry."

"The constant beat-down… constant neglect… all of it was *my* fault… My fault!"

Katie could tell from his fragmenting speech that his mind was rolling back to the beginning of it all.

He lifted a hand to regain his composure and quickly wipe the sweat from his eyes.

At that exact moment, Katie launched herself at him. He dropped his gun on impact and it skittered across the room and through a doorway opening.

CHAPTER FIFTY

When Katie hit the floor, Jerry took most of the impact beneath her. He didn't move, so she thought he was knocked out and lessened her grip on him. A mistake. That's when he struck, flipping her over on her back and punching her stomach. The oxygen left her body and she heard herself gurgle, trying to catch her breath after it was knocked out of her.

Jerry pinned her down and wrapped his fingers around her throat. She watched his pupils dilate, turning his eyes to almost black like a demon. His glee was evident in his effort to strangle her to death. Katie fought to stay conscious, lights flashed in her peripheral vision, and the sheer pain from him trying to crush her windpipe—feeling her throat compress against her spine—was overwhelming. Her hands couldn't overpower his around her throat.

Fighting to bring up her left leg, she finally managed to do so, kneeing him in the groin and stomach areas. He lessened his grip. She clasped her hands in a tight clenched prayer position and broke his arms away from her before managing to wiggle her body free. Jerry fell to the side, moaning and swearing. Without her gun or even her cell phone, she had no other choice but to run.

Staggering to get to a standing position, her head spinning, Katie fought the urge to fall down and sleep. Her exhaustion and lack of proper oxygen made her feel disconnected and weak. Her vision blurred.

Making it to the stairwell, she grabbed the railing for dear life. It was the only thing that held her upright so she squeezed her fingers tight, melding them onto the wrought iron.

A loud wild-animal snarl came from behind her and a moment later Jerry grabbed her and began pulling her back to the room.

"No!" she yelled, flailing her feet in the air. Remembering a tactic that one of her army trainers taught her, she pushed back hard as her boot caught the handrail. She continued pushing and managed to bring her feet over her head and come back down in a backward somersault.

Katie freed herself from him but had nowhere else to go except down the stairs. She hit them at full speed but missed the third step, causing her to tumble forward and stagger. She stopped herself about halfway down, trying to protect her head and neck. Fumbling for her footing, she was caught by Jerry again.

His continuing rage had turned him unpredictable, making him an impossible adversary to fight as his hand, fists, and feet caught her body endlessly. One more bash to Katie's head, and Jerry managed to claw a fistful of her hair and slam her forehead into the handrail. She took a deep breath and was about to retaliate—

Everything went black.

CHAPTER FIFTY-ONE

Drums pounded in Katie's head. The intense throbbing was almost unbearable as she touched her forehead and felt something sticky. She didn't need to see it or touch it; she knew it was blood, hot, viscous, slipping down her forehead.

She opened her eyes but saw nothing but blackness.

Leaning forward, at first she couldn't see anything or feel anything. Then she felt a flat wall in front of her and a stair underneath her body. Why couldn't she see it?

"Hello?" she said. Listening to the sound of her tinny echoing voice made her think of a long cavern, an endless abyss. She gulped down her fear.

Stairs, she thought. Her mind raced to figure out where she was as her memory cleared. Remembering what had happened came in bits and pieces. Jerry Weaver was not only psychologically damaged, but forever demented. He believed the girls of Elm Hill Mansion had used him. The result—they were going to pay with their lives.

She stood up slowly, not able to differentiate up or down due to dizziness. Stairs. No railing, just walls. She was in the secret staircase. Katie's fuzzy feeling began to clear and she was able to think more clearly. At that moment, she knew that Shane was tied up in the closet and Jerry Weaver was the killer. With all the evidence they had discovered, she had missed this link. Someone who had been in foster care, someone who had been abandoned, and someone who picked his work to get closer to those who would understand him.

Katie needed to get to Shane. Hands flat against the wall, she made her way up as best she could. Slow, steady, and using her hands until she reached the top.

Thunder shook the house as if an earthquake rumbled through it.

Katie stood still, listening intently in the darkness.

It boomed again—this time the violent shake felt like a train had hit the house.

The house—in its fragile condition and ready for demolition—was going to come down one way or another. There was no other alternative.

Katie's blood turned cold, her hands sweated, and a lump appeared in her throat, making it difficult to breathe. Her heart raced and her pulse thundered in her ears. No, she kept telling herself. She was not going to die alone beneath a pile of rubble. She hadn't lived through what she had in the army and her police work to die trapped in a rotten old house. Katie began pounding on the walls and the door at the top of the stairs. "Hey! Can anyone hear me?!"

She continued pounding with her fists and when she grew tired, she kicked at the door with her boots.

Then… there was a soft sound. She heard a knock, once, twice, and then a third time.

Katie wasn't imagining it.

"Can you hear me!" she yelled. "Help! Get Help!"

A very weak voice responded, "I can hear you…"

"Get help!" she yelled again.

"I can't."

Katie realized it was Shane. Poor Shane.

A crash hit the corner of the foundations, rocking the upper floor.

Katie bounced around the wall of the staircase like a ball.

"Katie," Shane said in a weak voice. "I'll try to get to you."

Moving back from the door, she heard pounding and then scratching up and down. It sounded like he was trying to unlock the door with his hands behind his back.

"C'mon, Shane, c'mon, c'mon," urged Katie. "You can do it, Shane!"

A low grumble came from underneath the second floor. It revved like a massive airplane engine and then a crash hit the building with a tremendous force—this time from another corner. Katie knew that Jerry was systematically taking out the structural parts of the building until it tumbled down into a pile of rubble—falling into itself.

"C'mon, Shane! You can do it!" she yelled through the wall.

More pounding and scratching came from the other side of the door. Until something clicked and the door opened an inch. "Get back!" she yelled, before kicking the door open the rest of the way.

Katie stumbled into the main room on the second floor. There she found Shane slumped on the floor, leaning up against the wall. Dried blood had stuck to the side of his head and face, he was missing his gold-rimmed glasses, and breathing hard.

"C'mon, we've got to get out of here now," she said, and began untying his restraints. "You okay?"

He nodded.

The room spun slightly for Katie and she had to steady herself as she pulled Shane to his feet. "We need to leave now," she urged. "Where's your phone?"

"Back pocket," he said.

Katie quickly reached for his cell phone and found it. Dialing 911, she explained the address and the line went dead. She frantically called McGaven's number and when he answered, "Get help to Elm Hill... we need..." The connection went dead.

It was perfect timing; the next impact against the house was larger than the previous ones, shaking the entire mansion like a combined explosion and 8.0 earthquake. The floor shifted and then tilted to one side. The groans and screeches emitted from the old house were deafening. The mansion tried to hold together, but ultimately its tired old construction began to let go.

Both Katie and Shane couldn't hold tight to anything and were left sliding across the main floor to the other side.

The rattling was unrelenting, deep groans, screeching, cracking, and crashing was heard all around them. There was nothing that Katie could do.

CHAPTER FIFTY-TWO

McGaven took the last turn on the road before the driveway to Elm Hill Mansion too fast and he fishtailed the car, barely getting it back under control. He was followed by four patrol cars, the sheriff's car, and soon the fire department would be arriving after the place was secured. He knew that he was putting his job on the line, but he also knew that there was no room for mistakes.

Within seconds, he drove up the driveway for Elm Hill Mansion and saw an earthmover still idling on the property. No one was around.

The main structure of the house was smashed to pieces.

Katie's car was there, along with another small vehicle.

McGaven drove all the way up to front yard area, slammed on his brakes and flung open the door.

The other patrol cars fanned out and took their backup positions, ready as needed.

McGaven stood in the middle of the property. Diesel hung in the air. There was an eerie quiet. "Katie!" he yelled. "Katie!"

Sheriff Scott, driving a department SUV, sped up to the property and stopped. He was out of the vehicle in seconds, running toward McGaven.

"What happened?"

At that exact moment, the entire mansion collapsed. Creaking, groaning, and crunching grew in sound as the structure slipped into its own grave. First from the middle inward, then the second and third floors crumbled and fell downward with a huge crash.

Each piece of carefully planned and designed lumber let loose and caved in at weird angles, leaving a pile of rubble.

Dust rose into the air.

"Back up!" McGaven yelled, and everyone ran from the spectacle until it was finished.

When it was done, the once beautiful house was now a pile of old wood and shattered dreams. Its history halted. Dust continued to float over to the police officers in swirls with the humidity. There was a distinct smell of old barn wood and wet earth mixed with surrounding forest.

McGaven stood next to Sheriff Scott and they both were speechless for a moment.

Scott turned to the officers and said, "We need rescue workers here now! Get the fire department out here *now*!"

"Do you think Katie's in there?" whispered McGaven, barely able to speak, still staring at the wreckage. "Do you think she even survived that?"

"If anyone can survive something like that—it's Katie." The sheriff left to coordinate the rescue, pushing his personal feelings aside.

McGaven stood still, gaping at the wreckage, but then he had an idea.

CHAPTER FIFTY-THREE

"Shane," said Katie with a raspy voice. "You okay?"

She sat up and was able to free herself from the larger beams of the house. They were lucky, she thought—at the final moment she'd dragged them both into the small closet and wrapped her arms around him to shield him. As the building collapsed, this little closet held fast, protecting them in a small pocket of air.

"I'm here," Shane said. He sounded strange, as if he were in another room.

"Where are you? I can't see much," she said.

Katie crawled slowly, mindful of pipes and wiring—she didn't know if there was electricity still coursing through the lines. She used her hands to feel her way. A tiny crack of light was above them—hopefully a good sign—with light and oxygen reaching them.

A hand grabbed hers, making her startle. "I'm here," he said.

As Katie neared him, she saw an outline of a body lying on its side with an arm pinned beneath timber. "Shane," she said. "Can you move?"

"A little, but my arm…" he said breathlessly. "I can't move my arm."

"Okay, I think we're close to the outside so let's see what I can do." She began feeling around to see if she could move the obstructive wood. "Wait, what's that sound?"

*

The deputies had all pitched in and began carefully pulling pieces of lumber and supports away from the outside, trying to find any area where there was an air pocket or chamber where Katie and Shane might be.

Soon, the fire department and volunteers arrived to help.

McGaven saw Chad drive up in his vehicle. He ran to meet him. Cisco was riding shotgun, panting and pacing back and forth as if he knew that Katie was in trouble. "Hey, man, glad you got here quickly."

Chad looked grave and barely keeping it together, but said, "Great idea. Cisco can find where Katie is before we do." He stopped McGaven. "Do you think that she survived that?" he said in a barely audible voice. He looked at the giant heap of rubble of a once large mansion.

McGaven gritted his teeth, and said, "The sheriff said if anyone could survive that it would be Katie."

*

"Wait," said Katie. "Hear that?"

"Yeah," said Shane weakly.

"Someone's here. They're here to rescue us. Help! Help!" she yelled. "We're here!" She waited but no one responded. "Help!" she yelled again.

"They can't… hear us…"

"Don't worry, we'll get you moved and try again. Okay? The important thing is that help is here."

He nodded and exhaled an agonized breath.

Katie surveyed her area just like she would do if she was out in the mountains or studying the crime scene. Keeping her focus, she did a 360-degree slow circle. It was tight and there were a few obstructions, but she managed.

"Okay," she said. "I'm being straight with you, okay? Don't answer, just nod or squeeze my hand if you understand."

He nodded.

"We're in a small cubbyhole with only a tiny crack of letting air, which means we only have so much oxygen. But we're fine for now, okay?"

A squeeze of her hand.

"Let me see if I can move this," she said. Trying to push or pull the wood amounted to not moving or budging it at all. It was clear that Shane probably had a broken arm, and maybe a shoulder or collarbone too. She didn't know how bad or if there were compound fractures.

She heard his ragged breathing.

"Shane, stay with me, okay?"

He barely squeezed her hand.

Katie leaned in and could see that he was fading and would be unconscious soon. She needed to find a way out—fast.

Dust trickled down, making the pocket of air heavy and difficult to breathe. Katie coughed and tried to clear her throat but it was becoming worse. She couldn't stop coughing and suddenly felt woozy so she leaned back and closed her eyes.

*

"Wait a minute, wait a minute," called one of the deputy sheriffs. "I thought I heard something. Quiet!"

Everyone stopped working and listened. Silence, but that didn't deter them as they kept working to pull wreckage away.

"Okay, let's get Cisco working," said McGaven to Chad.

"I can work him in a quadrant search. That's probably the most efficient way in this type of setting."

"Sounds good," he said. "Hey."

Chad turned to face McGaven.

"She's going to make it—if there's one thing I've learned about Katie—she's a fighter."

Chad gave a weak smile and turned to hike over to the other side with Cisco. "Okay, buddy," he said to the panting dog. "We've been here before."

Cisco barked. It was clear that he sensed a heightened urgency.

Chad unclipped the leash. "Cisco, search. Find Katie. C'mon, boy."

The dog barked again, spun two times and began systematically using his nose to find Katie in between boards, down in crevices, and across the top of piles. He became interested in a certain area, but moved on. The dog worked for about fifteen minutes and seemed tired. Chad stopped the dog and gave him some water.

"Good boy, good boy," he said.

Cisco's ears perked up, ears forward, and eyes intense. The black dog was like a statue as he strained his hearing. He began barking—incessantly barking. Some of the searchers stopped what they were doing and watched the dog.

Cisco ran up on one of the piles about ten feet high and began barking. He ran up and down the same area a few more times, barking the entire time.

*

The oxygen was dwindling faster than Katie had thought it would. She became excessively tired. She leaned against one of the supports and rested her eyes again. All she could smell was mold and dust.

She thought she was dreaming because she could hear Cisco barking. It was his loud bark when he found something, or a bad guy. Opening her eyes, she realized that she wasn't dreaming. She really *could* hear Cisco barking.

"Cisco…" she whispered. Moving to Shane, she could tell he was breathing but wasn't conscious, most likely due to the head injury he sustained from Jerry.

The barking continued and became louder.

"Cisco! Here, boy! I'm here!" she yelled as loud as she could, making her dizzy. Her voice sounded like it was inside a bottle and made her tone strange. She took several deep breaths.

"Cisco... Cisco..." she said and fainted.

*

Chad had moved toward Cisco, who was on the other side of the house that they were searching. "Hey! Over here!" he yelled. His anxiousness increased and he waited impatiently, moving a few boards out of the way. "Hey!"

The entire crew, made up of deputies, firefighters, and volunteers, came to Chad's aid. "I think she's over here."

They worked tirelessly. Even the sheriff worked with them.

One of the volunteers finally said, "They're over here." It was the area that Cisco was barking on top of barely fifteen minutes earlier.

Chad pushed his way past them and slipped down inside.

Cisco still barked, clawing at the area, trying to get inside—desperately trying to get to Katie.

Five minutes later, Chad appeared with Katie in his arms. Everyone helped to get her out. She had cuts and bruises, but she was semiconscious. Cisco licked her face and she moved her hand to pet him.

"C'mon, we need a gurney over here," said Chad. "There's another one down there, he's pinned. C'mon, let's go..."

*

With huge relief, Katie felt like she was drifting in a dream. She kept her eyes shut and embraced the fresh air and daylight on her face, along with kisses from Cisco. It was all like a warped fantasy—a once terrifying dream but with a happy ending as she felt the strong arms of Chad wrapped around her.

Hearing the familiar voices of her uncle, McGaven, Chad, and others made her anxieties diminish. She mumbled, "Shane needs your help… he needs your help…"

Sitting straight up on the gurney with a surge of anxiety as the medic tried to calm her, Katie looked desperately for McGaven.

Cisco jumped up and huddled next to her.

Her head cleared. "Gav," she yelled. "It's Jerry… she kept saying. "It's Jerry…"

He jogged up to her. "Take it easy, Katie." He tried to make her lie down and relax.

"No. You don't understand. Have you caught him?" she said, trying to catch her breath. It felt as if she had run a marathon.

"Who?"

"It's Jerry."

"Jerry," he repeated.

"Yes, it's Jerry Weaver."

"The social worker? Are you sure?"

"Yes, he trapped me at the house with Shane. And… and…"

McGaven grabbed a deputy. "We need officers at Jerry Weaver's house, he's a county social worker. Do it now. He's considered armed and dangerous." He thought about the options and said, "There could be a victim with him. Use caution."

The deputy began radioing the information and took off to his patrol car.

"NO… no, you don't understand," she said.

Chad and the sheriff approached.

"Take it easy," said McGaven.

"No, we don't have time. We have to get there."

"What do you mean, Katie?"

"I think…" she said, her mind spinning fast. His build, his access to the reports, his meetings at the house, and his contact and personal information with the girls. "It makes sense…"

"What are you talking about?"

Katie realized, of course, it had been Jerry Weaver at the prison, covering his face but readjusting the clipboard to sign in using his left hand, and he must've said something so threatening to McDonald that she killed herself.

And Candace's reluctance to say "Ray" was the social worker. She probably thought she'd get him in trouble or he might harm her. His wording about how he couldn't make unannounced visits, the bipolar assessment that was completely wrong, yet in reality he could have intervened if there was any indication of abuse.

Jerry Weaver used the abuse as a way to the girls—a twisted way that he was going to save them because he figured out how to survive his past through the Hunter-Gatherer book.

"It's him!" she said desperately.

"Who?" said McGaven.

"Jerry Weaver is Ray… Ray is Jerry Weaver."

CHAPTER FIFTY-FOUR

McGaven drove at excessive speeds—taking the corners with haste and expertise. Katie rode shotgun against all orders from paramedics, Chad, and the sheriff. She was fine, in her opinion, and promised that she would get checked out once Jerry Weaver was in custody. Once the killer had been caught and wouldn't hurt anyone else.

After hearing back from Spreckles PD, the fingerprints on a tea mug at Tanis Jones's apartment came back as Jerry Weaver's and everything became a blur from there. Weaver's house was found vacant. There was no clue to where he had gone.

Katie hung on to the arm rest and pushed away the pain that was now, ultimately, flooding her body. Her legs felt numbed to everything, but that didn't stop her. She gritted her teeth every time they drove over a bump as it jarred her neck, causing excruciating pain to explode down her back.

After Jerry Weaver's house was found empty, Katie knew exactly where he would be hiding and hopefully Tanis would be there too. Once she realized Jerry was Ray, it was easy to read his motives for doing things and how he manipulated his victims to fit his fantasy. When his victims saw right through him, he killed them. There was no other choice. Once they didn't fit his version of his fantasy—they were gone.

Katie recalled several of the clues that they had uncovered and ran them over and over in her mind. Shelly McDonald committing suicide after receiving a visit from a man that signed in as Ray

Roland, which just happened to be the name of the author of the "Hunter-Gatherer" series. Candace Harlan seemed genuine, but there were a few things bothering Katie about her statements. Her flippancy about Ray Conner, who didn't exist. Her being at the Elm Hill property during the time where Katie and McGaven were trapped in the metal storage container and almost killed. Candace's Ray was described as average, business type, quiet, older, and had helped her escape the conditions at the mansion. And Mary's Ray made her believe that he was the one—the perfect man for her.

Katie speculated that Weaver had had a horrible childhood and spent time immersing himself in a book series that most never heard of—but why would he want to kill the girls at Elm Hill and carve the title of his favorite books? It obviously satisfied an internal need, a fantasy, a way that he could be in control. By basing his life on a fictional character, it made him feel like he was finally in control, that he was important.

"You okay?" asked McGaven, who had been staring at her as they stopped at a traffic light.

"Of course. I'm fine." She forced a smile even though she wasn't.

McGaven kept driving, passing through downtown, and heading northeast to the outskirts of the area. Not much to see except for some industrial business and the railroad which drove right through it. They were heading to the Sunny Motel—the one where Candace Harland and Ray stayed for three months some five years ago. Patrol was on standby, ready for backup less than a mile away from the location when McGaven gave the word.

McGaven eased up on his speed when they saw the big motel sign with a red dot described by Candace Harlan. The sign was the only thing that looked decent and relatively new. The old two-story motel was an L-shape structure and bordered the property next to the railroad where there were dozens of old train cars stored. Most were heavily tagged with graffiti. Tall weeds had taken over all around them, contained only by a drooping barbwire fence.

McGaven pulled off the road next to an abandoned gas station. The car was blocked from view at the motel. He had called the motel and spoken with the manager, and after some finessing, he found out the largest room with two sleeping areas and a kitchen was rented by a Ray Roland.

"I want you to stay here," said McGaven with a serious expression. No smiles. No jokes. He was dead serious.

"You know I can't do that. We're partners. We have each other's back."

He shook his head.

"C'mon, I'll hang back. Just give me the shotgun," she said, almost matter-of-fact. As if it was any other day trying to finagle her way into the situation.

McGaven leaned forward. "I know you're tough, but think just for a moment what you've been through today. You should be resting at home or in the hospital under observation—resting."

Katie opened her mouth but decided not to say anything. She sat back and tried to relax.

"I'm not joking around." He stared at her, anticipating what she might say. Opening the door, he added, "I'll be back, I'm just going to have a look around." He left, not saying another word.

Katie watched McGaven move stealthily toward the motel. He went around the back way and disappeared from her view.

She spied the keys dangling in the ignition. Thinking for a moment, she swiped them and stepped out of the car. Opening the trunk, there were several duffel bags McGaven had packed. She knew he had one for stakeouts, but there was also another one with his backup pistol. Unzipping the bags, she quickly found the gun and made sure that the magazine was fully loaded. It didn't take her long to fully protect herself with firepower and a heavy sweatshirt as she closed the trunk. She thought about the bulletproof vest, but didn't want to waste another moment.

Katie didn't intend on running in like a banshee, she wanted to be prepared as backup. Surveying the property, so many variables were obvious to her. First, there were several areas where someone could hide and ambush the police, and there were also several exits making it more difficult if the killer fled and hid somewhere in the brush nearby.

The parking lot was in dire need of repaving, with several deep holes. Two orange cones had been placed near them, but they were faded from being in the sun for such a long period of time. There were only three cars parked—one pickup truck, an SUV, and another small compact car. She assumed one was the manager's and one of the other two was most likely Weaver's.

Two patrol cars rolled up and slowly drove around and parked just out of sight. McGaven must've called in for backup.

The two deputies jogged down the side of the property along a narrow trail in between the heavily overgrown area. They too disappeared with the weeds as cover.

Katie spied an area just above the motel near the storage yard where she could watch and move in if needed. Moving quickly, her muscles began to loosen up, making it easier for her advance. She observed the two deputies and McGaven priming themselves at the motel room door—it was last one on the end at the second level.

She heard McGaven give the law enforcement orders, "Jerry Weaver, this is the Pine Valley Sheriff's Department! Open the door!" McGaven stood strong with the two patrol officers beside him. "Kick it in," he said, and stepped out of the way.

With ease, one of the patrol officers stomp-kicked the door, allowing the frame to splinter and then the door burst open with a loud bang.

Each of the officers moved inside with furtiveness, their weapons trained in front of them ready to use force if needed. Katie heard them yell, confirming they had cleared the rooms.

"Clear!" The main living room.

"Clear!" The bedroom and bathroom areas—McGaven!

"Clear!" The kitchen and dining area.

To Katie's surprise, the two deputies and McGaven quickly exited. She watched the anguish on McGaven's face. He was angry, but upset by what he had seen.

Katie left her position and jogged up to the motel, taking the stairs two at a time.

McGaven saw her and said, "I knew you wouldn't listen to me." He was still visibly shaken and his voice remained low.

"What is it?" she said breathless.

"Jerry Weaver isn't here."

She glanced around. "Oh, he's around. There's no way he's not."

"Based on what?" he said.

"Based on the fact he thinks he's so smart. Look, he's outsmarted us twice before and got away. I bet he's watching right now. I'd bet my badge on it."

McGaven hesitated and thought about Katie's rationale, trusted her expertise, and then turned to the patrol officers. "Take a look around the property. Check every possible hiding place. Turn your radios down. Stay alert."

Katie pushed past McGaven and entered the motel room. She wanted to see for herself—Weaver's lair.

"Wait," he said.

She ignored him and went inside the cramped room with tattered and worn-out furniture. Everything appeared to be mismatched thrift-store buys. Food remains, flies, and miscellaneous wrappers were strewn all over the table, counter, and small sofa. Mouse droppings were scattered across the floor near a small opening at the end of the wall.

Katie walked through the cramped living area and moved into a small room. It was mostly dark, making everything obscured. The rancid food smell was overwhelming, but there was another smell vying for attention that caught Katie's senses, triggering her to slow her pace.

"Katie," said McGaven. This time with more urgency as he followed her into the room.

Looking at the other end of the dank room, to Katie's horror, there was a nude woman, tied to a chair and slumped over, and it was easy to see the letters carved into her back even in the gloom. She still approached with caution as the stench was overwhelming and growing in intensity with every step. Katie couldn't tear her eyes away from the woman. Her thin body didn't move. The skin stretched over bone was grayish and had a slight iridescent shadow about it. Her long dark hair covered her face. It was clear to see that the rope around her neck had been tightened too much. Looking down, she saw her feet, ankles, and calves were partially eaten away by rodents—tiny chew marks were visible.

Katie put her hand to her mouth, to some extent in horror and partially to keep the smell away from her nose.

McGaven moved closer to her. "Don't, Katie."

Dapples of the victim's blood were scattered across the floor in an almost intricate design of dots and then full-sized spatters. They weren't bright red, but dull, dark, and almost rust-colored.

With one hand, Katie slowly moved the woman's hair, noting that her face was extremely pale and gaunt. Katie recognized the resemblance to the lovely, quiet woman that she and McGaven had spoken to.

Tanis Jones appeared dead, but her skin was still warm.

On a small table, there were various bottles of shampoo and ink. In a large shallow bowl, there was a mixture of jewelry, fingernails, barrettes, and groupings of hair. His trophies.

McGaven touched Katie's arm. "C'mon, let's get out of here. We have to call it in for the homicide and forensics."

"Why?" she said. "Why did he need to do this?" She was devastated and weary as she looked around the room.

"Let's go outside," he said gently. "C'mon."

A quiet gasp of air. It was faint but discernible.

"Wait," said Katie. She knelt next to Tanis and gently pulled her hair from her face again. Pressing her fingers against Tanis's neck, Katie was able to detect a pulse. "She's alive!"

"What?" said McGaven.

"She's alive. There's a faint pulse. Call an ambulance." Hope filled her heart and she silently prayed for a miracle.

McGaven made the call.

Katie found a pocket knife on the table and began carefully cutting Tanis's restraints. "C'mon, Tanis, you got this. Keep breathing… Gav, get a blanket or sheet. Anything we can wrap her in until they arrive."

McGaven and Katie carefully wrapped Tanis and laid her on one of the beds. She began to make tiny noises and it became clearer that she was breathing shallow, but it was consistent.

Katie waited outside on the flimsy decking with a wobbly metal railing as McGaven stood next to her. She couldn't get Tanis's face out of her mind and the fact that she had been left to die in that condition. She couldn't imagine the horrors and suffering Tanis had been through. If only she had figured out who the killer was sooner, then they would have found Tanis sooner. She felt weak and defeated as she stood there trying to act like everything was okay—when it clearly wasn't.

She watched the deputies search the overgrown area and thought they were going to find only ticks and mosquitos.

Trying to calm her nerves, the only thing she could do was breathe and focus. The simple act of taking air in and out made things better. She kept her focus present and her mind on finding Jerry Weaver.

Something shiny caught Katie's attention—it flashed twice. She kept her head low but turned her gaze toward one of the train cars, not making it obvious. She knew instinctively that Jerry Weaver was hiding out there, and once they left, he would make his escape and maybe avoid law enforcement in the future.

She wasn't going to allow him to slip away again… He wasn't going to hurt anyone else—ever.

Katie walked up to McGaven and whispered, "He's in the fourth train car with the blue graffiti." She backed away. "I'll head back toward the car and go around the long way as backup. You and the deputies can confront him."

"We can take care of this," he said softly.

"I'm just the insurance that he's not going to get away this time. There won't be enough time to call in for more reinforcements. Besides," she said, "there will be cops coming here because of the crime scene, but that will ten or twelve minutes. Every minute counts."

McGaven gave her a look, a stern stare, before he jogged away to meet up with the two other deputies.

Dark clouds skirted across the sky, making the day darker than normal. A few drops of rain escaped and dappled the ground. Rolling thunder rounded out the gloomy day with a deep rumble. It seemed fitting to Katie as she moved silently through the weeds on the other side of the train yard.

Some of the area was piled with trash and plastic items wedged underneath the dried overgrowth. Katie kept her eyes focused on the train car. With no movement or voices, she thought that the deputies were searching farther away than the area she had explained to McGaven.

She came to a clearing where there were discarded canned goods and a pot. Looking closer, she found blankets and large trash bags filled with what she presumed were clothes and more bedding.

It was a place that transients occupied and that made her pause. Where were they now?

Looking around cautiously, Katie realized that she was exposed and needed to take cover. She pulled McGaven's gun from underneath her jacket and moved faster, zigzagging around old machine parts and equipment until she faced one of the train cars. She continued moving until she was behind the car in question.

Katie waited.

She heard steady heavy footsteps approaching. Pressing back against the train compartment wheel, she readied herself for an attack, or to become backup for her colleagues.

More thunder reverberated all around her, making her startle.

"Come out now!" yelled McGaven, shattering the quiet. "Let's see some hands now!"

"I see you, Deputy," came a voice Katie recognized. She knew that her assessment was correct and Weaver was hiding out, watching and waiting for his opportunity to slip away again.

"Put down the weapon, Weaver!" yelled McGaven again.

That's all Katie needed to hear—that her partner and two other deputies faced being shot. With desperation she looked around the area, spying a ladder on the train car. Pocketing the gun, she climbed up the ladder without making a sound. It was rickety and she wasn't sure if it was going to hold her weight, but she made it to the top.

Lying on her belly, she inched forward until she looked down on the top of Weaver's head; he was waving a gun as McGaven and the deputies had their weapons trained on him.

"I'm not going to ask you again. Put the gun down!" demanded McGaven.

"You can't tell me what to do," said Weaver. "I have rights."

"Your rights are going to be revoked. What you did to those women is despicable."

"Deputy, I pity you. You are so delusional and quite defenseless, even with your gun aimed at me. Nothing can defeat me."

Katie was listening to utter madness; it was clear that Weaver was beginning to unravel and he was capable of anything.

"Vi compatisco deputati. Io vinco. Hai perso," Weaver said in Italian almost singing his reply of how he had won and they had lost.

The tension around them heightened with his eerie Italian words still hanging in the air. His desperation could mean catastrophe for anyone around him. Katie had to think quickly. There wasn't a good enough shot to get him from her vantage point, so that meant she had to go to plan B.

Katie moved her aching body into a crouching position, but her foot slipped, making a scraping sound.

Weaver looked up, along with the deputies and McGaven.

It was a split second that meant life or death. Katie's training taught her that was all you had at times, and you had better make peace with it.

In that split second she regained her balance, then pushed up and jumped off the train compartment roof. Within two seconds, she saw Weaver rotate and bring up his arm to shoot her. Katie landed directly on him, taking them both to the ground. The gun fired. Thunder crashed. Deafening explosion in her ears. She had let out a Comanche yell, not realizing it as she dive-bombed the killer, hitting the ground hard and rolling several times out of McGaven's and the deputies' views.

Loud voices hollered different orders. "Drop the gun! Let's see some hands! Stay on the ground NOW!" There was a frenzy of chaos as they scrambled to save Katie.

She landed on her back a few feet away from Weaver. He had already stumbled to his feet with the gun still in his hand—turning his focus on Katie. His face contorted, full of rage, wanting blood to spill. He was going to kill her.

Her hearing hadn't cleared as her ears still buzzed from being next to Weaver as he fired the gun. The side of her face burned. Her left eye watered uncontrollably.

With a shaky hand, anchoring her feet against the ground from her lying position, she managed to pull her gun and fired once—missing Weaver. A bullet whizzed by her head simultaneously as she fired a second shot, hitting Weaver directly in the chest. He crumpled over and hit the ground—not moving, with his gun still hooked on his fingers.

Katie readied herself to fire again—she watched—waiting for Weaver to get up.

"Katie, Katie," came a familiar voice, although it was muffled.

She looked up as McGaven scooped her to her feet, holding her tight.

The deputies made sure Weaver was dead and gathered his gun, handcuffing his hands behind his back, as procedure, until the shooting investigation began.

Katie couldn't take her eyes away from Weaver—the two cases were closed and Tanis was going to the hospital.

"You okay?" said McGaven, holding his hand to her face.

Katie could hear him clearer. "I'm okay," she said.

"You know how close that bullet came to doing some serious damage?"

"No, how close?" was the only thing that Katie could think of to say.

McGaven tore a piece of his shirt and pressed it against her cheek. "Too close. It grazed your cheek."

"That wouldn't even need a Band-Aid on the battlefield."

McGaven shook his head.

Katie finally averted her eyes, tearing them away from the killer lying on the ground, wrists handcuffed behind his back—as his eyes stared fixed at the sky.

Katie thought that was too good for Jerry Weaver—he got off easy.

Sirens sounded.

Cars screeched up to the rundown motel.

McGaven hugged Katie and then helped her walk up to the motel and to the parking lot as they met reinforcements.

The sky finally released the rain.

CHAPTER FIFTY-FIVE

A week later...

Katie heard the car pull up her driveway and when she looked out the window, she saw a black Lincoln Town Car slowly ease in and stop. She had no idea who it was until Candace Harlan jumped out and ran to the front porch.

Katie opened the door still wearing her robe, with Cisco at her left side.

"Hi, Detective Scott," said Candace, who was all smiles.

"You can call me Katie," she said. "What's going on?"

"I wanted to… I mean, *we* wanted to say thank you."

"Who?" Katie was puzzled at first then she saw Mrs. McKinzie step from the car. She was dressed casually in a pair of slacks and a yellow blouse, still looking elegant.

"Ms. Scott, I thought long and hard about what you said that night of the gala. And I took your advice. You made quite an impression."

"Yes, she did," chimed Candace. "And guess what?"

"What?" said Katie. Even though she had an idea of what the news was going to be.

"She's my mom—my *real* mom," said Candace.

Katie looked at Mrs. McKinzie who nodded.

"Well, we had the mitochondrial DNA testing done. And yes, Candace is definitely my daughter. Candace and Carol are my daughters. We're going to stop by Carol's grave today."

"And we're going to visit Tanis at the hospital too. She's doing much better," said Candace.

"I'm so happy for you, both of you. That you were able to find each other."

"We just wanted to come by and see you and tell you the good news in person," said Candace. "Thank you, Detective Scott—I mean Katie." She hurried back to the car. "I hope you're feeling better," she yelled over her shoulder.

Katie watched mother and daughter get back in the car and leave. She waved and watched the sleek car disappear.

"Well, Cisco. That's the best news that could have come out of these investigations." She tightened her robe and returned inside her house to rest and to contemplate some serious questions that were weighing heavy on her mind.

CHAPTER FIFTY-SIX

A month later...

The fall was stunning in the Pine Valley Mountains along the Sagebrush Lake. Sunny days this time of year were some of the most memorable. The best sunsets. The most picturesque clear water. The most beautiful dense forests with equally lovely wildlife.

Katie returned to the camp from a brief walk dressed in jeans and a heavy cream sweater. She loved this area and the time of year, and especially sharing it with Chad. Sitting next to their tent, she smiled and said, "Does it get better than this?"

"Nope," he said. "Not in my book."

"I just keep thinking that—"

"Nope."

"What?"

"No thinking, no contemplating, no investigating, just relaxing."

She snuggled into him, feeling the warmth of his body. "You're absolutely right."

They watched McGaven and Denise play with Cisco along the shore of the lake. Denise's young daughter Lizzie ran around laughing before throwing the ball for the dog. The three of them looked happy together playing tag.

Katie laughed. "They are going to wear Cisco out." She turned to Chad. "I'm glad that you suggested this trip with them. This is one of my favorite places—if not my favorite."

"Of course, I thought we all could use a break. And what better place?"

She gazed at the water.

"Have you heard from your friend Shane?" he asked.

"Yes. His physical therapy is going well. He'll make a full recovery. And Tanis is doing well. She's staying with the McKinzies and Candace Harlan."

Chad nodded. "That's good to hear."

"And I closed my cases." She smiled.

"How are you feeling now with everything?"

"I'm on to my next cold case."

"Hey, who wants hot dogs?" said McGaven as he hoisted Lizzie on his shoulders.

"I do, I do," said the little girl with absolute delight.

"Sounds good to me," said Chad. "I'm hungry."

"Count me in," said Katie as she got up. "C'mon, Denise, let's have some wine before the boys burn some hot dogs."

"You got it," she said.

"Hey, I heard that," said McGaven.

"Don't pay any attention to them," said Chad.

"I don't burn hot dogs. Well, maybe once."

Katie sipped her wine and watched her friends joke with one another and just have fun. She knew that this was home. It was where her family was and where she was supposed to be.

CHAPTER FIFTY-SEVEN

Katie sat down on her couch, taking a deep breath several times before opening her laptop computer. She glanced at the clock and it was 6.58 p.m., two minutes before Dr. Carver was to log on for their appointment.

She was nervous, wringing her hands and feeling the moisture of perspiration. As usual, her heart rate increased and pounded in her chest. Her anxiety took a backseat, but it was still there—hovering.

Taking another deep breath, she looked around the room and realized how lucky she was with friends, family, and a job that suited her.

Cisco whined and snuggled in next to her—her constant and loyal companion.

A chime resonated, indicating that her appointment was logged in and ready to go.

The smiling face of Dr. Carver filled the screen. She had a calming effect on Katie with her low voice—it soothed her. "Hello, Katie," she said.

"Hi, Dr. Carver."

"It's good to see you, Katie. How have you been feeling?"

"I've been doing well."

"And work?"

"It's been more routine and not as stressful. I've been learning to pace myself."

"Is there something that you would like to talk about today? Something that happened this week?" she said, and gazed down to make some notes.

"Yes," said Katie. "I want to talk about something that happened, but not this week."

"That's fine. An incident that happened this month?"

"No. It was an incident that happened in Afghanistan," said Katie. She felt her mouth go dry, but she was going to talk about it, get it out in the open, so that she could begin to heal.

Dr. Carver looked directly at Katie with a slightly surprised look on her face. "Of course. You can talk about anything."

"Well," began Katie with a little bit of shakiness to her voice. "It was a typical morning, extra hot and dusty, it was soon going to reach a temperature of over 110 degrees, but that was normal. We were going out on patrol as a team because we had received our special orders from the Pentagon and the President. So Cisco and I took point as usual..."

A LETTER FROM JENNIFER

I want to say a huge thank you for choosing to read *Last Girls Alive*. If you did enjoy it, and want to keep up to date with all my latest releases, just sign up at the following link. Your email address will never be shared and you can unsubscribe at any time.

www.bookouture.com/jennifer-chase

This was a special project and series for me. Forensics and criminal profiling has been something that I've studied considerably and to be able to incorporate them into a crime fiction novel has been a thrilling experience for me.

One of my favourite activities outside of writing has been dog training. I'm a dog lover, if you couldn't tell by reading this book, and I loved creating a supporting canine character for my police detective. I've had the incredible opportunity to train with my local police K9 association, which includes several counties throughout California. My dog is certified in trailing, scent detection, and advanced obedience. It's been exciting pulling from my own experiences to create specific scenes. I hope you enjoyed it as well.

I hope you loved *Last Girls Alive* and if you did I would be very grateful if you could write a review. I'd love to hear what you think, and it makes such a difference helping new readers to discover one of my books for the first time.

I love hearing from my readers—you can get in touch on my Facebook page, through Twitter, Goodreads or my website.

Thanks,
Jennifer Chase

AuthorJenniferChase

JChaseNovelist

authorjenniferchase.com

ACKNOWLEDGMENTS

I want to thank my husband Mark for his steadfast support and for being my rock even when I had self-doubt. It's not always easy living with a writer and you've made it look easy.

A very special thank you goes out to all my law enforcement, police K9, forensic, and first-responder friends—there's too many to list. Your friendships have meant the world to me. It has opened a whole new writing world and inspiration. I wouldn't be able to bring my crime fiction stories to life if it wasn't for all of you. Thank you for your service and dedication to keep the rest of us safe.

This continues to be a truly amazing writing experience. I would like to thank my publisher Bookouture and the fantastic staff for helping me to bring this book and the entire Detective Katie Scott series to life. Thank you, Kim and Noelle, for your unrelenting promotion for us authors. To my fantastic copyeditor, Liz Hatherell and my proofreader, Jon Appleton, who made the story shine. A very special thank you to my editor Jessie Botterill—your amazing support and insight has helped me to work harder to write more adventures for Detective Katie Scott.

Printed in Great Britain
by Amazon

86834497R00194